tangled in Ivy

ASHLEY FARLEY

ISBN Print: 978-1-7346294-0-8

ISBN: Hardback: 978-1-7346294-2-2

ISBN Ebook: 978-1-7346294-1-5

To my faithful readers,
for giving me the inspiration to keep writing

LILLIAN

SEPTEMBER 2019

A sliver of afternoon sunlight streams through a crack in the heavy brocade drapes, falling across my father's ashen face. He's sixty-three going on ninety. His hair, once thick and brown, has gone completely gray. His glasses, the same wire-rimmed frames he's worn as long as I can remember, are on his bedside table. He will never again need them to see.

Through cracked lips, his tongue coated in white, he mutters, "Hemingway knows."

I lay my head on his chest. I can hear his heartbeat, slow and labored, and his lungs rattle, a sign the end is near. "What're you trying to say, Daddy? What does Hemingway know? Tell me. I'm right here. I'm listening."

He's been going on about Hemingway for hours. The hospice nurse has warned me not to read too much into what he says, that he's in a morphine-induced delirium, but I can't ignore the feeling he's trying to tell me something. Dad's a veteran professor of American literature. Hemingway is his favorite author. We even had a cat once named Hemingway. But I don't think Dad's talking about the cat.

When he speaks again, his voice is surprisingly loud and clear. "Hemingway knows. The truth about my life."

I raise my head to look at him. He's staring at me with glassy eyes. "Hemingway," he says one final time and blinks his lids shut. Seconds later, a peaceful expression settles on his face.

My gaze shifts to the hospice nurse who is asleep, sitting up in the chair beside his bed. "Rose! Wake up."

She startles awake, her hazel eyes wide. "What is it? Did something happen?"

"My father was alert when he spoke to me just now. But he's so still. I think maybe . . . Is he . . ."

Rose reaches for his wrist, feeling for a pulse, and gives her head a solemn shake.

I can't believe this is happening. I've known for months that this moment would come. I thought I was ready. "Are you sure?" I ask, hoping she's mistaken.

"Yes, I'm sure. I'm so sorry, Lillian." Rose lifts her clipboard from the bedside table and begins jotting notes.

Tears sting my eyes, and a pain grips my heart. I feel the urge to flee the room, yet I'm glued to my chair. I kiss my fingertips and press them against his lips. He's still warm to the touch, but not for long. He's gone. There's nothing I can do for him now.

Willing my legs to support me, I stand, turn my back on my beloved father, and pass through the double glass-paned doors to the piazza. I breathe in the heavy salt air. Now that my father is gone, the humidity and view of Charleston Harbor are two of the few remaining constants in my life.

I've devoted the last three months to taking care of my father. How do I move on from here? Dad left a file with detailed instructions for his funeral. I'm to call the minister, funeral director, and head of the English department at the College of Charleston. But then what? Do I return to my job at the art gallery? Move back into my studio apartment above said gallery?

A dark blue sedan turns off East Battery and passes through our iron gates. Trudy's eyes focus on the narrow brick driveway. I wave at her, but she doesn't see me when she passes below. As she circles the courtyard, I notice the three-tiered stone fountain has gone dry. One more thing in a long list that needs fixing around here.

Trudy parks at the back door near the kitchen and gets out of the car with a single bag of groceries. She left an hour ago to pick up a missing ingredient for my dinner. She insists I have a hot meal every night, even though I rarely eat more than a couple of bites. Watching one's father's internal organs being eaten alive from pancreatic cancer has a way of zapping one's appetite.

I can't remember the names of all the maids and cooks and gardeners my family has employed over the years. But Trudy and her husband, Isaac, our part-time fixit man, are more than household staff. They're family. It pains me to watch Trudy shuffling toward the back door. She's slowed down these past months. Dad's illness has taken its toll. And I dread breaking the news to her.

I reenter the house through the dining room and pause in front of my mother's portrait hanging above the sideboard. Dressed in a white polo shirt and khaki shorts, she's leaning against a live oak tree with the marsh in the background at our cottage on nearby Wadmalaw Island. Her wavy golden hair frames her sun-kissed face, highlighting eyes that are as blue as the deepest part of the ocean. She's in her early twenties, but she has an innocent, almost childlike, quality about her. Even though she died when I was six, my father has done a commendable job of keeping her memory alive. She was adventurous and athletic and loved the outdoors. I have a few blips of memories as well. Of her lighting birthday candles and presenting me with a baby kitten. Of the lingering scent of her flowery perfume after she tucks me into bed at night. Although I barely remember her, even after all this time, I get an aching feeling in my gut whenever I think of her.

Forcing myself away from the portrait, I exit the dining room and tread down the hall to the kitchen. To call our kitchen outdated is an understatement. The appliances came over on the Mayflower and the red Formica countertops trimmed in metal are vintage 1950s. But it's all I've ever known. The kitchen is the hub of family life in our home. From the doorway, I watch Trudy scrubbing an imaginary spot on the counter with her dish towel.

Two years ago, for no apparent reason, Dad fired all the staff except for Trudy and Isaac. The burden of the extra duties has fallen on Trudy. At seventy-two, her hair is completely gray, and the freckles dotting the bridge of her nose have darkened, but her caramel skin is still taut across her face. Despite her slight build, she's the strongest woman I've ever met spiritually, physically, and emotionally. And the closest thing to a mother I've ever known.

When I call her name, my voice breaking the silence, her head jerks back and she clutches the front of her apron. "Lord, child. You scared me. Don't go sneaking up on me like that."

"Daddy's gone. He died a few minutes ago."

Her body sags. "God rest his soul. He was a kind man, a good human being."

"If you need some time with him . . ."

"Nah." She waves off my offer with her towel. "I said my goodbyes when I got here this morning. You were still asleep." She hangs her towel on the oven handle. "I had a feeling today would be the day. Your daddy never liked Sundays."

I smile, thinking back on all the Sunday afternoons Dad isolated himself in his study with strict instructions for no one to bother him. "Why do you think he got the Sunday blues so bad?"

"It was harder for him to hide from his memories on Sundays when he didn't have his work or household duties to think about." Trudy crosses the room to me, taking me in her arms. "How are you holding up, sweet girl? Your daddy loved you so much. You know that, don't you?"

I nod into her shoulder. "Aside from being relieved he's no longer in pain, I'm not sure what I feel."

"It'll take some time to process." She holds me at arm's length. "You should call your sister."

"I've been calling her for a week. She's had plenty of time to get here. Atlanta's not that far."

"Still. You need to call Layla. To let her know he's gone."

The slamming of the front door is followed by footfalls on the hardwood floors and my sister's voice echoing throughout the house. "Lillian!"

My body tenses. "Speaking of the devil."

"She's not the devil. She's your sister."

"She's the devil," I repeat. "Layla, Princess of Planet Stoney, has returned. We might as well get this over with."

I start off toward the front of the house. When Trudy doesn't follow, I say, "Aren't you coming?"

"This is family time. I'll be right here if you need me."

"Chicken." I leave her standing in the doorway, snickering into her apron.

Layla and her husband and their ensemble of matching Tumi luggage are waiting at the top of the stairs outside the drawing room. My sister, a fashion designer, looks the part in her black jumpsuit and leopard skin booties. She has expensive highlights in her blonde hair now, but growing up, our hair was the exact same shade of blonde—beach blonde Dad called it when it bleached out in the summers. I've allowed mine to darken naturally to what some call dirty blonde.

5

Standing next to Layla, two heads taller than she, Roger, her husband is sporting a gray crew neck sweater and tapered jeans with designer sunglasses embedded in his thick head of dark hair.

"How was the drive?" I ask, kissing each of them on the cheek.

"It was five hours of bliss, Lil. What do you think?" Layla's arm shoots out, a black lacquered nail pointing at Dad's hospital bed. "Why'd you put him on display in the drawing room?"

My gaze follows her finger. Our father lies perfectly still. His skin is translucent, and his lips have turned blue. If she'd allowed her glance to linger for even a few seconds, my sister would have realized he's dead.

"Dad insisted on it," I say. "He wanted to be close to his study. Three flights of stairs are a lot to manage for a man riddled with cancer."

Squinting, Layla says, "He looks so pale. He's okay, right?"

"Actually, he's not," I say in a tight voice. "I'm sorry, Layla. You're twenty minutes too late."

"Wait a minute, what?" My sister, the great Houdini of emotions, shakes off disbelief and slips into anger. "You never told me the situation was urgent."

My jaw hits the floor, and I shift my gaze to my brother-in-law who shrugs as though he, too, can't believe the absurdity of his wife's comment. "Seriously, Layla? I called you no fewer than twenty times in the past seven days. When we spoke yesterday afternoon, I told you that Dad's hospice nurse"—I sweep my arm at Rose, who's talking on her cell phone in the corner of the drawing room—"predicted he wouldn't make it through the weekend."

A flush creeps up my sister's neck to her cheeks. "We had an important function last night. We couldn't get away until this morning."

"You didn't mention an *important* function when we spoke on the phone." I'm tempted to ask her if she deems saying goodbye to one's father on his deathbed unimportant, but I hold my tongue. "Whatever Layla. I'm sure you'll want some time alone with him now."

Brushing past her, I hurry down the stairs and out into the sultry afternoon. I cross East Battery Street to the seawall and lean against the railing on the promenade. The sight of the sail-boats gliding across the Cooper River has a calming effect on my nerves. The Lowcountry is in my blood—the marshes, the oak trees, the cuisine. Following his diagnosis, my father talked obsessively about my future, as though he could not rest in peace until he knew for certain I had a clear-cut path in mind.

"After I'm gone, I want you to pack your easel and leave this town," he said, repeatedly. "You have no obligations tying you down. Go explore the world, paint until your heart's content."

Contrary to what my father wants . . . wanted for me, I can't imagine ever leaving Charleston. As for artistic inspiration, the number of enchanting scenes for me to paint in this town and the surrounding areas is infinite.

Placing my back to the harbor, I stare across the street at our home. Just as I can't imagine moving away from Charles-ton, I never want to leave this house. My ancestor, my too-many-greats-to-count grandfather, built the gray-stuccoed three-story Federal-style house in the 1820s. One member of the Stoney family after another has lived here ever since.

Narrow on the street side, the house extends deep into the property. Informal sitting rooms occupy the first floor of the main house, but we spend the majority of our time on the upper two levels, which allow for more scenic views. Back in the olden days, kitchens were built separate from the main dwelling for fear of fire. That dependency is now attached to the main house, providing space on the first and second floors for kitchen and laundry and the third floor for rarely used bedrooms. At the far back of the property, the original carriage house offers a fully equipped apartment that has been used by many over the years. A visitor to our home needs a map to find his way from the front door to the kitchen through our conglomeration of chopped-up rooms.

I've always assumed I would be the one to inherit the house, but when I got up the nerve to question my father about it a month ago, he said, "You'll have to work that out with your sister."

"But she lives in Atlanta," I argued. "She's never expressed any interest in moving back to Charleston."

"I can't explain it now, sweetheart. You'll understand everything in due time."

Due time has now come.

A white van whips into our driveway and comes to a screeching halt in front of the main entrance on the first-floor piazza on the side of the house. Two men dressed entirely in gray get out. I don't need to see the logos on their uniforms to know they've come to collect my father's body. I long to run after them, to beg them not to take him away, but I'm frozen to my spot on the railing by a sudden vision. A bird's eye view through a rain-splattered window. A much-younger version of my father pacing the driveway, raking his hands through a thick head of dark hair. The transfer vehicle in my vision is not a van but an ambulance. The sheet-draped body on the stretcher can only be my mother. The tiny figure in the third-floor window is my six-year-old self on the day she died.

LILLIAN

For the next two days, I hide out in my room away from my sister. Layla's always been domineering, but she's grown difficult and more demanding since we last spent any real time together. Besides, I've been managing our father's care for the past three months, including his brief and ineffective regime of chemotherapy. It's time for her to do her share. She's in her element, anyway, socializing with friends she hasn't seen in years who stop in to pay their respects.

Because Dad had the foresight to plan his own funeral, Layla and I have only one fight over the specifics. She wants to bury him in a navy-blue suit she discovers in his closet that I've never seen him wear. But my father had specified his favorite tweed blazer with the suede patches on the elbows and his worn brown corduroy pants. It dawns on me that our father left his list of instructions, not to make things easier for my sister and me but to prevent arguments over the details.

I'm deeply touched by the outpouring of sympathy—the lush bouquets of flowers and the endless platters of cold cuts and casseroles—not only from friends of the family but from Dad's coworkers as well. When the head of the English department cancels classes on Wednesday, the day of the funeral, faculty members and hordes of students pack the church for the service and migrate to Magnolia Cemetery for the burial afterward. I'm humbled by these kids who care enough about my father to attend his funeral. I'm studying their youthful faces gathered around the perimeter of the tent at our family gravesite when I notice an elegant woman at the far edge of the crowd. She's dressed in black, from the hat and veil covering her head down to her spike-heeled boots.

"Who's that woman with the veil?" I whisper to Trudy, with a slight nod in the woman's direction.

Trudy lifts her hand to shield her eyes, and I feel her body go rigid. "What woman? I can't see without my glasses."

I cut my eyes at her. Trudy wears glasses to read, not for distance. I've never known her to lie. And I can't imagine why she is now. I lean in close, preparing to interrogate her, when the minister announces the benediction. The mysterious woman in black slips from my mind as the assembly begins to disperse and I'm besieged by people.

Layla has arranged a catered reception at the house after the funeral, and the place is already mobbed when we arrive. I'm pleased to see my friend Bert Edmunds, the owner of the art gallery where I work . . . worked . . . whatever . . . wearing a slim-fitting black suit and standing just inside the drawing room.

He envelops me in a hug. "Lil, I'm so sorry, sweetheart. It's been a tough road for you."

Fresh tears fill my eyes. "Everything happened so fast. I'm grateful he didn't suffer for long." I draw away from Bert. "How're things at the gallery?"

He runs his hand across his slicked-back dark hair. "Busy. We have three openings scheduled for October. We could really use your amazing organizational skills whenever you're ready to come back to work."

I chew on my lip. I hate disappointing him. "I'm sorry, Bert. You've been so understanding, but I need a little more time."

"No worries. I get it." He gives my arm a pat. "Your apartment's still available too, if you're interested in moving back in."

"I . . . I don't know what to say. Everything about my life is so uncertain at the moment. I need to sort a few things out."

He raises a hand. "You don't have to give me an answer now. Think about it, and let me know when you decide."

"Has anyone shown any interest in my work?" Bert has three of my paintings for sale in the gallery. A marsh view from our family's cottage on nearby Wadmalaw Island. The steeple of St. Phillips church at dusk. And the famous Rainbow Row on a sunny day.

"Everyone who comes into the gallery expresses interest. But no one has made an offer. At least not yet."

"Because you have the paintings priced too high."

He fingers a lock of hair off my cheek. "Come on, Lil. We've talked about this ad nauseam. We've priced them appropriately for the quality of your work. You are one of the most gifted young artists I've ever encountered. Your paintings will start to sell, and when they do, you'll be an overnight success. You have to trust me on this. I know what I'm doing."

Tingling feelings of excitement dance around in my belly at the prospect of someone buying my work. "I do trust you, Bert. No one knows the art business better than you. I'm just impatient."

"Tell you what. Let's give it a few more months. If nothing's sold by"—he glances upward, as if to find the right date written on the ceiling—"say February, we'll consider lowering the prices."

February is four months away. Which, at the moment, seems like an eternity. "All right, then. You have until February first. But not a single day longer."

Bert's green eyes grow wide as he spots someone behind me.

"Ooh, I see the McGees across the room. I need to speak with them. Stay in touch, Lil. Too-da-loo."

He leaves me standing alone in a sea of people. The sickly sweet scent of a gardenia plant overpowers the room, and while I find the fragrance suffocating, it stirs in me some emotion I can't identify. What will we do with all the flower arrangements sent by well-meaning people after today?

Eyeing the staircase, I consider sneaking up to my room. Then I remind myself these people are here for my father. I owe it to them, and to him, to be cordial. I have countless brief conversations as I make my way through to the dining room. There's very little food left on the table, and I'm snagging the last broken pieces of cheese straws for my plate when I sense someone behind me. "Hello, Lillian," a familiar voice says near my ear.

I turn to face the man I almost married ten years ago. His face has matured, his jawline stronger and auburn hairline receding slightly. But his penetrating green eyes haven't changed. He looks at me now, and it's as though he knows everything I'm feeling. "Marcus. I heard you'd moved back to town. So nice of you to come."

"Of course. I wouldn't have missed it."

We step away from the crowd at the table for privacy. "I'm sorry about your father, Lil. I admired Graham a great deal."

I offer him a polite smile. "And he thought a lot of you as well." *Until you broke my heart by hooking up with my sister.*

He tosses a quarter-size sweet potato biscuit into his mouth and sets his plate on the sideboard. "Normally I wouldn't bring this up at a time like this, but I have a matter of some urgency to discuss with you. I'm a junior partner at Cross, Ball, and Stanley, and your father specifically requested that I be assigned to his team. We need to meet with you and Layla sooner rather than later."

I frown. "If this is about his estate, can't it wait? We only just buried him today."

His hand grazes my arm. "I'm sorry, Lil, but the matter is pressing. I've spoken with Layla. She's planning to return to Atlanta on Friday, so we'll have to meet tomorrow. Three o'clock in our office. Trudy will need to be there as well, since she's mentioned in the will."

What is wrong with me that I care that he spoke to Layla first? He's successful and good-looking, living proof that ginger men are sexy as hell. But is he married? While I'd overheard my friends talking about him being back in town, no one mentioned a wife. I risk a glance at his ring finger, and a wave of relief washes over me when I see that it's bare.

Don't go there, Lil. He broke your heart once. He doesn't deserve a second chance.

Our minister appears in the doorway, providing my escape. "I'm sorry, Marcus, but I need a word with Reverend Lewis." I walk away without so much as a goodbye.

I thank the minister for the flattering things he said in his eulogy about my father and move into the drawing room where Roger is offering drinks to our few remaining guests. From the slur in his words, he's poured himself a few too many already. Even though Layla and I had agreed to no alcohol at the reception, I accept the glass of red wine he offers me and take it out to the piazza. I'm a million miles away, lost in my own thoughts, when a woman who looks vaguely familiar but I can't quite place approaches me.

"You don't remember me, do you?" the woman says. "It's been a long time."

I study her more closely. She's in her seventies, attractive with silver hair and a nice tan. I see kindness in her brown eyes and hear it in her voice. I admit, "I can't place you, but I have the strangest feeling I once knew you very well."

She extends her hand. "I'm Elizabeth Hudson. *Doctor* Elizabeth Hudson. Your father was one of the good guys. I got to know him pretty well while you were under my care. I'm a child psychiatrist. You were once my patient."

Suddenly lightheaded, I grip the porch railing for support. "Are you sure you don't have me confused with my twin sister?" I ask, even though Layla is the last person who would ever need to see a shrink.

"No, sweetheart. I'm positive it was you. I helped you sort through your emotions after your mother's death. At least, I tried. Your mind had a mighty powerful lock on your memories from that day."

I know her answer before I ask the question. "What day?"

"The day she died."

I get a whiff of the gardenias wafting through the open doors, and a wave of nausea engulfs me. My vision blurs red and I drop my wine glass. Fragments of glass scatter across the wooden floor and wine splashes on my black suede pumps.

Fingers on lips, she says, "Oh dear. Are you okay?"

"I'm fine. But I need to clean this up before someone cuts themselves." Pressing my hand against the woman's back, I hustle her off the piazza, closing the door behind us. "Thank you for coming, Dr. Hudson. If you'll excuse me."

"Let me give you my card in case you ever want to talk." She digs in her bag, but I don't wait for her to find her card.

I go to the laundry room for the broom and dustpan. The silence there is a welcome relief. I lean against the closed door and slide to the floor, landing with a soft thud on my bottom. The harder I try to wrap my mind around my loss, the more overwhelmed I feel. I keep telling myself to take one day at a time. This one's almost over. If I can get through the meeting with the lawyers tomorrow and see Layla off to Atlanta on Friday, I can begin to cope with my grief.

I remain on the laundry room floor for a long while. When I finally drag myself back to the drawing room, Dr. Hudson is gone, along with all the other guests. Trudy is in another part of the house, and Roger and Layla are nowhere in sight. I clean up the mess from my shattered glass and stretch out on the sofa. When I close my eyes, the gardenia fragrance assaults my nose, and the backs of my eyelids burn red, the same bloodred from before when I was out on the porch with Dr. Hudson. There's something beyond the red, but it's too dim to tell whether it's a person or a thing. Am I having some sort of premonition? Or am I remembering something from the distant past? Dr. Hudson's words come back to me. *Your mind had a mighty powerful lock on your memories from that day.* Is it possible that seeing her again released one of those memories? Or did the gardenias trigger the vision?

A voice startles me out of my reverie. When I open my eyes, a strange woman is standing over me. I spring to my feet. "I thought everyone was gone."

"Most everyone is. I've been outside in the courtyard talking with Trudy for over an hour. It was good to catch up with her after all these years." The woman pauses, as if waiting for me to respond. When I don't, she says, "You don't know who I am, do you?"

Ugh. The ghosts are coming out of the woodwork today. Are all funerals like this?

This woman isn't even vaguely familiar. Her appearance is unremarkable. Auburn hair streaked with gray. Hazel eyes that look at me but don't see me. "I'm sorry. I've met a lot of people today."

"I'm Alice. Alice Browder. I'm your godmother, yours and Layla's. Your mother was my best friend."

My mother's best friend? I'm intrigued. But I don't believe her. Something is sketchy about her. "If that's so, why don't I know you?"

"You knew me once," she says. "When you were a little girl. I moved to the West Coast twenty-seven years ago, right after your mother died. Did your father never talk about me? I sent you birthday and Christmas cards every year. Didn't you get them?"

"I did not." I'm certain of this. I would've remembered receiving greeting cards from my godmother, my mother's best friend.

"I can't say I blame your father for keeping you from me. But I loved you girls like my own. I was never able to have children. In many ways, I thought of you as my own."

"If that's the case, why didn't you ever call or come for a visit?" My tone is accusatory, even though I don't mean for it to be. It's been a long day.

"That's a fair question. Unfortunately, the answer is complicated. May I?" She gestures at the sofa and sits without waiting for my answer.

Once upon a time, I would've relished having a godmother, a female figure I could relate to, my mother's best friend who could tell me girly secrets about her. But that time has passed. If this woman cared about me, she would've done more to stay in touch than send a Hallmark card twice a year.

"Honestly, now is not the best time for a heart to heart."

Seemingly surprised at my rudeness, she rises slowly to her feet. "I have an early flight out tomorrow morning." She hands me a business card. "Call me sometime. We'll have a nice long chat."

I look down at the card that states she's an attorney at law and lists the contact information for her firm in San Francisco. I pocket the card, but I don't agree to call her, because I'm not sure I will. "Thank you for coming to the funeral," I say in a softer voice.

After showing Alice Browder to the door, I return to the drawing room for the gardenia plant. I walk it down the hall, through the kitchen, and outside to the trash can. For the purpose of writing thank you notes, I remove the white envelope from the plastic holder and read the card inside. *In deepest sympathy, Alice Browder.*

Is there a hidden meaning behind the gardenias? Is Alice sending some sort of message? Or am I delirious from exhaustion and reading too much into everything?

Back inside the kitchen, I retrieve an unopened bottle of white wine from the refrigerator and retreat to my bedroom. Despite the early hour, I'm in for the night. I aim to drink until I forget about Marcus Mullaly and Alice Browder and Dr. Hudson.

After changing out of my funeral dress and into my shorty pajamas, I take the wine out to the piazza and cozy up in my hanging rattan chair. My bedroom is on the back corner of the original house with a view from the piazza overlooking the courtyard below. Three hinged wooden shutters separate my little corner from the rest of the porch. I finish one glass of wine and I'm pouring another when I hear a door on the other side of the screen open and angry voices spill out.

"You're drunk, Roger."

"Damn right! Being drunk is the only way I can tolerate being with you."

Ouch, I think. That's harsh. Especially coming from Roger. He's by far their better half. True what they say about opposites attracting. Dad and I were thrilled when Roger entered Layla's life. His calm demeanor has always provided a stabilizing influence for her erratic personality. His tolerance has run its course. I must say, he lasted longer than I thought he would.

"I can't do this anymore," he says.

Desperation creeps into Layla's voice. "What're you talking about?" asks Layla, with desperation creeping into her voice. "What can't you do anymore?"

I should make my presence known. But I'm way too curious.

"I can't stay married to you, Layla. You've changed. Your success has gone to your head."

"I don't understand, Roger. Why are you so mad at me?"

"I'm not mad," Roger says with a note of resignation. "I'm disappointed in the way you handled your father's illness. In the three months since his diagnosis, you've only visited him one time."

"I'm not a doctor!" she snaps. "How did I know his disease would've progressed so fast?"

"If you'd listened to your sister, you would've known. But you don't listen, Layla. You only hear what you wanna hear. Who passes up the opportunity to say goodbye to their father on his deathbed for a Juvenile Diabetes benefit?"

"I'll have you know, those tickets cost me five hundred dollars apiece."

He lets out an exasperated groan. "This is exactly what I'm talking about."

Their voices fade, and the door slams shut.

While I'm not my sister's biggest fan, I feel sorry for her. I certainly don't want to see her marriage fail. She is, and always has been, her own worst enemy.

My desire to get drunk has passed, and I set my glass down on the table beside me. I don't know what to think of any of it. The visits from the past. My sister and her marital problems. The visions. This day has turned my world upside down, and I have no clue how to go about setting it right again.

LILLIAN

I hear Layla and Roger arguing throughout the night, and when I go down for breakfast at eight the following morning, Roger has already left for Atlanta.

A bewildered Trudy says, "He was in such a hurry to get out of here, he didn't bother with breakfast. Not even a cup of coffee. Your sister couldn't be bothered to come down and see her husband off. I reckon she'll fly back to Atlanta when she's ready to go home."

When I mumble, "I hope that'll be soon," Trudy gives me the stink eye.

I eat a bowl of oatmeal and spend the next couple of hours helping Trudy clean up from the reception. Around noon, I change into shorts and a T-shirt and walk up the road a few blocks to the Charleston Yacht Club where we keep our daysailer. I haven't been out on the water in weeks and the fresh air helps clear my mind. I'm on the water for over an hour before my thoughts shift to Dr. Hudson and Alice Browder.

My father would never have prevented Layla and me from knowing our godmother without a good reason. Alice said she didn't blame him *after everything that happened*. She moved to

California twenty-seven years ago, right after my mother died. Did this thing that *happened* drive her to move to California? Did it have something to do with my mother's death? Is it the reason I suppressed memories from the day she died?

Closing my eyes, I lift my face to the sun. I try to summon the red vision, but the day is bright, and I see only the cobalt-blue color of the sky through my eyelids. Why tamper with the powerful locks on my memories when they are protecting me from something unbearably painful? Don't I have enough suffering in my life already with mourning the death of my father?

I return home to shower and dress before heading to our meeting with the attorneys. A grim-faced Layla slides into the back seat of my Subaru with Trudy beside me in the front. None of us speak during the drive to the law firm's offices on Broad Street. We ride the elevator to the third floor where a receptionist directs us to the conference room. Marcus is seated at the mahogany conference table with Daddy's senior attorneys, Messrs. Cross and Ball. I've known these gentlemen all my life. Even though Layla and I spoke with them at length at the funeral, they express their condolences again as we take our seats opposite them.

I feel Marcus's green eyes on me. I'm an ugly duckling in plain khaki pants and a white cotton crew neck sweater next to my sister who, despite the turmoil in her marriage, presents herself as a seasoned professional in gray slacks and a powder-blue silk blouse.

Ball opens a file in front of him. "Let's get started. I believe Marcus explained to you that we have urgent business to discuss. Let me start with a bit of positive news. Graham has bequeathed a nice sum for your retirement, Trudy."

When he announces the amount, Trudy's brown eyes grow wide. This is no surprise to me. Dad told me he'd taken care of Trudy in his will.

Ball continues, "In terms of the remainder of his estate, however, I'm afraid there's not much left. At least in terms of liquid assets after funeral expenses are paid. On the bright side, there's no mortgage against either the house in Charleston or the cottage on Wadmalaw. Combined, even in their current state of disrepair, the properties are worth several million dollars."

Silence settles over the conference room and the attorneys stare down at the table. Sweat trickles down my back, and I find it difficult to breath. When I look to my sister for help, she shrugs. She's at a loss for words as well.

I fold my hands on the table to keep them from shaking. "I don't understand. Are you saying the Stoney family fortune is gone?"

Marcus's lips part in a sympathetic smile. "Except for the equity in the houses, yes."

"How did this happen?" Layla asks.

"The portfolio took a considerable blow in the last recession," Cross says. "Your father, on his teaching salary, couldn't begin to pay the staff and maintain two houses."

Everything suddenly makes sense. Why Dad fired the staff and why, when I asked him if I would inherit the house, he said, "You'll have to work that out with your sister." He didn't leave either of us the house. He left us a mess.

The room falls silent again, and the three attorneys cast uncomfortable glances at one another. "Are there additional questions?" Cross asks.

I know I should be asking something. I'm just not sure what. Layla pushes back from the table, and the rest of us stand.

"We're here to support you in any way we can," Ball says as he escorts us to the door.

We're halfway to the elevator when Marcus calls, "Wait!

Lil, I forgot I have something for you. It's in my office, if you have a moment to spare."

Goose bumps break out on my arms. What could he possibly have to give me?

I tell Trudy and Layla I'll meet them at the car, and then follow Marcus back down the hall in the opposite direction. His office is spacious with a dark wooden desk positioned in front of a large window overlooking Broad Street.

"I neglected to tell you yesterday at the funeral that your father summoned me to your house three weeks ago. You were at the dentist, having your teeth cleaned, at the time. He asked me to give you this after he was gone." Marcus presses a small silver key in the palm of my hand.

I stare at the key. "What lock does it fit? Did he say?"

"The bottom desk drawer in his study. The one that holds his files."

"I always assumed Dad kept files relating to college business locked in that drawer. Is there something specific he wants me to see?"

"He didn't say. But he wanted me to be sure to give the key to you and not Layla."

I slip it in my pocket. "Now I'm really curious."

"I'm here for you, Lil." His face reddens. "Professionally, I mean. Call me if you need anything." He hands me his business card with his cell number.

I take the card from him and hurry out of the office to the car.

On the way home, Layla, who is now in the passenger seat, says, "I'm not at all surprised. Dad was a great teacher. But he sucked at managing money."

From the back seat, Trudy says in a tight voice, "I want you girls to take my share. I wasn't expecting this, and I don't need it. Isaac and I been saving for our retirement for years."

I smile at her in the rearview mirror. "That's very generous of you, Trudy, but that money is for you. Dad didn't give it to you because he thought you needed it. He gave it to you because he wanted you to have it. You've earned it taking care of us all these years. This is our way of taking care of you in your retirement."

When we get home, I follow my sister through the house to the drawing room. She grabs two glasses and a bottle of chardonnay from the minifridge and takes them outside to the piazza. We sit side by side on the small sofa. I can't remember when I was last in such close proximity to my sister, and the scent of her expensive perfume is a reminder of her success.

Layla fills both glasses with wine and hands one to me. "It's never good news when an attorney requests a meeting immediately following a funeral."

"I admit, I'm floored. I was not expecting this." Reality hits me like a bombshell, and I fall back against the cushions. "I'm flat broke, Layla. I have less than a thousand dollars in my checking account."

"You're going back to work, aren't you?"

"I was hoping to take some time off to sort out my life. The past few months haven't been easy, and I'm having a bit of a professional crisis." I think out loud as I sip my wine. "My salary won't begin to cover the costs of upkeep on a house this size. Commissions from the sale of some of my paintings would help, but there's little hope of that happening anytime soon. I'll have to figure out some other way."

"Hold on a sec, Lil. If you're thinking of keeping the house, you can forget it. We own it together. You would have to buy me out, which you obviously can't afford to do."

I shift my position so I can look directly at her. "Our forefathers built this house, Layla. Our mother loved this house. She loved Charleston. Her heritage meant everything to her. This house is our legacy. For crying out loud, she named us Lillian Stoney and Layla Stoney to ensure that legacy lives on."

Layla fell back against the sofa. "Jeez. I didn't mean to touch on a sore nerve. None of that legacy stuff means anything to me. I dropped the Stoney name when I married Roger. I'm Layla Alexander Payne now."

"Seriously? We never even met our Alexander grandparents." Shaking my head, I mutter, "How are we even twins?"

Layla punches me playfully in the arm. "You have no idea how many times I've asked myself that very thing. Maybe we were switched at birth."

"Puh-lease. Have you looked in the mirror lately? We're not identical, but we look an awfully lot alike."

"Except that I'm the princess and you're Cinderella."

Layla says things like this in jest, but they hurt my feelings nonetheless. Maybe because there's truth to them. "Bottom line is, we can't sell the house."

"We can, and we will. We have no choice."

I scowl at her. "Your husband's right. You have changed. Your success *has* gone to your head."

Her nostrils flare as she glares at me. "How'd you know that? Were you eavesdropping on us?"

I drain the rest of my wine and slam the glass on the coffee table in front of her. "Hit me again. Being drunk is the only way I can tolerate being around you," I say, repeating what I overheard Roger tell Layla on the porch last night. I immediately hate myself for being cruel. I never intend to hurt my sister. She just brings out the worst in me.

Layla jumps up. "God, I hate you, Lillian."

I grab her arm. "Wait, Layla! Please, don't go. I don't know why I said that."

She jerks her arm away. "But you did, and you can't take it back. Why are you always such a bitch to me?

I stand to face her. "That's the cat calling the kettle black."

She looks away from me. "In my case, it's different."

24

"How so? Because you're Layla, Princess of Planet Stoney?"

She used to laugh when I called her that. Now her lips spread into a sad smile. "Because I'm mean to everyone. You're only mean to me. Why is that?"

"I honestly don't know," I say flopping back down on the sofa. "Sometimes you get under my skin, and I can't help myself."

She sits back down beside me and refills both of our glasses. "Now is as good a time as any to talk about the problems in our relationship."

"Ha. Where do we even start?"

She thinks about it for a minute. "Maybe we should talk about the good times we had with Dad first."

"I like that idea," I say. And once we get started, we can't stop. We cry and we laugh and we cry some more. We finish off the bottle of wine and open another. The orange ball of sun is beginning its descent below the horizon when Trudy arrives with a tray of sandwiches.

I jump up and take the tray from her. "I thought you'd already gone home. What're you doing here so late?"

"I can't bring myself to leave." Her face is scrunched up, and I can tell she has something on her mind. "Your family has been good to me over the years. And now it's my turn to pay it back. I'm gonna work for free until you figure out what to do about the house."

"No way! We can't ask you to do that." I've been too self-absorbed to think about how recent developments might affect Trudy. Sure, she got a windfall today, but she earned every penny of it, taking care of three generations of Stoneys. She's like my mother, but she's not my mother. It has never occurred to me that our relationship might one day come to an end.

I burst into tears and fall into her arms.

"Come now, child," she says, stroking my hair. "What's this all about?"

"Everything's changing," I sob. "I don't know what I'll do without you. Please, don't leave me."

"I'm not going anywhere, baby. I will always be here for you."

I cry for a few minutes in the safety and comfort of her arms before finally pushing her away. "I'm sorry for my outburst. I'm letting my emotions get the best of me."

"And the wine," Layla says.

Trudy cuts her eyes at Layla. "It's good for you to get it all out, sweet girl." She removes a tissue from her apron pocket and dabs at my eyes. "Your daddy is smiling down on you from heaven, seeing you girls sitting out here together on such a pleasant evening. You have some important decisions to make. If you listen to your hearts, you'll know what to do." She hands me the tissue and moseys toward the door. "I'll see you in the morning."

I wait for Trudy to leave before reclaiming my seat. I haven't eaten since breakfast, and I'm famished, but I can't stop crying. With tears streaming down my face, I stuff half an egg salad sandwich in my mouth at once.

Layla leans into me. "You're blubbering like a fool. I wish I could cry. I have yet to shed a tear."

"Like you said, it's the wine." I reach for another sandwich, pimento cheese this time.

"Or maybe I am the heartless person Roger thinks I am. Do you think I've changed, Lil?"

"I haven't seen you enough in recent years to make that judgment. I will say this." I point my sandwich at her. "I don't blame Roger for being disappointed in you for not being here for Dad. That is time you will never get back."

She looks away from me, toward the setting sun. "I was afraid to see him. I wanted to remember him healthy and vibrant. When I woke up on Sunday morning, I realized I'd made a mistake. I got here as fast as I could. But it wasn't fast enough." Her eyes are back on me. "Was it awful?"

"You have no idea." A chill travels my spine when I think back to everything I went through with Dad. I did things for him no daughter should ever do for her father. But I wouldn't change a thing. And we grew closer because of it.

"I will forever regret not coming sooner. I only hope Dad will forgive me."

I don't have the power to absolve her of her guilt, but I can see she's genuinely remorseful. I choose my words carefully. "Talking about him with you, reliving all those memories, really helped. Thank you for that. From now on, I'm only going to think about the happy times."

We sit in silence for a while with our bodies touching, the closest contact we've had in years.

"I'm scared, Lil. I think I really blew it with Roger."

"Roger loves you. That's the most important thing. You can fix your problems if you try."

Layla exhales a contented hum. "This is nice, us being here together like this. I've missed having a sister. Now that Dad's gone, you and I are all each other has left. I'd like for us to have a real relationship, if you can stop being mad at me."

Heat flushes through my body at the memory of her betrayal. "I have a right to be angry, damn it. I caught you kissing my fiancé. And that's not something I can easily forget or forgive."

"Come on, Lil. It started way before the thing with Marcus, and you know it. It started when Mom died. Even though you *claim* to remember nothing, I recall everything about that day in vivid detail."

A chill travels my spine. "Tell me, Layla, what exactly is it that you recall?"

Layla rolls her eyes. "Stop faking, Lil. Your so-called amnesia was nothing more than an act to get attention."

"I'm not the one who plays games to get attention!" I leap to my feet so fast my head spins. I limp over to the railing, gripping it tight as the vision flashes before me. I close my eyes shut, willing it to go away. The scent of gardenias is in the air, even though I threw the plant in the trash can. This time, I sense a presence in the red mist, a person, or maybe a thing, lurking in the background.

Layla is at my side. "Are you okay, Lil? You look as though you've seen a ghost."

"The wine made me dizzy. If you'll excuse me." I flee the porch without so much as a glance at my sister.

LILLIAN

$\mathcal{I}$ go up to my room, but the key Marcus gave me is burning a hole in my pocket. Although I've had too much to drink to go snooping in Dad's study, I need the liquid courage to face whatever is so important for *my eyes only*. After I hear the soft click of Layla's door closing, I wait thirty minutes before sneaking back down to Dad's study. Locking the door behind me, I sit down in his leather chair at his desk, an English antique with secret compartments that has always fascinated me. Running my hand across its beautiful mahogany wood, as I often do when I'm working here, I think about the generations of Stoney men who've paid bills and written correspondence, both business and personal, for nearly two centuries.

I insert the key in the silver lock on the inside of the desk and slide open the drawer. An envelope addressed to me in my father's neat cursive is lying across the hanging file folders.

My dearest Lillian,

If you are reading this letter, our time together has come to an end. Don't be sad. Celebrate the happy times we shared.

You brought great joy into my life. We are kindred spirits, you and me. My hope is that you'll one day experience the same unconditional love for your own child.

I'm devastated over having to leave you in financial trouble. I did my best to be a responsible custodian of the Stoney fortune. Unfortunately, the downturn in the economy during the recent recession wiped us out. I was in the preliminary stages of putting the house on the market when I fell ill. In this same drawer, you'll find a file with the contact information for the real estate agent I've been working with. The proceeds from the sale of the house will free you from debt and give you a considerable nest egg to start anew, to spread your wings and fly. Be free, my darling. Find your happiness. You deserve it.

I'm also leaving behind unfinished business relating to your mother's death. Something happened to you on the day she died, something so traumatic you buried it deep in the recesses of your mind. I have a strong suspicion your sister was somehow responsible for that something. And that something is the reason for your deep-seated animosity toward her.

Dr. Hudson and I have kept in touch over the years. I trust you have heard from her by now. She's a good friend and a wonderful listener, should you ever need either. After three years of therapy, when Dr. Hudson failed to connect with the ghosts from your past, we agreed to leave you be in the hopes you'll one day have a breakthrough on your own. I believe in my heart that It's not too late for that breakthrough.

One good thing came from your therapy. Dr. Hudson discovered your talents in the drawings she requested of you. You can find your first masterpieces in another file folder in this drawer. While you may find them disturbing, perhaps the drawings will enable you to reconnect with the past and move toward recovery and reconciliation with your sister.

This is your journey, Mouse. Do with it as you will. If you

choose to proceed down this path of discovery, you'll need to know more about my life with Ivy. Look to Hemingway to guide you.

Love,

Daddy

I fall back in my chair. *Mouse*. That was Dad's childhood nickname for me. He never would tell me why he called me that. "Don't you remember?" he'd say when I asked.

"Damn it, Dad! Of course I don't remember. Why are you making this so difficult for me?" I sit up straight again. "Right. Because it's my journey, my discovery to make. But I don't get what Hemingway has to do with anything. Why didn't you ever mention Alice Browder or the missing greeting cards?"

I run my fingers across the hanging file folders, reading the labels. There's nothing much here of interest to me. The balance sheets and brokerage account statements are over my head. I find the file for the Realtor, but I'll have to be desperate before I contact her. I come across the thick folder with my drawings and spread it open on the desk. They are organized in chronological order beginning in June of 1993, seven months after my mother's death.

The first few show nothing more than red crayon scribbles. But as the dates progress over the next two years, my talent emerges and the compositions transition to finger paints, pastels, and watercolors. As I flip through the pages, I realize the illustrations tell a story. I'm alone in the upstairs hall calling for Trudy. My mother, with angry face and halo of golden hair, is wagging a finger at me. In another one, I'm peeking from behind a door. In another, I'm staring down from a rain-soaked window as Layla, in a red rain slicker and matching boots, skips off hand in hand with another little girl. The child's name comes to me out of the blue. *Sally.*

Warmth spreads throughout my body as I study the pastel drawing of me curled up in a ball in the cavity of Dad's desk. This I remember. Before and after my mother's death, I spent a great deal of time at my father's feet, reading books and coloring, protected from my sister.

The last in the file is a watercolor in shades of reds and pinks. The faint scent of gardenias causes an explosion of red to go off inside my head, and I scramble under the desk. Voices surround me. Layla's. Trudy's. My daddy's. One I don't recognize — it must be mama's. Some are shouting. Some speak to me in threatening tones. But their words are too jumbled for me to understand. I cover my ears and squeeze my eyes tight. There's something or someone else there, beyond the red. I dig deep in my brain, but I can't remember who or what it is. The red dissipates and I open my eyes wide.

My mother died from an accident that happened inside this house. I've always assumed she fell down the stairs. Did someone push her? Maybe *I* pushed her. That would explain why my subconscious blocked it out and why my dad refused to talk about it.

I fall asleep under the desk, and in my dreams, my sketches come alive, playing over and over in my mind. When I wake to the first rays of pink sunlight streaming through the window, my sister's venomous tone from my dreams is still echoing in my mind. "You'd better not tell."

Better not tell what, Layla?

Crawling out from beneath the desk, I gather the sketches and stuff the file into the drawer, making sure to lock it. I fold Dad's letter into my pocket and go to the kitchen where I find Trudy making inventory of the funeral casseroles in our freezer.

"Tell me the truth, Trudy. How did my mother die?"

"Oh, Lord." She slammed the freezer door shut. "Your

father warned me you'd be asking some hard questions. Sit down. Let me fix you some breakfast."

When she palms my cheek, I brush her hand away. "I don't want breakfast. I want answers."

"Don't get sassy with me, young lady. Sit." She jabs her finger at the table, and I sit.

"Coffee only, please."

"Coffee it is." She fills a mug from the carafe, adds a splash of cream, and places it on the table in front of me. She sits down in the chair on the other side of the table. "Talk to me."

I explain about Dad leaving me the key to his desk. I tell her about the drawings and show her the letter. "Why did I need to see a shrink after my mother died? And why is her death an off-limits subject in this household?"

A pained expression crosses her face. "Losing your mama was traumatic for all of us, but mostly for you. You became withdrawn, and you had horrible nightmares. We know you were in the house when your mama died, and we know something bad happened to you that day. But we don't know what. Only that it was something so terrible your mind blocked it out."

No wonder my soul is tortured. "It would help if I knew how she died. Did I push my mother down the stairs?"

Trudy's neck snaps as she jerks her head back. "What? Where'd you get that cockamamie idea?"

"I'm not sure." I rub my chin until my skin is raw. There's a memory floating off in the distance, but I can't reach it. "All my life, I've had this feeling, this burden of guilt, that whatever happened to my mother was somehow my fault."

"You were a dear, sweet child. You weren't capable of violence."

I give her a hard stare. "Then how did she die?"

Trudy looks away from me. "I can't tell you. Dr. Hudson says it's better if you remember on your own."

"Were you in the house when it happened?"

Trudy's chin trembles and her eyes fill with tears. "I was at a teacher's conference at my daughter's school. By the time I got here, it was too late."

"What else can you . . . will you tell me?"

She shakes her head. "I promised your daddy I wouldn't tell you anything."

"Why now, Trudy? Why is it so important that I remember now?"

"Your daddy always hoped you'd remember in your own time." Trudy wipes her tears with a napkin. "But he got desperate when he found out he was dying. He worried that, with him out of the picture, you and Layla would be lost to each other forever. Like he says in his letter, he was convinced you would never make your peace with your sister until you remember the events of your mama's death. He wanted so much for the two of you to mend your relationship."

"That's nothing new. He was always trying to get Layla and me to make nice." He made me feel guilty for not calling my sister or visiting her in Atlanta. On Layla's rare trips home, he planned corny family outings that always ended up with one of us mad at the other.

"Being broke complicates the situation," I add. "I'm sure he realized we'd fight over selling the house." I get up from the table and pour myself another cup of coffee. "Did you know about his money problems?"

"He never mentioned a word. I'm not surprised, though. Your daddy was a proud man. Be just like him to carry a secret like that to his grave."

"Look where that pride got us," I mumble and leave the room knowing little more than I did thirty minutes ago.

Returning to Dad's study, I carefully examine each of his many Hemingway novels. I have no idea what I'm looking for. Another note from my father? A hidden meaning in the words themselves? A treasure map pointing me to more clues. When I learn nothing from Hemingway, I tear through Dad's office like a maniac. There are hundreds of books by other authors lining the shelves. I give each a quick once-over before tossing it onto the growing pile on the floor.

By the time I finish my search, my blouse is soaked through with perspiration and my frustration has morphed into annoyance. "What the heck, Dad? It would've been so much easier if you'd just told me what you want me to know."

It dawns on me that while Trudy won't give anything away, there's someone who might.

I text Marcus. *I need to see you. Can you spare a few minutes?*

He responds immediately. *I'll meet you at the fountain in Waterfront Park in 15. Should I grab some coffees?*

None for me. I've had too much caffeine already.

I leave the house without a jacket, but it's warm out. Warmer than it should be in early October. I racewalk up East Bay Street and cut over on Tradd Street to the waterfront. When I reach the fountain, I crouch down and dip my fingers into the cool water. The fountain bears the pineapple motif—the symbol of hospitality found all over the city. It was erected in the spring of 1990, six months after Hurricane Hugo devastated much of the Lowcountry. I vaguely remember the destruction from the hurricane. The debris in the streets and having to stand in long lines for supplies. Oddly, I recall it being a happy time. We had strangers living in our house. My mother was always in a good mood. And I felt close to another woman. Was that woman Alice?

The sight of Marcus walking toward me in casual gray cotton pants and a blue-striped button-down steals my breath. *Get over it, Lil. He ripped your heart out and stomped all over it.*

As he leans in to kiss my cheek, I'm acutely aware of my appearance. I'm still wearing the same rumpled khakis and blouse from our meeting the day before. I haven't brushed my teeth since yesterday morning, and I smell of sweat and stale coffee.

Removing an elastic from my wrist, I tie my greasy hair back in a ponytail. "Thanks for coming on such short notice. I need to know everything Dad told you when he gave you the key."

"He made me promise to look out for you after he was gone."

With head bowed and chewing on a thumbnail, I walk in little circles in front of Marcus. "I don't understand why he would ask that of you. Why he would have you assigned to his team of attorneys."

"Because he trusted me."

My head shoots up and I stop walking. "He didn't trust you. You broke his daughter's heart."

"There's something I need to tell you." Marcus walks me to a nearby bench, and we sit down side by side. "After we broke up, before I left for law school, I went to see Graham at his office at the college. I confessed the truth about why I broke up with you."

My heart skips a beat. "What truth? You betrayed me by hooking up with my sister. My *sister*, of all people." I raise my voice and people around us stare. "Don't try to deny it, Marcus. I saw you kissing Layla with my own eyes."

He lets out a deep breath. "Okay, first of all, Layla kissed me. I didn't kiss her. She was in a mood that night. She was pissed because she didn't have a date to the party. As usual, you were her target."

I'm shocked, and yet I'm not. Vintage Layla. "Why didn't you tell me this then? You could've salvaged our relationship."

"Because I used the situation to make a clean break. I was a coward, Lil. I realized after we got engaged that I wanted to experience the world outside of Charleston before I got married. I never told you that I'd applied to law schools up north. When I got accepted at Columbia, I knew I would forever regret not going to New York."

"Did you ever consider taking me with you?"

He cocks an eyebrow at me. "Would you have gone?"

"Probably not, but it would've been nice if you'd asked. Then again, it would've been difficult for you to discover the real you with a wife hanging around." Leaning forward, elbows on knees, I stare across the marsh grass at the river. "So, all this time, I thought I was the one who broke off our engagement because you hooked up with my sister when it was all about you finding yourself."

"That's the thing, though. I wanted you to find yourself as well. I wanted you to get out from underneath the hold your sister had over you. I thought maybe, you being angry at Layla for kissing me would give you the nerve to stand up to her."

I snort. "I stood up to her, all right. And we've hardly spoken since then."

None of this makes any sense. I think back over the years. Dad comforted me in those dark days following my broken engagement, but he never once said a negative thing about Marcus. Why would he keep Marcus's confession to himself when he knew I would've forgiven Marcus if I'd known the truth? Because Dad was a man of honor, the greatest secret keeper of all times. He would never have betrayed Marcus. He loved Marcus like a son. And, because Dad would've agreed with Marcus that I needed time alone to sort out my relationship with my sister.

I straighten. "Whatever, Marcus. This is all ancient history. I have too much else on my plate to worry about this now."

"Talk to me, Lil. Maybe I can help."

I remove Dad's letter from my pocket and hand it to him, sitting quietly next to him while he reads it. He looks up when he's finished, his auburn brow knitted in confusion. "Sounds like Graham sent you on a wild goose chase."

"Yep. Pretty much. I need to find this truth he's talking about. Although I have no clue what Hemingway has to do with it. I've already turned Dad's study upside down. There's nothing there."

"What about the cottage? Doesn't he have a home office down there?"

I toss my hands in the air. "Of course! Why didn't I think about the cottage? He has an extensive Hemingway collection down there. Bigger even than here." I get up and walk away without saying goodbye.

"Hey!" Marcus calls after me. "Where're you going?"

"To Wadmalaw," I toss over my shoulder and take off running toward home.

LILLIAN

When I enter the house, I hear voices in the drawing room. While I appreciate the outpouring of sympathy from friends and neighbors, I'm in no mood for company. There's no way to bypass the drawing room to get to my bedroom. I hold my breath and hug the wall as I inch down the hall, but Layla spots me anyway.

"Lillian, come here! There's someone I want you to meet."

I exhale my breath with a sigh and reluctantly enter the room. A handsome man with the healthy glow of an outdoorsman crosses the room to greet me. "Nice to meet you, Lillian. I'm Bennett Calhoun." Elegantly dressed in poplin slacks and a knit polo, I estimate him to be in his forties despite his prematurely gray hair.

"Bennett's a Realtor," Layla explains. "He's here to talk to us about selling the house. I was just showing him around."

She crosses the room to Dad's study. She's reaching for the doorknob when I say, "I wouldn't go in there if I were you."

She swings the door open anyway, gasping at the sight of the mountain of books in the center of the room. "What the hell happened in here?"

"I was looking for something." I elbow her out of the way, pulling the door tight. I turn to the real estate agent. "My sister asked you here under false pretenses. The house isn't for sale."

Hands on hips, Layla let's out an exaggerated huff. "What're you talking about, Lil? The house is totally for sale."

My eyes remain on Bennett Calhoun. "Am I correct in assuming that, since Layla and I are joint owners of the house, you'll need both our consents to put it on the market?"

"That's correct." Although he does a good job of hiding it, I can tell by Calhoun's tone of voice that he's disappointed.

"Then we have a problem, because I'm not giving my consent." I leave the room without further discussion.

Upstairs in my room, I pack enough clothes for the weekend in a duffle bag and toss in my toiletry bag. Layla is still conversing with the real estate agent in the drawing room when I come back down. I sneak past them on my way out the back, and head to the utility room to retrieve my canvas tote bag. It contains the art supplies I used when I last painted weeks ago.

I throw my duffle and tote bag in the back of my Subaru and go in search of Trudy. I have a hunch of where to find her, and I'm right. She's in the hidden garden behind the carriage house clipping herbs.

From over the fence, I say, "Trudy, I'm going to Wadmalaw for the weekend."

She straightens slowly, grimacing as she places a hand on her back as though in pain. It's time for her to retire, to enjoy life while she still can.

"This is sudden," she says. "Is something wrong?"

"No, I just need to get away by myself for a while."

She removes her tattered straw hat and wipes the perspiration from her forehead with the back of her hand. "If you give me a minute, I'll pack you a cooler."

"No need. I'll stop at the grocery on the way."

A worried expression crosses her face. "When are you coming back?"

"I'm not sure. I'll call you. Don't worry, though. Everything's fine." I blow her a kiss. "By the way, I made a huge mess in Dad's study. Leave it. I'll clean it up when I get back."

The traffic is surprisingly light for an early Friday afternoon as I drive out of town. After crossing the Ashley River, I merge onto the highway and set my cruise control on seventy. I have no business chasing ghosts when I should be trying to save our house. If I'm not careful, my conniving sister will find a way to sell it out from under me. But I can't put the worms back in the can. And I have this nagging gut feeling the two are somehow related. That the search to find out more about my father's past and my mother's death will help me make the decisions regarding my uncertain future. Including what to do about the house.

I stop at the Food Lion on Johns Island for a few staples before continuing on to the island. Arriving a few minutes before one, I unload my car and place my perishable food items in the refrigerator. I take a container of strawberry Greek yogurt out to the porch and eat it while sitting on the steps and staring out at Bohicket Creek.

Our cottage is a two-story white frame farmhouse built in the early twentieth century and updated with modern conveniences in the mid-1980s. A center hallway separates casual living spaces downstairs while the second floor has four adequate size bedrooms. When we were growing up and my father was on summer break from the college, we spent Memorial Day to mid-August on the island. Those were the happiest days of my life, a reprieve from the constant bickering with Layla. We found it easier to tolerate each other down here with plenty of outdoor activities and our friends from neighboring cottages constantly coming and going. A feeling of dread settles over me at the thought of having to sell this place.

Setting the empty yogurt container on the wooden floor beside me, I hug my knees to my chest. My life is changing drastically, and I have no power to stop it. My father is gone. Trudy is retiring. And Layla will eventually return to Atlanta. Maybe I should do as Dad suggested and paint the world. But why would I do that when I'd rather be painting scenes of Charleston? Am I the only person on the planet not consumed by wanderlust?

The urge to paint hits me, and I set up my easel in the front yard. I've painted this scene dozens of times, but today, my canvas remains blank. I can't see the trees and marsh clearly from the flashbacks I'm having of days spent here with Dad. No one would ever buy a painting of a man pushing his pig-tailed daughter on a tire swing. Or would they?

I pack up my art supplies and change into my bikini. There are no boats on the water today. I dive off the end of the dock and swim back and forth across the creek until my restless energy is spent. Like a seal, I hoist myself out of the water and onto the dock. I stretch out on the warm wooden boards, and as the sun dries my body, my thoughts turn to Marcus.

Our wedding had been set for June of the year following our breakup that December. The invitations had been ordered, the save-the-date cards sent. I'd bought my wedding gown and planned the reception. Marcus had been accepted to law school at the University of South Carolina, and I'd been interviewing for jobs teaching art at area high schools. How differently our lives might have turned out if only he'd confided in me about his desire to go to college up north and his yearning to experience the world on his own. I loved him. I would've given him the space he needed. I can't deny that I still have feelings for him. I will always have feelings for him. But I'll never be able to trust him again. Him wanting me to stand up to my sister, to escape her hold over me, was nothing but a convenient excuse to ditch me.

With a slight breeze across my face and the waves gently lapping the side of the dock, I fall into a blissful sleep. When I wake again, the sun has begun its descent. I shower and dress in cutoff jean shorts and a sweatshirt. I make an omelet for dinner and eat it standing at the kitchen counter. After rinsing my plate, I turn on the coffee maker, and as I watch the slow stream fill the pot, I brace myself for a long night ahead.

I take my coffee to Dad's small office at the front of the house where, surprisingly, I find what I'm looking for in the third book on the shelf dedicated to Hemingway. In a hollowed-out, hardback copy of *For Whom the Bell Tolls*, I discover another note from Dad as well as a thumb drive marked with a Sharpie: *For Lillian.*

Instead of his creamy embossed stationery, this note is written on a folded sheet of notebook paper with jagged edges as though ripped from a composition book.

Dear Lillian,

I have written these pages to tell the story of my life with your mother. I began writing this memoir within days of her passing, and it has taken me nearly two decades to complete, 1,040 Sunday afternoons spent holed up in my study with my ghosts. You will find some events are more detailed while others skip through a longer span of time and deserve only a bird's eye view. I found the work therapeutic, enabling me to keep your mother alive in my mind and in my heart. I hope my story enables you to recall the events from the day your mother died and ultimately make peace with your sister.

Love,
Daddy

Between the Realtor's visit, which left me addled, and my eagerness to get to the island, I realize I'd forgotten to grab my laptop. Luckily, Dad's desktop is here. I sit down at his small pine desk and power on the computer. Several years ago, when he upgraded his hardware in Charleston, he brought this old desktop down here. It was antiquated at the time. It's a dinosaur now. When the machine finally comes to life, I insert the thumb drive into the tower. The drive contains only one PDF file titled *My Life with Ivy*.

I open the file and begin to read.

GRAHAM

AUGUST 1984

*M*y first official duty as newcomer to the faculty was to attend the annual reception celebrating the kickoff of another year of academia. The crowd—made up of teaching staff, administration, and benefactors—was packed together like sardines inside the president's home, the oldest building on the College of Charleston's campus. The cacophony of animated voices and laughter grew louder with each round of alcohol consumed.

I spoke with the few professors I knew and the distinguished head of our illustrious English department as I inched my way through the crowd to the patio. Exiting the french doors, I met with a wall of heavy air. A New Englander by birth, I had not yet acclimated to the oppressive heat and humidity of the Lowcountry.

Draining the last of my drink, I crossed the patio to the linen-draped bar table. I was waiting patiently in line for a drink when a man stumbled into the gentleman standing next to me. The gentleman lost his balance and fell into me, the last of the amber liquid in his glass sloshing down the front of my white Oxford shirt. The gentleman wiped at my shirt with his cocktail napkin, but instead of sopping up the liquid, he made the stain bigger.

"Sorry, my boy. This function is entirely too crowded for my liking. President Collins invites more and more people every year." The gentleman took a closer look at me. "But you wouldn't know that, because you're new here."

I squint at him from behind round metal eyeglass frames. "How'd you know that?"

"I read my alumni mail." The man extended his hand. "Edward Stoney, class of 1946."

I remembered seeing the Stoney name chiseled in the stone on one of the academic buildings during my campus tour. "Of course, Mr. Stoney. I'm Graham Alexander. Delighted to meet you."

"Please, call me Edward."

When it was our turn at the bar, we moved forward together, placing our drink orders with the uniformed bartender —Glenlivet on the rocks for Edward and vodka tonic for me. Cocktails in hand, we stepped away from the drinks table to the edge of the patio. Edward studied the crowd while I studied him. With a headful of thick salt-and-pepper hair and skin leathered from years in the sun, I guessed him to be around sixty. He wore his gray beard closely trimmed and wrinkles gathered at the corners of his deep blue eyes.

Edward shifted his attention from the crowd to me. "If my memory serves me correctly, you're a Harvard man."

"Yes, sir. After graduating from Harvard, I continued on there for several years as an associate professor before taking the job here."

Edward leaned back against the lattice brick wall as though settling in for a long conversation. "Why the College of Charleston?"

I felt as though I was being interviewed all over again. I gave him my well-rehearsed answer. "A smaller college means less competition, which equates to more opportunity for promotion."

Edward clapped my shoulder. "I applaud your ambition. If I remember correctly, you're with the English department."

"That's right. I have a master's degree in Liberal Arts. I teach American literature and an introductory course in creative writing."

Edward smiled. "Good man. I'm a fan of American literature. Who's your favorite author?"

Without hesitation, I said, "Hemingway. And yours?"

"Mark Twain, although I have great admiration for Tennessee Williams as well."

A stunning woman appeared at Edward's side. She was way too young to be his wife. Was this exotic creature his daughter?

Tugging on the sleeve of his seersucker sport coat, she said, "Are you ready to go now, Daddy?"

Edward patted her arm. "Not yet, sweetheart. We just got here. I'd like you to meet our newest member of the English department. Graham Alexander, meet my daughter, Ivy."

Ivy gave my proffered hand a firm shake. She wore the casual elegance of the extremely wealthy in a navy linen sundress, but there was an innocence about her that fascinated me. She was fresh faced and vibrant, as though spawned from the earth, a goddess from the sea with the long, tanned limbs of an athlete and a thick mane of wavy blonde hair.

Never before had I experienced such an instant attraction to a woman. When she turned her lovely face up at me and her deep blue eyes met mine, a fluttering sensation danced across my chest.

"When do classes start, Professor? "she said with a hint of a smirk on her rosy lips. She was totally flirting with me. But I had no doubt but what she flirted with every member of the opposite sex.

"On Monday. And, please, call me Graham . . . unless, of

course, you're a student." The thought of having this magnificent woman in one of my classes sent a trail of perspiration down my back. "*Are* you a student here?"

She let out a high-pitched shriek of laughter that some would think obnoxious, but I found infectious. "I'm way too old to be in college."

"You can't be that old. Certainly no more than twenty-five." Now I was the one flirting.

She jutted her chin out at me. "I'll have you know, I turned twenty-eight on June fourteenth. I'm one of those crazy Geminis."

A stupid grin spread across my face. "What a coincidence! I'm a Gemini as well. My birthday is June seventh."

Her blue eyes twinkled. "We're kindred spirits. We'll have to celebrate together next June."

I relished the idea that we'd be friends next summer. If all the stars aligned, perhaps we'd even be lovers.

"Your father and I were discussing American literature before you joined us," I said. "Do you have a favorite author?"

Ivy tapped her chin. "Hmm, let's see. If we're talking classics, I actually prefer British to American. But I'm a bigger fan of more contemporary literature like Pat Conroy. Do you know Conroy's work, Graham?"

"Only by name. He's much revered by my colleagues. One of them lent me a copy of *The Lords of Discipline,* although I've been too busy preparing for classes to read any of it."

Ivy looped her arm through her father's, leaning in close to him. "Conroy is a friend of Daddy's. They go way back."

Edward kissed the top of his daughter's head. "My daughter is exaggerating, as she so loves to do. I knew Conroy briefly when he was at The Citadel."

She looked up at Edward adoringly. "And my father is being his humble self. Conroy dined at our house several years ago when he was in town."

Meeting Pat Conroy in person would make me the envy of my department. "I'd love to meet him sometime."

"He's a busy man," Edward said. "Perhaps we can work it out the next time he's in town."

We were interrupted by an older couple who stopped to speak to the Stoneys. When Edward introduced them to me, I recognized their name as yet another of the college's generous benefactors.

Once the older couple had moved on, out of the blue, Ivy suggested her father take me sailing sometime.

Edward's face lit up at the idea. "You're right. I should. I assume you sail since you're from Boston. Where'd you spend your summers, Graham? The Cape? Martha's Vineyard? Or are you a Nantucket guy?"

I'd learned early on at Harvard that it was best to say the least. "I've spent a fair amount of time at all three." Which wasn't a lie. I'd frequently gone with friends to their family cottages for long weekends during the summers.

"What you don't know, I'll teach you," Edward said. "Any chance you're free tomorrow?"

I considered my agenda, the back-to-back faculty meetings that made up most of my morning and early afternoon. "Not until later in the day. Around four."

"Four is perfect," Edward said. "According to the forecast, the wind is expected to pick up late afternoon."

Ivy brought her fingertips to her lips, pretending to stifle a yawn. "That's my cue to leave you gentlemen to make your plans."

"So soon?" Edward asked, visibly disappointed. "Where are you heading off to?"

"To meet Alice and some others at East Bay Trading."

"Can we count on you for sailing tomorrow?" Edward asked.

"Sorry, Daddy, but I can't. I'm already playing tennis. But I'll join you for dinner afterward. That is, if Graham is free."

What fool would turn up the chance to dine with Ivy Stoney? "I'm available. I'd like that very much. Thank you."

As Edward and I watched Ivy's tall form disappear into the crowd, I said, "I admire her spontaneity."

Edward chuckled. "Spontaneity? My daughter has no impulse control whatsoever." He then turned to me and said, "So, we have a date for tomorrow. We'll meet at my house at four." He recited his address and I jotted it down in the small notepad I kept in my pocket for ideas that often popped into my head.

We chatted for a few more minutes before parting. After saying goodnight to my host, I cut through Porter's Lodge, the arched entrance to the Cistern Yard, and made my way across campus to the house I shared with three other unmarried faculty members. I was ashamed of myself. I'd moved to South Carolina to start a new life. I was tired of hiding from my past. I was a fraud, pretending to be a man of wealth and privilege when I was nothing more than the son of a poor lobsterman from Maine. I'd been acting the role for so long I'd totally lost sight of the real me. Problem was, I feared the real me was a very boring person. What did I have to offer the world except my knowledge and appreciation of literature? Men like Edward Stoney didn't have time for paupers like me. I certainly wasn't the kind of man he wanted for his daughter.

But I was good at pretending, and Edward Stoney was in an excellent position to further my career. What harm would come from one sailing expedition? Besides, I was thrilled to have the opportunity to see Ivy Stoney again.

Edward was waiting for me at the wrought iron gate at the end of his driveway when I arrived promptly at four o'clock the following afternoon. We were dressed similarly in khaki shorts, polo shirts, and deck shoes. But he was a dashing captain in aviator sunglasses with his gray beard and pipe clinched between his teeth while I was merely his lowly deckhand.

"Ready, mate?" he said. "I'm eager to get out on the water."

Without waiting for my reply, he took off north on East Battery, and I had to work hard to keep up with his long stride during the short walk to the Charleston Yacht Club. His sail-boat was a mint-conditioned 1973 thirty-five-foot sloop cruiser that bore the trademark navy hull and teak trim of the Hinckley brand.

With majestic sails flapping in the wind, we glided across the smooth waters of the Charleston Harbor to Fort Sumter where the first shots of the Civil War were fired. Venturing farther, we skimmed the coast of Sullivan's Island, which provided an up-close look at the series of fortifications that made up Fort Moultrie.

Upon our returned to the yacht club, we swabbed the decks with soapy water and dried the chrome railings to prevent them from spotting. It was nearing seven o'clock by the time we retraced our steps to the Stoney's home.

As a history enthusiast, I was thrilled with the opportunity to tour one of the magnificent antebellum houses on the Battery. We entered through the main front door on the southern side of the house and climbed a wide flight of stairs to the second floor. Passing through the drawing room, which was appointed with fourteen-foot ceilings and European antiques, we exited onto a wide veranda, known to Charlestonians as a piazza. A grouping of wicker furniture—loveseat, rockers, and coffee table—made up one end of the porch while a marble-topped table, set for dinner with linens and flatware, occupied the other.

I was so drawn in by the panoramic view of the harbor, I failed to notice a uniformed black woman hovering nearby with a tray of drinks until she cleared her throat. "May I offer you a drink, sir?"

As she extended her tray to me, Edward said, "I hope I remembered correctly that you were drinking vodka and tonic at the reception last night. If you prefer something else—"

"Not at all. Vodka tonic is perfect." I smiled at the woman as I lifted the sweating silver tumbler off the tray. Her skin was the color of butter toffee and her warm smile set me at ease.

Edward accepted his drink from her. "Trudy, I'd like you to meet our college's newest professor of American literature, Graham Alexander. Graham, this is the love of my life, Trudy Jackson."

Trudy cut her brown eyes at him. "You know better than to talk like that in front of your guest. You're liable to scare the poor man away."

Edward rested a hand on her bony shoulder. "Once Graham samples your cooking, I'll never get rid of him. Trudy's the best cook South of Broad. I stole her away from my neighbor down the street. Had to double her wages to get her to come work for me."

"Mister Edward is telling a big fat fib. I've lived in this house all my life and worked for this family almost as long."

"That's truly remarkable," I said.

Edward's demeanor sobered. "My wife, Virginia, died giving birth to Ivy." He gave Trudy's neck a squeeze. "Ivy and I would never have survived without Trudy and her parents, Hazel and Herbert, God rest their souls."

I was taken aback at the mention of Edward's wife's death. I'd assumed Mrs. Stoney would be joining us for dinner.

Pressing the back of her hand to her eyes, Trudy tucked the tray under her arm. "Excuse me. I need to check on dinner."

When she entered the house, Edward called after her, "What's for dinner, by the way?"

Trudy's muffled response came from within. "Shrimp and grits."

I shake my head in disbelief. "Grits again. I've been in South Carolina for a month now, and I still don't understand the obsession for grits."

Edward laughed. "You will when you sample Trudy's grits. They're stone-ground and slow-cooked with heavy cream and butter."

Edward and I stood side by side at the railing in companionable silence while we sipped our cocktails. As a gentle ocean breeze ruffled my salt-crusted hair, I had an odd sense of déjà vu, as though I'd come home after a long journey.

Trudy returned with the dinner cart and a much younger maid wearing the same black dress and white apron. Edward and I sat down opposite each other and waited while the maid placed three silver-domed plates on the table.

Eyeing the third place setting, Edward said, "Any word from Ivy?"

"Yes, sir," Trudy said. "She just got home from playing tennis. She'll be down soon."

Trudy had no sooner spoken the words than Ivy arrived on the piazza dressed in madras shorts and a pink polo, her hair still damp from the shower. She said a friendly hello to me and kissed the top of her father's head before sliding into the chair between us.

"This looks delicious, Trudy. Thank you." She smiled up at Trudy before shifting her gaze to her father. "And before you ask, no, I did not beat Alice."

"But you will," Edward said in a confident tone. "Eventually."

"You've been saying that since Alice and I took our first tennis lesson at age seven. We need to face the fact that *eventually* may never come in this case."

"O ye of little faith," Edward said.

Ivy snorted. "O me of facing reality."

As I witnessed the exchange between father and daughter, I couldn't help but wonder how difficult it must have been for Edward to raise Ivy alone. From what I'd seen, which admittedly wasn't much, he'd done an exemplary job. "Who's Alice?" I asked.

"My best friend." Ivy snapped her linen napkin open as though challenging a bull. "She's good enough to take the US Open title from Martina Navratilova."

Edward laughed out loud. "You give her too much credit. You've defeated every other female tennis player in the city of Charleston. You're letting your obsession with beating Alice get to you, mentally." He tapped his temple.

"You're probably right. Let's talk about something else." She stuffed a shrimp in her mouth. "Actually, before we move on from the subject of Alice, she invited me to spend Labor Day with her family on Sullivan's Island. Can I go?"

Edward maintained his composure, but his disappointment was evident in the deepened creases around his eyes. "You're a grown woman, sweetheart. You don't need my approval. I'll be awfully lonely without you, though."

"Wadmalaw is just so rustic," she said, some of the enthusiasm gone from her voice. "Sullivan's is much more civilized. I wouldn't mind so much if you'd update the plumbing and electrical."

Edward scooped up a forkful of grits. "The cottage is fine the way it is."

"I've got a great idea," Ivy said. "Why doesn't Graham come with us for Labor Day?"

I nearly choked on a shrimp. *So now she wants to go to Wadma-Whatever-Wherever? And she wants me to go with her?* The rapid rate at which Ivy changed her mind gave me whiplash. I sat in stunned silence as she babbled on.

"I assume that since you're an English professor, you like to read. Be sure to bring a stack of books. If you have any papers to grade, bring those too. There's not much to do on the island except watch the grass grow."

"There's plenty to do," Edward said. "Fishing, swimming, sailing, tennis."

Ivy tossed her hands in the air theatrically. "Great! More tennis. Maybe Graham will take pity on me and let me beat him."

Edward dabbed at his lips with his linen napkin. "Slow down, Ivy. Graham hasn't accepted your invitation yet. If you want to call that an invitation."

Ivy's neck snapped as her gaze darted from her father to me. Pressing her hands together, she said, "Say you'll come, Graham. We'll have so much fun. I promise."

I smiled. A minute ago, she was complaining about their island being boring. "Count me in. I'm sure we'll have a wonderful time. And don't worry. You won't have to work very hard to beat me." While I didn't particularly care for chasing a yellow ball around, I would make the sacrifice if it meant seeing Ivy's long legs in a short white skirt.

"Awesome!" Ivy said, coming up out of her chair a little.

In a warning tone, Edward said, "Don't expect anything fancy, though. We'll have to fend for ourselves without the staff. Trudy and her husband, Isaac, are taking their little girl to visit her family in Beaufort and the rest of the staff has the weekend off."

We talked on about the upcoming holiday weekend while we devoured our main course. Trudy appeared with a Key lime pie for dessert, but when she tried to serve Ivy a slice, Ivy held up her hand in protest.

"None for me, Trudy. I'm already late for a meeting." Popping the last piece of cornbread in her mouth, she pushed back from the table, handed her empty plate to Trudy, and disappeared inside.

I watched her go. "What kind of meeting does she have at this time of night?"

Edward rested against the back of his chair with his hands clasped on top of his stomach. "She's involved in a lot of volunteer work. She's currently helping to plan the Junior League's fall festival they hold every year for underprivileged children in Charleston. I imagine this meeting has something to do with that."

"Does she have a full-time career?" I asked, and then realized I was being rude. "I'm sorry. That's none of my business."

"Not at all, my friend. We're an open book around here. After graduating from Sweetbriar in Virginia, Ivy studied to become a paralegal. She even got a job in a local law office." Edward laughed. "But that didn't last long."

From her pushcart where she was slicing pie, Trudy chuckled under her breath. "Sitting behind a desk all day is not my Ivy's cup of tea."

"She's like a hummingbird, dropping in for nectar at one party before moving on to the next." Leaning across the table toward me, in a teasing tone with a serious face, Edward added, "Something you should know about my daughter. She's always well-intentioned, but her impulsive, devil-may-care personality often lands her in trouble."

I let out an awkward laugh. "That sounds like a warning."

Edward nodded. "It is. Of sorts. I say this with sincere affection, but if you let her, Ivy will rope you into robbing a bank."

I experienced firsthand Ivy's devil-may-care attitude during Labor Day weekend on Wadmalaw Island. But she was so much fun to be around, I would volunteer anytime to be her partner in crime. She was too slender to have much of a figure, but her graceful limbs and powerful strokes in action were a sight to behold. A great blue heron cutting back and forth across the wake on waterskies. A cheetah chasing down tennis balls on the hard court behind their cottage. She was an excellent player. While I gave her a good match, she beat me in straight sets.

As for the cottage, she'd been right about it needing updating, but despite the outdated plumbing and electrical, I found everything about the house and surrounding property charming. Built in the late 1830s, the clapboard two-story farmhouse boasted sunshine-yellow shutters and a central hallway to allow salt-infused breezes to flow through from front to back when the doors were open, which they almost always were. Live oaks sprawled across the landscape from the house to the dock, while beyond the body of water known as Bohicket Creek, a lush green marsh was home for numerous wildlife species.

Because we were in constant motion during the day, we went to bed early at night and slept late in the mornings. We ate eggs, bacon, and biscuits for brunch, and cooked hotdogs and hamburgers on the grill every night.

"Have you started *The Lords of Discipline* yet?" Ivy asked me on our last night on the island.

Our bellies stuffed with s'mores, we were gliding to and fro on the bench swing on the wide front porch. Edward had retired right after dinner, which came as no surprise to either of us. For much of the weekend, he'd seemed content to let Ivy and me have all the fun while he lazed in the hammock, reading the summer's blockbuster novel, *The Hunt for Red October* by Tom Clancy.

"I'm halfway through, as a matter of fact. I'd hoped to finish over the weekend, but despite your claim that there isn't much to do on the island, I've been anything but bored since arriving."

She raised a sun-bleached eyebrow. "And? Are you enjoying it?"

We'd talked a lot about literature over the past two days. As with everything else, Ivy had turned our discussions into contests to see which of us knew the most. I beat her every time in this competition, but that didn't prevent her from trying.

"Very much. I plan to read some of Conroy's other novels."

Ivy sent an elbow crashing to my ribs. "See! I told you."

"You were right. Conroy's poetic way with words allows me a greater appreciation for the Lowcountry's wildlife and scenery."

"You're exactly right. Having lived here all my life, I take all of this for granted." Ivy spread her arms wide. "Conroy reminds me to stop and study the beauty around me."

"Are his protagonists always so preachy? Will McLean's soliloquies get tiresome at times, if you know what I mean." On the other hand, and I wouldn't admit this to Ivy, but Conroy's leading man in *The Lords of Discipline* was affording me a better understanding of the mindset of the honorable Southern gentleman.

She stared up at the porch ceiling while she gave this a moment's thought. "I agree about that particular character. But all of his books are different. You, being a teacher, might want to read *The Water is Wide* next. It's a memoir of Conroy's early days as a teacher on Daufuskie Island, an island down near Hilton Head." She settled back on the swing. "What's it like being a professor, being responsible for imparting your vast wisdom to impressionable minds?"

I burst into laughter. "Imparting my vast wisdom," I repeated. "I'll have to remember that the next time one of my students asks me a question I can't answer."

Ivy rolled her eyes. "As if that ever happens."

"It hasn't happened yet, but I'm certain it will." I thought back over my first week of classes. "The teaching part is everything I'd hoped it would be. But, as it turns out, I was worried about all the wrong things."

She angled her body toward mine. "How so?"

"Well . . . I was concerned I'd have trouble finding my voice in the classroom, to express my love for literature in an organized fashion so as to impart said wisdom to my students. Surprisingly, though, that part has come easy. At least for the handful of students who come to class regularly. The biggest obstacle I face is attendance. Based on my experiences as an assistant professor at Harvard, I designed a rigorous attendance policy. They get three unexcused cuts before I penalize them. So far, the kids aren't taking me seriously, but they'll learn soon enough, when midterm grades come out."

She raised a balled fist. "That's the fighting spirit. They can't learn if they don't come to class."

I smile at her enthusiasm. "Let me guess. You were a straight A student."

Her chin high, Ivy said, "From kindergarten all the way through college."

"You have your fair share of wisdom to impart. Have you ever considered teaching?"

"I have, actually. I love children. Elementary school would be my preference." Her body sagged. "I doubt parents would be thrilled about turning over their little darlings to a space cadet like me."

"What're you talking about, Ivy? I don't think of you as a space cadet."

"I am, though. I have a terrible time staying focused. That's why volunteering works for me. If I grow bored with one project, I move on to the next. And I get to hang out with my friends. Or I used to. Before they all started getting married and having babies."

Her expression was guarded, and I couldn't tell if she envied her friends their marriage and children or resented them for abandoning her.

"Why aren't you married, Ivy? Pretty girl like you, surely you've had marriage proposals."

She inched closer to me. "Do you really think I'm pretty, Graham?

I smiled. "I think you're fishing for compliments. You're pretty, and you know it." She was not only beautiful on the outside, her inner beauty, her joy for life, shown from within, surrounding her like a halo. Although she was no angel. "I'm sure you've had a long string of boyfriends."

"Plenty of dates. No serious boyfriends. Every time I get interested in a guy, I find myself comparing him to my father. So far, none have ever measured up."

I'm curious what the poor saps lacked that prevented them from measuring up to her father. But before I could ask, she leaped off the swing. "Let's go for a swim." She sprinted across the small lawn and down the dock, stripping off her clothes along the way. She dove into the water and emerged twenty feet away, the light from the moon shimmering on the water around her.

When I dove in naked after her, she paddled backward, splashing me when I got too close. "Keep your distance, Graham Alexander, else I'll holler for help at the top of my lungs."

I laughed out loud. "Need I remind you, Miss Stoney, that you started this?"

She splashed me again. "Because I got caught up in the moment. I forgot you were a man."

"You forgot I was a man?" I repeated, insulted. "What did you take me for? If you say a woman, I'll drown you right here and now."

She looked away from me, as though embarrassed. In a soft

voice, she said, "I thought you were a friend. Maybe I was wrong?"

And I thought she was a tease. Either that or extremely naive. She'd been toying with me all weekend, flirting one minute and being an ice princess the next. I found her irresistible, and whatever game she was playing, while maddening, intrigued me.

"Not at all," I said. "I'd like very much to be your friend."

She splashed me again. "And I'd like for you to go inside before I call my daddy."

My hands shot out of the water. "I'm going!" I turned and swam back to the dock.

GRAHAM

$\mathcal{A}$s we moved from summer into autumn, Edward and I established a standing date for Thursdays to go sailing late afternoon and have dinner together afterward. Out on the water, we sometimes spoke of current events and politics, but for the most part, we sailed along in companionable silence. I used the time to reflect on my performance in the classroom, what was working and how I could become better engaged with my students.

I especially looked forward to the fleeting moments with Ivy over dinner, when she dropped in long enough to gobble down her food before rushing off to a meeting or to join friends at one of the downtown bars for drinks. While she continued to flirt shamelessly with me, I accepted the fact that if she was romantically interested in me, she wouldn't run off before dessert.

I was shocked when, one day in mid-October, Edward prompted me to ask Ivy for a date.

"I can tell you're interested," he said. "I've seen the way you look at her."

A thunderstorm with severe lighting and driving rain had forced us in off the water, and we were sipping cocktails in

Edward's study while waiting for dinner in the dining room. I hung my head in response to Edward's suggestion. "I don't think she's interested in me that way."

He raised his hands, palms up, as if to say who knows. "Maybe she is. Maybe she isn't. I gave up trying to figure my daughter out a long time ago. She sure does flirt with you an awful lot."

"I assumed that was her nature. Is she not like that with everyone?"

Edward considered his answer. "Only with people she admires and trusts. Ask her to the movies or out for pizza. So what if she says no? At least you tried."

I left the plush velvet sofa and crossed the Oriental rug to the bookshelves lining the walnut-paneled walls. Removing a hardback copy of Stephen King's *Salem's Lot*, I opened the front cover and read the handwritten inscription from King to Edward. "You know Stephen King?"

"I met him at a friend's house in Nantucket one summer," Edward said. "But you're avoiding the subject at hand."

Returning the book to the shelf, I faced Edward. "If I ask Ivy out and she says no, won't that ruin our friendship?"

"Not at all. Ivy's not one to let things like that get to her."

"I'll think about it," I said, but I'd already made up my mind. Edward had all but given his blessing. If he thought I had a chance with Ivy, I was totally going to ask her for a date.

When Trudy called us to dinner, we proceeded through the drawing room into the formal dining room, taking our seats in ladder-back chairs at one end of the mahogany table. This was my first time in the dining room, and I couldn't take my eyes off the oil portrait of Ivy hanging above the sideboard, a twenty-one-year-old rendition of her lovely self fittingly composed in the natural habitat at Wadmalaw island.

Seconds later, I was still staring at the painting with a lovesick expression on my face when Ivy, raincoat dripping wet and hair hanging in damp strands around her face, stuck her head in the doorway. "Y'all start without me. I need to change into dry clothes."

Trudy and one of her many assistants arrived promptly with the dinner cart. They were serving warmed plates of fried pork chops, crispy okra, and brown rice when Ivy returned, dressed like one of my students in jeans and a gray University of Virginia sweatshirt, her wet hair tied back in a high ponytail.

While we ate, Ivy monopolized the conversation with talk of Alice's new love interest. She'd met Heath Jordan for the first time earlier in the evening over drinks at East Bay Trading. "He rubs me the wrong way," she said. "I can't decide whether I simply dislike him or whether I question his feelings for Alice."

Edward said, "If Alice likes him, you should give him the benefit of the doubt until he proves otherwise."

"I guess you're right." She pushed back from the table. "If you'll excuse—"

Edward stood abruptly. "I've just remembered I need to make a quick phone call. Ivy, darling, do me a favor and sit with Graham until I'm through."

This was my cue to ask Ivy for a date, and I waited for Edward to leave the room before casually broaching the subject. "The new movie *Amadeus* has gotten rave reviews. Would you like to see it with me this weekend?"

She toyed with her strand of pearls. "Me? But what about Daddy? I'm sure he'll go with you."

Placing my clasped hands on the table, I addressed her as one might a child. "But I didn't ask your father. I'm asking you."

Her eyes brows shot to her hairline. "You mean like on a date?"

I smiled. "Yes, like on a date. What about tomorrow night?"

Ivy's eyes darted about the room as though searching for an escape. Her unease confirmed my suspicions about her lack of interest in me. "I can't tomorrow night. I have a friend's birthday dinner."

I pressed her. I had nothing to lose. "What about Saturday night?"

"Sorry. Daddy and I watch football on Saturdays." I was about to give up when she surprised me by saying, "But we could go to an early matinee, and you could come back here with me afterward to watch football."

And so, our courtship began with Edward as our chaperone. During the weeks that followed, I felt as though I was dating both father and daughter. My few stolen moments alone with Ivy consisted of goodnight pecks on the lips. While my desire for her was fierce, I was completely besotted and willing to wait as long as necessary.

I spent Thanksgiving with the Stoneys, gorging myself on Trudy's roast turkey and all the traditional side dishes. That weekend marked the beginning of a seemingly endless round of holiday cocktail parties to which I was included. I met Alice and her now-steady beau for the first time that Saturday night at an informal gathering in honor of the state's annual football rivalry between the University of South Carolina Gamecocks and the Clemson Tigers. Ivy had described Alice as exotic with curly auburn hair, creamy complexion, and green eyes. But I found her hair orange, her complexion washed out, and her hazel eyes lifeless. Heath was plump and a good two inches shorter than Alice, but his seemingly jovial personality made up for what he lacked in looks.

After the round of introductions were made, Ivy scurried me away to the TV room in the back of the house. During the game, she sulked for no apparent reason, and nothing I said could lighten her mood. But when I returned from using the restroom after the game ended, I found Alice and Ivy standing off to themselves, whispering and giggling like schoolgirls. Ivy's animosity toward Heath became apparent to me in that moment. She didn't doubt his feelings for Alice or dislike him for any reason. She was jealous of him for monopolizing Alice's time.

"I'm glad to see you're feeling better," I said to Ivy as I approached them.

"I'm happy because the Gamecocks won, Graham." She held her hand out to Alice. "And you owe me twenty dollars."

Alice slapped her hand. "I was rooting for the Gamecocks all along. You know I hate the Tigers. You insisted I bet against you." Cupping her hand around her mouth, Alice whispered to me loud enough for Ivy to hear. "Everything's a competition with her."

Ivy gave me a sheepish grin. She looked adorable in an Icelandic sweater and blue jeans, a wide navy headband holding her golden hair back from her face.

"Don't I know it," I said with a laugh. "She beats me every time at tennis. She pedals harder and faster on a bicycle. And she can man a sailboat better than Edward. I consider myself an excellent shot, but I refuse to go hunting with them for fear she'll show me up."

"You'll have to get over that, Graham," Alice said. "Every Southern gentleman hunts."

"I'm not Southern. And I'm no gentleman," I said in a teasing tone. "Truth be told, though, I've killed enough ducks and geese with my college friends to last a lifetime. And freezing my ass off in a duck blind at daybreak is not my idea of fun."

Alice laughed. "I know what you mean. Heath keeps begging me to go with him, but I prefer to leave the hunting to the men."

Ivy's face turned sour. "You've been hunting with me before."

Alice leaned into her. "And I hated every minute of it."

Heath joined their threesome, handing Alice a glass of red wine. His adoration of her was written all over his ruddy face.

Originally from Raleigh and a graduate of the University of North Carolina at Chapel Hill, Heath, now an investment adviser for high-net-worth individuals, was making a reputation for himself among the Charleston elite. While Alice and Ivy carried on their own private conversation, Heath and I moved from one topic to the next with relative ease. By the end of the night, I felt as though I'd made my first true friend since moving to Charleston. Aside from Edward, of course, whom I thought of more as a mentor than a friend.

I was exhausted by the time I'd finished administering exams and posting grades. It was the Friday before Christmas, which would fall on the following Tuesday of that year, and all the students and my roommates had left campus for the holidays. I'd been looking forward to having the house to myself, but with everyone gone and our two weeks of vacation stretching out ahead of me, I felt lonely and restless.

I deemed my first semester as a college professor a success, and I admitted as much to Edward that evening when I arrived at their house for drinks prior to the evening's event. "According to our registration department, all of my classes for the spring semester are full. Many of them even have waitlists."

Edward clinked his glass against mine. "Good man. I knew you'd be a success."

We were in the drawing room, admiring Ivy's and Trudy's work. They'd spent untold hours decorating the twelve-foot Christmas tree with mini-colored lights and generations of the Stoney family's treasured ornaments. I felt like a college student in my worn blue blazer and khaki pants standing next to Edward, the epitome of good taste in what Ivy referred to as his elf suit—a green wool sport coat and gray flannel pants embroidered with holly leaves.

Ivy was upstairs dressing for what was reported to be the largest and most elaborate of the season's parties being held at Alice's parents' house on Legare Street. The Browders were rumored to have more money than Edward, if that was even possible, and I was looking forward to visiting their home.

"When are you heading to Boston for Christmas?" Edward asked.

I still hadn't told him I was from Maine, not Massachusetts. It was an explanation I wanted to avoid for as long as possible. "Actually, I'm staying in Charleston for Christmas."

Lines creased Edward's forehead. "Really? I assumed you would be visiting your folks."

"I'm not close with my family, Edward," I said in a curt tone, hoping to discourage him from pushing me for more details.

"Family is family, Graham. Close or not, you should spend Christmas with them."

"I don't like to talk about my family, Edward. I have few happy memories of my childhood."

In a stern voice, he said, "If you're going to date my daughter, I need to know about your family." He glanced at the mantel clock. "We have time." He led me over to the sofa and we sat down side by side.

Edward's jaw was set in determination. There was no escaping. The time had finally come to have the dreaded conversation. While I was afraid it would spoil the festive mood, I was ready to put an end to the charade. I'd felt like a phony these past months, dining in grand style and attending elaborate parties as though I were one of them.

I looked away from him. I couldn't bear to see his disappointment when I told him the truth. "I didn't hail from Boston aristocracy as I led you to believe. My father is a lobster fisherman from Maine. A mean son of a bitch who took his unhappiness with his life out on his wife and five kids."

Edward sat back on the sofa, crossing his legs. "Go on."

I'd rehearsed in my mind what I'd say to him when the time came, and I let the words spill from my lips while I had the courage. "I was a good student, unlike my four older brothers. While they were stealing cars and getting girlfriends pregnant, I was using my brain to forge a better life for myself. I went to Harvard on scholarship. I studied my classmates and learned to mimic their speech and mannerisms and the way they interacted with one another. They invited me home with them for the holidays to Connecticut and New York and to Nantucket and Martha's Vineyard for long summer weekends. They assumed, and I never corrected them, that I was like them."

I paused to sip my vodka and tonic. "I got the worst beating from my father, not as a child, although there were plenty back then, but as a young man. When I graduated from Harvard, I invited my parents to the ceremony. I'd worked so hard, and I wanted them to acknowledge what I'd accomplished. I felt I needed their approval to validate the life I'd chosen. When they failed to show, I drove home to Maine the following weekend to visit them. When I asked my father why they didn't come to graduation, he turned on me. He called me a candy-ass coward. He said I should be working with my hands instead of my head. That I'm no better than him. That I come from a long line of blue-collared workers, and I should stop trying to be someone I'm not. He beat me senseless that night. Broke three ribs. Blackened both my eyes. Split open my temple." I pointed at the scar above my left eyebrow. "I crawled out of our house that night and drove myself to the nearest hospital. An ER doctor, a wise old man who'd seen more than his share of sorrow, patched me up and sent me on my way. He told me to live my life for me and the rest will fall into place. I haven't spoken to anyone in my family since that night. Turns out he was right. I am a candy-ass coward for not fighting back."

Edward, his face softer now, said, "Gentlemen don't fight with their fists, Graham."

"I'm no gentleman, Edward. My dad was right about one thing. I shouldn't try to be someone I'm not. I'm tired of hiding. I came to South Carolina hoping to start anew, a fresh slate where I could merge my past and present into my future. But then I met you and Ivy and . . ." My voice trailed off.

Edward got up and refilled our glasses. "Did you not feel you could be yourself with me?"

"If I'd told you my father was a lobsterman when we first met at the president's reception, would you have invited me to go sailing with you?"

Edward handed me back my glass, but he remained standing. "Probably not. Which makes me an insufferable snob."

"You're not a snob, Edward." Unlike some of the pompous asses I knew in college, Edward possessed the quiet confidence of a man who'd never had to worry about money. He never put on airs. Was never unkind to anyone. And he was always willing to lend a helping hand. He was the real deal, a true gentleman.

Edward went over to the fireplace and began stabbing the logs with a brass poker. "I'm disappointed, Graham. Not that you misled me into believing you came from a wealthy family, but that you didn't trust me to tell me the truth."

I hung my head. "I know, sir. And I'm sorry."

He jabbed at another log. "I'm sorry too, Graham. For what you went through as a child. I don't blame you for disowning your father, and I admire you for working hard to make a better life for yourself. We will not speak of your family again unless you bring them up. I assume Ivy doesn't know any of this."

"No, sir." I doubted Ivy would be as understanding as her father.

"I'll let you decide when the time is right, but at some point, I'll expect you to tell Ivy the truth."

"I will, sir."

"I want you to feel like you can be yourself in my home." He turned to face me. "Spend Christmas with us. I'll have Trudy make up the guest room first thing in the morning. You can move in tomorrow and stay through New Year's. We'll have a wonderful time."

Relief washed over me that Edward wasn't kicking me to the curb, and that I wouldn't have to spend Christmas alone in my dismal rental house. "I'd like that very much, Edward. Thank you."

Ivy glided into the drawing room in an elegant long-sleeved black velvet dress that hugged her slim figure. "You look stunning, my dear," Edward said, taking her by the hand and giving her a ballerina spin.

She plopped down on the sofa so close to me she was nearly in my lap. "Did I overhear correctly? Will you be spending Christmas with us, Graham?"

I touched the tip of my finger to the end of her nose. "If that's all right with you."

She batted her mascaraed eyelashes at me. "Better than all right. We'll have so much fun."

I longed to be alone with her, to hold her tight and kiss the shimmering gloss off her lips. "I'm glad you approve."

Ivy leaped up and pulled me to my feet. "Then what're we waiting for. Let's get this party started."

The Browders' house was decked with red poinsettias, creamy candles flickering a soft glow, and bows of fresh magnolia, pine, and holly. While I thought the decorations lovely, I wished for a city sweep to remove it all so I could explore the true beauty of the rooms—the intricately carved moldings, random-width oak floors, and priceless antiques. A fourteen-foot Fraser fir with white lights and sterling silver ornaments filled the two-story entryway. With Heath at her side, Alice stood with an older couple at the base of the sweeping staircase, talking and gesturing with her left hand.

When I felt Ivy tense beside me, I followed her gaze to the enormous solitaire diamond on Alice's left ring finger. Placing a hand at the small of Ivy's back, I leaned in close. "Why don't we grab a drink? We can catch up with them later."

Her blue eyes glistened with unshed tears. "I'll wait. I need to talk to Alice now."

"Fine," I said. "We'll wait."

We inched closer to Alice and Heath. By the time our turn came to speak with the newly betrothed, the color had drained from Ivy's face and her chin was trembling. "Why didn't you tell me?"

"Because it only just happened. Heath surprised me right before the party." Alice thrust her left hand out, fingers splayed. "Oh, Ivy. Can you believe it? I'm getting married."

"You'll make a lovely bride. I wish you all the best." Ivy spun on her heels, swiping at her eyes as she fought her way through the crowd.

I snagged two champagne flutes from a passing waiter and shepherded her down the center hallway to a glass-enclosed atrium at the back of the house.

"Come now," I said handing her a glass of champagne. "It's not the end of the world. You're not losing your best friend. You're making a new one in Heath. It's not like they're moving away from Charleston. They're lives are here."

"You don't understand, Graham." She drained the champagne in one gulp, handed me the empty glass, and excused herself for the ladies' room, leaving me alone in the atrium surrounded by tiers of red poinsettias.

When Ivy failed to return within a few minutes, I roamed the rambling Federal-style home, speaking to the few guests whom I knew and grabbing appetizers from trays as servers passed. I kept an eye out for Ivy, but I wasn't really worried when I didn't see her. I figured she needed some time to herself. But two hours later and still no sign of her, I began my search in earnest. I finally found her in the game room with some of her guy friends, beating them at pool despite her obvious intoxicated state.

I sent one of Ivy's pool partners to locate Edward, and the two of us managed to get her out of the Browders' home without causing a scene. We'd walked to the party because of the unseasonably warm weather and now found ourselves navigating the sidewalks back to the East Battery. With Edward and me on either side of her, Ivy babbled on as she fought to break free of our grip. "Alice doesn't wanna get married. She doesn't love Heath. She just wants to have children."

I helped Edward get Ivy in the house and up the stairs to her room. He walked me back out into the hall. "I apologize for my daughter's behavior. You should know Ivy well enough by now to realize this is out of character for her. She and Alice have been joined at the hip since childhood. This sudden engagement has come as something of a shock."

"She'll feel better in the morning," I said with more conviction than I felt.

"We won't let this spoil our Christmas. Don't forget to bring your hunting gear when you come tomorrow. We'll have ourselves a jolly old time."

I don't own any hunting gear, I thought as I let myself out. Just as well. I had no intention of going hunting.

To give Ivy a day to recover, I postponed the start of my extended holiday stay with the Stoneys until Sunday. I spent Saturday morning doing laundry and the afternoon shopping for gifts. I bought Ivy a dainty gold necklace with a tennis racket pendant from Croghan's Jewel Box and Edward a coffee table book with stunning photographs of sailing yachts on the open water. I chose a trio of lavender sachets for Trudy and a cardboard book, *The Very Hungry Caterpillar*, for her eight-month-old baby girl whom I had not yet met.

When I joined Edward and Ivy for church and brunch on Sunday, Ivy had returned to her jovial self, and she chattered on about errands that needed running and presents that needed wrapping. That afternoon, Ivy hounded Trudy until she agreed to let Ivy and me help bake cookies. I'd never been in the Stoney's kitchen before, and I found it the coziest room in the house. Aromas of cinnamon and nutmeg filled the air and a fire crackled in the fireplace on an exposed brick wall. In the center of the room, a rack of copper pots hung over a butcher block, and a scattering of worn Oriental rugs in brick red tones adorned the pine floorboards. A farmer's table and six chairs occupied the side of the room opposite the stove in front of a large window overlooking the brick courtyard.

"Do you take any time off for Christmas?" I asked Trudy as we sprinkled red sugar on the first batch of cookies.

"Yes, sir. We leave after brunch on Christmas Day to visit my family in Beaufort for the week. I don't like to be gone that long from Mister Edward and Miss Ivy. They count on me. I trust you to keep them in line until I get back."

I laughed. "I'm pretty sure they'll be the ones keeping me in line."

We were decorating our third batch of sugar cookies when Trudy's husband arrived with Ruthie on his hip.

Ivy dropped her icing bag on the counter and went to greet them. Standing on her tiptoes, she kissed Isaac's cheek, wishing him a Merry Christmas, and snatched the baby out of his arms. "Look at you, big girl. You're growing up so fast." Lifting the baby over her head, she spun her around in circles until Ruthie squealed in delight.

I went over and introduced myself to Isaac. "I've heard an

awful lot about you," I said. While he often did odd jobs for the Stoneys, he was head of the grounds crew at The Citadel.

I winced in pain when he gripped my hand. "And I've heard a lot about you."

Over six feet tall with a powerful build, Isaac stared at his wife with the tenderness of a gentle giant. "I got off work early today. Ruthie and I are gonna make a quick trip to the market before it closes. Do you need anything?"

Trudy thought for a minute. "Nah. We're in good shape. But thanks."

Ivy walked Isaac to the door, reluctantly returning the baby to her father's arms. Watching from the window, she had a faraway look on her face as Isaac buckled his daughter into the back seat and drove out of the driveway in his pickup truck. I thought back to what she'd said about Alice in her drunken state after the Browders' party on Friday night. *Alice doesn't wanna get married. She doesn't love Heath. She just wants to have children.* Was she talking about Alice? Or was Ivy the one eager to start a family?

GRAHAM

*J*elected to sleep in on Christmas Eve instead of joining Edward and Ivy for an elaborate hunt at a friend's spread of land near McClellanville. Late morning, I was dozing in the queen-size mahogany rice bed in the guest room, with a copy of John Jakes' *Love and War* spread open on my stomach, when I heard Edward's Jeep Wagoneer rumble in the courtyard below. I got up, went out to the piazza, and observed as father and daughter unloaded guns and gear along with their kill—at least a half dozen mallards. I'd witnessed similar relationships with college friends and their parents, and I envied them their special bond. While I'd missed out on that closeness with my parents, I vowed to one day have that with my own children.

After a quiet afternoon, we devoured a dinner of standing rib roast, scalloped potatoes, and a medley of roasted vegetables before retiring to the drawing room for dessert. Ivy, who was toying with her bread pudding beside me on the sofa, suddenly sprang to her feet and announced in a childlike voice that it was time for bed.

She moved over to her father's chair, and standing behind

him, she leaned down and hugged his neck. "Should we put cookies out for Santa?"

Edward rubbed his belly in a circular motion. "Santa's getting fat. He doesn't need any cookies."

She tightened her arms, her lips close to his ear. "Is Santa bringing me something special this year?"

"You'll have to wait and see." He patted her arm. "Now off to bed with you."

Ivy strolled out of the room, as though floating on a cloud, blowing a kiss at me as she passed close behind the sofa.

"We must seem silly to you," Edward said when she was gone. "We've been playing this game since Ivy was old enough to realize I'm Santa Claus. In the past, my special gifts were elaborate—new automobiles and jewelry and expensive trinkets she'd asked for but never fully appreciated. But I've never given her anything like what I have planned for tomorrow. It's a total surprise. She has no idea."

I leaned in close to him. "Tell me."

Edward chuckled. "Not on your life. Even Trudy doesn't know what I'm giving Ivy this year." He rose out of his chair and went to the bar, filling two tumblers with cognac. "I fancy myself a smoke. Let's go to my study."

I dutifully obeyed, although I hated to leave the comfort of the Christmas tree and the warmth of the fire. I sat down opposite Edward at his leather-topped desk. "Do you love my daughter, Graham?" he asked, packing his pipe.

I was taken aback by his directness, but I answered without hesitation. "Yes, sir. I do. Very much."

"I've been thinking a lot since we spoke the other night about your background." He paused to light his pipe. "And I think you should ask Ivy to marry you."

My eyes bulged and I was temporarily rendered speechless. "But . . . but, we've only been dating a couple of months."

"True." Edward jabbed the shank of his pipe at me. "But you said yourself, you love her."

I moved to the edge of my chair. "But does *she* love *me?* That's the bigger question. I have nothing to offer her, Edward. I can think of any number of men better suited."

Pipe clenched in teeth, Edward leaned across the desk toward me. "You have more to offer her than you think. Wealth doesn't make a man, Graham. It's what's inside his soul that matters. You have a good heart. And I trust you. I already think of you like a son."

"I'm flattered, Edward. But are you sure you want me as a son-in-law?"

"Damn sure!" he said and pounded the desk with his fist. "We're talking about my daughter. Don't think for a second I haven't thought this thing through." He straightened in his chair. "You stand to gain a lot here, Graham. Ivy and I have plenty to offer you. She's my only child, and as her husband, you'll never want for anything. All I ask in return is that you treat her in the manner to which she's accustomed."

Sipping my cognac, I stared into the adjacent room at the magnificent Christmas tree. While belonging to the Stoney family would definitely have its perks, being a kept man was not at all what I'd envisioned for my life. Then again, I'd dreamed of success bigger than what a college professor would afford me. I was finding teaching both challenging and rewarding, and I wanted to see it through for at least a few more years.

From the top drawer of his desk, Edward produced a velvet ring box and slid it across the desk to me. "I gave this to Ivy's mother when I proposed to her. I'd be honored if you'd give it to Ivy."

Opening the box, my eyes grew wide at the sight of the emerald-cut diamond flanked by triangular-shaped sapphires. I dropped the box on the desk. "I can't. It's not right."

"Of course, you can. Happens all the time in families like ours. As far as I'm concerned, you can tell people you purchased it yourself. Same goes for your background. That is your business. You decide how you present yourself to Charleston society as long as you tell Ivy the truth."

I raked my fingers through my coarse brown hair. "I'm sorry, Edward, but I have to ask. Does this sudden urgency for Ivy to get married have anything to do with Alice's engagement to Heath?"

A vein in Edward's neck began to pulsate, and I knew I'd gone too far. He sat back in his chair and puffed on his pipe, blowing smoke rings while I waited anxiously for his response. "You're very astute, Graham. I'm a lot of things, but I'm not a liar. Ivy is ready for the next phase in her life. Of that much, I'm certain. Ivy and Alice have always done everything together from the time they were young girls. Now that Alice is getting married, Ivy wants to get married. But who am I to meddle in my daughter's love life? If the timing is wrong, forget I asked, and we'll move on."

"Thank you for your honesty," I said, rising out of my chair. "I hope you understand that I can't make a decision about something so important on the spur of the moment."

"Of course, you can't. You wouldn't be the man I believe you to be if you did."

"I love your daughter with all my heart, and I want to do right by her. I want her to marry me for the right reasons, not because she's competing with Alice to have a bigger or better wedding."

"You have a valid point." He chewed on his pipe for a minute as he mulled this over. "I've said my piece. You can decide whether or not to proceed." Edward gestured at the velvet box with his pipe. "But take the ring with you. I'll be gone for a couple of hours in the morning. I have to drive over to Summerville to collect Ivy's present." His blue eyes twinkled with mischief, and I was more curious than ever about the gift. "My absence will give you a chance to propose, if you decide to do so. And I hope you will."

Pocketing the velvet box, I drained the last of my brandy and climbed the stairs to my room. I felt as though I'd simultaneously won the lottery and been sentenced to life in prison. The latter confused me. Why did I feel trapped when I was certain about my feelings for Ivy? Because I knew in my heart she didn't love me back. And because, by marrying Ivy under these conditions, I'd be relinquishing control of my life to Edward. Edward, who would no longer be my friend and mentor but my father-in-law, a relationship that came with a whole new set of rules.

I never closed my eyes that night and was sitting at the kitchen table in my flannel pajama bottoms and undershirt, an empty glass of milk in front of me, when Trudy arrived for work on Christmas morning.

"Uh-oh," she said when she saw me. "Judging from the look on your face, disaster struck in this house after I left last night."

I couldn't help but smile. "It's nothing like that. I'm just faced with the biggest decision of my life."

She gave a curt nod. "I'll put on some coffee."

While she started the coffee maker and placed an almond Kringle in the oven to warm, I gave her a brief rundown of my conversation with Edward. "Do you think there's any chance Ivy will fall in love with me over time?"

Trudy placed a steaming cup of coffee and the fixings in front of me and joined me at the table with her own mug. "There's a good chance she loves you already. My Ivy's not one to show affection. Except when it comes to her daddy, babies, and puppies."

"I disagree, Trudy. She beams like the North Star in Alice's presence. Her adoration for you is written all over her face every time you enter a room. Yesterday, she planted a kiss on your husband's cheek as though he was her best friend returning home from war."

Trudy blew on her coffee and took a tentative sip. "It's not always about love, Mister Graham."

"Isn't it, though?" I stirred a rivulet of cream into my coffee. "I guess the hopeless romantic English professor in me wants to believe it is."

"I grew up in the carriage house apartment with my family," Trudy said. "Isaac and I even lived there for a while after we got married, before we got a place of our own. This is my home. The Stoneys are my family. There's a lot of meanness in the world outside that front door." She gave a nod of her head toward the front of the house. "A lot of corruptness and bigotry. My Ivy and Mister Edward ain't perfect, but they're good people. The timing's right for the two of you."

"You mean because Alice is getting married."

She lifted a shoulder. "Something like that. Mister Edward loved Virginia dearly, and when she died, he bestowed all that love on Ivy. She's spoiled—"

"And petulant at times," I added.

"And God knows that child can find her way into some trouble. But she's as good-hearted as they come. If you really and truly love her, don't let this opportunity slip away. And if Ivy asks me, I'm gonna tell her the same thing. I have a good feeling about you, Mister Graham. She could do a lot worse."

I smiled across the table at Trudy. Having her around was another perk of belonging to the Stoney family. "Thank you, Trudy. You've helped me make my decision." I waggled my finger at her. "But if things don't work out for us, I'm blaming it all on you."

She wagged her finger back at me. "And if you hurt my Ivy, Mister Graham, you'll have to answer to me."

I laughed. "Fair enough."

I went upstairs to shower and dress. When I returned an hour later, Ivy, wearing lime-green wide-wale corduroys and a cream-colored sweater, was pacing back and forth behind a flustered Trudy who, with smudges of flour on her cheeks, was rolling out biscuit dough on the counter.

"Daddy's not here," she announced when I entered the room.

"Merry Christmas to you too," I said.

"Sorry. Merry Christmas." She kissed my cheek. "But he's never not been here on Christmas morning."

"He's gone to meet an elf," I said with a smirk.

She stuck her tongue out at me. "Haha. Do you know where he went?"

"Nope. He wouldn't say." I retrieved our windbreakers from the rack beside the back door. "Why don't we get out of Trudy's hair for a while and go for a walk on the seawall?"

"Good idea! Daddy will surely be home by the time we return."

We strolled down the driveway, across East Battery, and mounted the concrete steps to the promenade. We stood at the railing looking out over the harbor. The sun beamed bright in a cloudless vibrant blue sky, its rays sparkling off the smooth waters of the Cooper river.

Closing my eyes, I tilted my head back and felt the warmth of the sun on my face. "I'm not used to such pleasant weather on Christmas Day. I don't even miss not having snow for the holidays."

"It is, indeed, a glorious day. Think about all the children, Graham." Turning her back to the water, Ivy spread her arms wide at the homes lining the Battery. "Inside all these houses. Their faces bright and shiny with the merriment of Christmas as they tear open their presents. The bicycles and doll houses and board games. All my life, all I ever wanted was to be a mother. Is it so wrong of me, Graham, to have such a simple ambition?"

"Not at all, Ivy. Especially since you grew up with only a father." I took hold of her hand. "You're going to be an excellent mother."

She leaned against me. "Do you really think so?"

"I really think so." Placing an arm around her, I drew her in close. I felt the soft thumping of her heart against my rib cage. Would she have room in that magnificent heart for me? Kissing the top of her head, I whispered into her hair. "I love you, Ivy. If you'll let me, I'd like to spend the rest of my life making you happy. More than anything in this world, I want you to be the mother of my children."

She put some distance between us so she could see me. "Marriage, Graham? Really? Aren't you getting ahead of yourself? We haven't been dating very long."

"While that may be true, we're not getting any younger. I'm ready to settle down and have children. I think you are as well."

Her blue eyes traveled from my face to the river behind me, and for the longest time she didn't say a word. Certain she would turn me down, I presented the trump card I'd promised myself I wouldn't use. "Your father gave his blessing."

Her eyes dart to me. "You asked him?"

More like he asked me, I thought.

"Not only did we talk about it . . ." I removed the velvet box from my jeans pocket and opened it. "Your father gave me your mother's engagement ring to give to you." I took the ring out of the box and slid it on her finger. "It's a perfect fit. That must be a good omen. But if you'd rather have your own ring . . . I certainly can't afford anything like this, but we can go shopping."

She held her hand close to her face, examining the ring.

"I've always loved this ring." She looked up at me with tears in her eyes. "Are you sure about this? You really want to marry me?"

"I've never wanted anything more in my life." Taking her face in my hands, I pressed my lips against hers, kissing her with all the love I felt for her in that moment.

When we drew apart, she looked at me with those deep blue eyes. "I promise, I'll try to make you happy, Graham."

"You won't have to try very hard."

When she caught sight of Edward's Wagoneer on the road, she abruptly pushed away from me. "Look! There he is! Let's go tell him the good news."

Hand and hand, we took off running back down the promenade toward the house. When we rounded the gate into the driveway, we slowed at the sight of Edward holding a tiny Labrador retriever puppy in his cupped hands.

Ivy's hands flew to her cheeks. "Daddy! You didn't."

Edward grinned from ear to ear. "I did. She's all yours. But I insist she go back for obedience training in a few months."

Ivy ran to him, taking the puppy into her arms. "This is the best day ever." She held the puppy in the air. "Aren't you the cutest thing. I'm gonna call you Bessie." She snuggled the puppy against her neck, kissing its head while it licked her chin with its little pink tongue.

"Guess what, Daddy? Graham asked me to marry him. It means so much to wear my mother's ring."

"She would want you to have it, sweetheart. I know the two of you will be very happy together." As he hugged his daughter and her new puppy, Edward winked at me over the top of Ivy's head and mouthed, "Good man."

I didn't feel like a man at all. I felt like a puppet. But I wouldn't let that dissuade me from marrying the woman of my dreams. While I didn't have a prayer of ever owning a piece of

Ivy's heart the size of the one belonging to her father, I would settle for a sliver for now and hope that, in time, she would carve out more for me.

GRAHAM

*I*vy invited Alice over to the house on Christmas night to tell her our exciting news. Heath had yet to return from Raleigh where he'd gone to be with his family for the holiday.

Alice let out a squeal and engulfed Ivy in a hug. "See, Ivy! I told you! We'll get married together. Have babies together. Grow old together."

Ivy dragged Alice down to the sofa beside her. "Would you be terribly upset if we got married in June? Your big day is the eighth. We would wait a couple of weeks. I'm thinking the twenty-second." When disappointment crossed Alice's face, Ivy stroked her arm. "Don't worry. My wedding will be nothing like your extravaganza. Eloping would be way more adventurous, but Daddy would have a fit. I'm thinking of a small church service with a garden reception here at the house."

Ivy had discussed none of this with me. I cleared my throat, reminding them I was in the room, standing by the fireplace.

Ivy looked over at me. "June works for you, doesn't it, Graham? You have the summers off from classes, right?

Daddy's treating us to a month-long honeymoon in Africa. I've always wanted to go."

We'd been engaged for eight hours, and she'd already planned the honeymoon. I told myself that I'd bargained for this. Life with Ivy would always be about Ivy.

When word of our engagement spread throughout Charleston Society, friends and acquaintances were naturally curious about the Yankee college professor who'd stolen Ivy Stoney's heart. As promised, Edward left it to me to decide how I presented myself, and after careful consideration, I chose not to lie about my past. I hinted at a modest New England upbringing and left it at that. I told my fiancée little more than that. I explained that I wasn't close with my parents and siblings, and they wouldn't be attending the wedding.

One afternoon in late May, I overheard Alice and Ivy talking in the garden behind the carriage house. They didn't see me walk up, and when I heard them mention my name, I eavesdropped from around the corner of the carriage house.

"Aren't you concerned about Graham's upbringing?" Alice asked.

"You mean because he comes from a modest family? Why would that concern me?"

"Be serious, Ivy. There are certain people in this town who do not accept others from backgrounds unlike ours. They could cause trouble for you down the road."

"Then let them. I'm not a snob like you, Alice."

I smiled to myself. I'd experienced Alice's snooty side many times during the previous hectic months. She'd intentionally omitted from guest lists those she deemed unworthy and been blatantly rude to others she thought beneath her.

Much to my surprise, there'd been little catfighting between the brides-to-be. Every time Alice got her nose out of joint about something—when Ivy unknowingly picked the same china pattern and when they accidentally scheduled engagement parties for the same night—Ivy gave in to her. Ivy was more interested in the honeymoon than the wedding. When she wasn't rolling around on the floor with Bessie or teaching her rapidly growing puppy to obey, she was reading travel guides and meeting with the travel agent.

I, too, was more interested in the honeymoon, except for the part of the ceremony where the minister announced us husband and wife and I got to kiss my bride, who looked ravishing in an off-shoulder cream-colored satin gown. While Ivy wanted adventure, I wanted sex. My patience had run out and my desire for her was all consuming. I felt a burning need inside my body, and I feared I might explode, if that need wasn't soon fulfilled.

Alice's wedding was an elaborate affair with six hundred people in attendance at the church ceremony and reception at the yacht club. Ivy, the maid of honor, cried when Alice walked down the aisle. I wanted to believe hers were happy tears, but from where I was seated in the fourth pew back on the bride's side, my fiancée appeared miserable, as though she were at her best friend's funeral and not her wedding.

Two weeks later, after our afternoon ceremony and reception, my bride and I took a late evening flight from Charleston that landed us in Atlanta in time to catch an overnight plane to Amsterdam. From there, we flew to Nairobi, Kenya, where we transferred to a single-engine Cessna for the one-hour trip to the airstrip nearest our tented camp. I'd been dreading the final leg of the journey, and while Ivy craned her neck to see out of the window, I sat ramrod straight with eyes shut tight, gripping the armrest of my seat and praying I didn't vomit all over the back of the pilot. When I felt my new wife's hand on my arm, I cracked an eyelid.

Pointing out her window, she shouted, "Look!" above the roar of the plane's engine.

Spread out beneath us for miles in every direction was the

endless savanna grasslands of the Serengeti National Park. From the airstrip, a guide dressed head-to-toe in safari khaki drove us in a Land Rover to our camp. Our host, Mack Chapman, a jolly older gentleman with a British accent, presented us with flutes of champagne and then showed us around the site. The open-air salon comprised the camp's lounging, dining, and reception areas and was adorned with tasteful furnishings and Turkish rugs covering the aged brick floor. After a brief tour of the camp—pool, spa, and upscale boutique—Mack showed us to our quarters, private rooms that mirrored the elegance of the main lodge.

Giddy from champagne, Ivy kicked off her heels and hopped onto the mosquito-netted king-size bed. "This is simply marvelous!" she said jumping up and down on the mattress. "What should we do first? Pool or spa? I don't know about you, but I could go for a massage after our exhausting trip."

"I have a better idea," I said, tackling her. "Why don't *I* give *you* a massage?"

She squirmed beneath me. "Can't we wait until after dinner tonight for that?"

"No way. I've waited long enough." I unbuttoned her cream silk blouse and tugged off the skirt of her yellow tweed suit. She was a sight to behold with her slim body, pert breasts, and blonde mound of pubic hair. "You're lovely," I said, my voice thick with lust.

"Be gentle, please, Graham," she whispered in a childlike voice.

"I will. I promise."

I ran my hands up and down her body, pinching her nipples lightly and palming her taut abdomen. She tensed when I entered her, her body remaining rigid as I thrust deeper and faster until I finally came.

Her body trembled beneath mine. I'd wanted so much for our first time to be special, but I was only moderately skilled in the art of lovemaking myself, and despite my best intentions, I'd hurt her.

"That wasn't what I expected," she said, her blue eyes glistening with tears.

Sliding off of her, I wrapped my arm around her, bringing her close. "Next time will be better."

She lay her head on my chest. "I was hoping for . . . you know, the earth to move or something."

I barked out a laugh. "That's a pretty tall order for our first time. Be patient, sweetheart. Honeymoons are for getting to know each other, in more ways than one."

She ran her finger across my lower lip. "Do you think we made a baby?"

We'd agreed not to use protection, to let nature take its course. I kissed her forehead. "Sometimes it happens that easily. But it usually takes a few tries."

She stuck out her lower lip. "I really want to have a baby, Graham," she said, as if I could wave a magic wand and zap a baby into her arms.

"I know you do, honey. But would it be so bad if it didn't happen right away? I, for one, would like to enjoy a few months to ourselves before becoming parents for life. We don't even know where we're going to live yet."

"Oh yes we do!" she said, her tone full of mischief.

Pushing her away, I sat up in bed. "Since when?" I'd broached the subject numerous times in recent months, but I could never get her to discuss our post-wedding living arrangements.

"Since the other day when I overheard Daddy talking to his contractor on the phone. He's planning to surprise us. While we're gone, he's having my bedroom and the room next to it converted into our own suite, complete with marble bathroom and one of those spa tubs. Isn't it wonderful, Graham? We can continue to live on the Battery."

Wonderful wasn't the word that popped into my head. Baffling was more like it. How could Edward make such an important decision without first consulting me? I thought back to my conversation with him on Christmas Eve. *All I ask in return is that you treat her in the manner to which she's accustomed.* I'd signed away my life to my new wife and her father. But was that all bad? Not only did my new lifestyle come with perks, including the ability to live rent-free in one of Charleston's most beautiful homes, I also felt a closeness with Ivy's father that I'd never felt with my own.

I fingered a lock of her hair. "I'll be happy living anywhere as long as you're there."

A dreamy expression settled on her face. "I've always wanted my children to grow up in that house. Did you know that Alice and Heath are living with her parents?"

"Only while they remodel their house." I sank back down in bed, snuggling close to her. "One day, we'll be able to buy our own house too, with all the money we save by living with your father."

Ivy ignored my comment, as she often did when the subject wasn't to her liking. "And when Alice and Heath move to Church Street, they'll be even closer to us. Did I tell you they're trying to get pregnant too?"

"I believe you mentioned it." I flashed her a wide grin. "A few gazillion times."

"Stop making fun of me," she said, smacking my belly. "Alice is my best friend. We want to raise our children together."

"Then we should give it another go." Beneath the sheet, I slid my hand between her legs.

She rolled off the bed, taking the sheet with her, leaving my erect manhood exposed.

"Jeez, Ivy. Give me back the cover."

"No!" She said, wrapping the sheet tighter around her breasts. "Get up and get dressed. I want to go exploring."

"We've been traveling for over twenty-four hours." I patted the mattress beside me. "Come back to bed. Let's take a nap first."

"We can nap by the pool. Seriously, Graham." She reached for my hand, tugging on it. "I don't want to waste a single minute of my time in Africa."

Her excitement was contagious. "All right. You win." I swung my feet over the side of the bed. "Let's go exploring."

And explore we did. For the next two weeks, we lived each moment to its fullest as we traveled from one luxurious camp to the next, following the great migration of land mammals from Tanzania to Kenya.

Ivy made friends easily with the others in our safari group. Charmed by the Southern belle with the lazy drawl from South Carolina, they flocked to our dinner table at night and competed for the opportunity to be included in our activities during the day.

Ivy and I were deeply moved by the beauty of Africa. Witnessing the animals in their natural habitat—males and females whose sole purpose in life was feeding and protecting their young—restored in me some of the faith in God my father had taken away. For the first time in years, I began to write again. While Ivy photographed prides of lions, parades of elephants, flocks of exotic birds, and herds of countless species of animals, I penned in my writing tablet short stories inspired by my admiration and respect for my surroundings.

Ivy and I grew closer during this time, challenging each other to athletic conquests, debating world issues, and discussing literature at length. But emotionally, we were both guilty of holding something back. While Ivy remained timid when it came to sex, I had yet to tell her about my abusive father and the beating he gave me that landed me in the hospital.

"Why don't you ever talk about your past?" she asked me late one night when we were lounging by the campfire after the others had retired.

I shrugged. "Because you never asked." Which was true. She rarely questioned me about myself.

When she set her blue eyes on me, I felt as though she was looking into my soul. "I didn't ask, because I figured you would tell me what you want me to know."

I raised my brandy snifter to her. "That's very perceptive of you." I decided right then and there never to tell her about my horrible childhood for fear she'd think lesser of me. "There are some things you're better off not knowing. Suffice it to say, my father is nothing like yours."

I applauded Ivy for knowing when not to pry. "Everyone should have a father like mine."

"I agree. I hope I'm as good a father to our children as yours has been to you." I chuckled. "I remember you said once that every time you get interested in a guy, you find yourself comparing him to your father. And that so far, none have measured up. By marrying me, does that mean I've measured up?"

She shrugged. "Daddy likes you. That's good enough for me."

My stomach knotted. "What kind of answer is that?"

"Just what I said. My father's opinion of you is important to me."

"Okay . . . so, I measure up to your father's standards. But does that mean I measure up to yours?"

She nestled her head against my shoulder. "Of course, silly! I married you, didn't I?"

I pushed her head off my shoulder. "I'm serious, Ivy. What are your standards of measurement?"

"Okay, I'm sorry," she said and put on her serious face. "You're honest and hardworking and I trust you. And you always let me have my way."

Just like you always let Alice have her way.

I let the subject drop after that. I'd gotten my answer, not in what she'd said but what she didn't say. My wife didn't really love me. At least not with her heart.

When our safari ended, we flew to the Seychelles for ten days of adventure of the oceanic variety. The day before we flew home to South Carolina, Ivy started her period.

With shoulders slumped, she sat on the side of the bed, staring at the orange carpet on the floor. "I don't understand, Graham. Why didn't it work? We did everything right. Why didn't I get pregnant?"

I sat down beside her. "Your body is not an electrical device you can turn off and on, Ivy. We're dealing with mother nature. Have faith that it will happen in time."

"But what if it never happens? What if I'm barren? What if I'm too old to have a baby?"

Draping an arm around her shoulders, I pull her in tight. "You're being ridiculous. You're not even thirty. You're in good health. You get plenty of exercise and eat well."

"Is it because I stink at sex?"

I burst out laughing, although I was encouraged that she at least recognized her inhibitions. "You don't stink at sex. We're newlyweds. We have to keep practicing. Regardless, the process of making love has little to do with making a baby. You'll get pregnant soon."

"You promise?" she asked, staring up at me with that wide-eyed look of innocence that melted my heart.

"You know I don't have the power to make that promise. But I can promise that, one way or another, we will have a child."

Ivy's spirits plummeted every month with the onset of her period. Her failure to conceive wasn't for lack of trying. Nestled in our new opulent suite of rooms on the third floor of the Stoney house, every night and sometimes when we woke in the mornings, I made love to Ivy—such as it was with me doing all the work. The one salvation that gave Ivy hope was that Alice and Heath had also failed to conceive.

On Friday afternoon the week before Thanksgiving, I was in my office on the third floor of Randolph Hall when I received an urgent phone call from my wife.

"Graham! Thank God I caught you. Daddy went out sailing hours ago and hasn't come back. I'm worried sick. Can you come home, please?"

Tossing my pen on my desk, I sat back in my chair. "Wait a minute, Ivy. Back up. Are you saying Edward went sailing in this weather?" Hurricane Kate had made landfall on the Florida panhandle during the early hours of the morning and was cutting a path of destruction across Alabama and Georgia, into South Carolina."

"Yes! Damn him. I begged him not to go. He said the weather wasn't bad. In his defense, when he left the house before lunch, it wasn't even raining and the wind was barely blowing. But now it's really bad out."

"Let's not panic. Remember, your father is an experienced sailor. He probably got caught in the weather and docked at a friend's house to wait out the storm. I'm sure he's three scotches in by now."

"I hope you're right, Graham, but I have a bad feeling."

I walked the phone to the window and stared out in disbelief at the driving rain and heavy wind swaying the live oaks in the Cistern Yard below. I, too, had underestimated the potential for severe weather from this storm. "Go to the yacht club and have the dock master try to raise him on the radio. I'll meet you there."

Luckily, I'd had the foresight to drive to the college instead of walking, which had become my habit on days when the weather permitted. I navigated my way to the yacht club on the flooded streets of downtown in my rusted-out, ten-year-old Toyota Celica. I found Ivy and the dock master, Woodie Lawson, in his office, hovered over a staticky VHF radio.

"Any luck?" I asked, draping my dripping raincoat over the back of a chair.

"No!" Ivy rushed into my arms. "We can't get him on the radio. Trudy's at home with his address book, calling anyone who might have seen him. I'm scared to death, Graham. If his boat capsized . . ."

"He shouldn't have been out in this weather," Woodie said. "And definitely not alone."

I glared at him over the top of my wife's head. While this was true, saying it in front of the man's obviously distraught daughter did nothing to help.

Ivy shoved me off and went to stand in front of the wall of windows, looking out at the choppy waters of the Cooper River. "Poor Daddy. The storm is really raging."

"I don't want to alarm you, honey, but I think we need to call in the Coast Guard." Woodie was an old salt of a man with shoulder-length gray hair and leathery skin, and I trusted him to make the right moves.

As she chewed on the tips of three of her fingers, Ivy gave him a nod.

Woodie notified the Coast Guard, who went immediately into action, searching past dusk and well into the night.

I stood next to my wife at the window, uttering reassurances that neither of us believed.

Ivy twirled strands of her golden hair until they sprung out from her head like corkscrews. "My father wouldn't worry me like this," she claimed, repeatedly.

I knew this to be true about Edward. His precious daughter was always at the forefront of his mind. He would never burden her unnecessarily.

"Why don't we go home?" I suggested to her around eight o'clock. "We'll be more comfortable waiting for word there. Woodie will call us the minute he hears anything."

"You go ahead," she said with a stiff jaw. "I'm not leaving."

"Then neither am I."

Trudy arrived around nine o'clock with thermoses of coffee and a basket filled with an assortment of sandwiches wrapped in wax paper. "I've called everyone I know," she said. "The whole of Charleston is looking for your daddy. Over in Mount Pleasant and Sullivan's Island too."

Ivy collapsed into Trudy's arms. "He's gonna be okay, isn't he Trudy?"

Trudy's face was pinched with concern, but her voice remained positive. "There's a logical explanation for his where-abouts. And when he gets himself home, I'm gonna take a switch to his behind."

This brought a hint of a smile to Ivy's face. "Do you mind going back to the house and staying by the phone?"

"Not at all. And I've already told Isaac I'm gonna stay the night." Tugging the hood of her red raincoat over her head, Trudy bustled out of the office.

The sandwiches remained untouched, but we drank every drop of the coffee during the hours that followed. Around two in the morning, when a heavy fog settled over the harbor, the Coast Guard called off the search for the night and we had no choice but to go home.

Bessie greeted us at the door, and Ivy dropped to her knees, burying her face in the dog's furry neck. At the sound of Ivy's muffled sobs, Bessie looked up at me with concerned brown eyes. Ivy suddenly jumped to her feet and, without a word, took the dog upstairs to Edward's room, closing and locking the door behind her.

I had no idea if my wife slept that night. I certainly didn't. Trudy, who spent the night in the apartment out back, was the one to answer the door to the young Coast Guard officer at seven the following morning. When I joined them in the foyer, he was explaining that the fog had lifted, and they'd resumed their search a couple of hours earlier.

"We found some debris we believe belonged to the missing vessel—a large remnant of the main sail and a life preserver bearing the name of the boat—*Miss Ivy*."

We heard a gasp, and the three of us looked up to see Ivy standing at the top of the stairs. "You can't give up!" she said, as she dashed down. "He's alive! I know he is. Daddy's an excellent swimmer. Please, keep looking."

"Ma'am." He tipped his orange cap to her. "We have no intention of stopping our search."

"I'm going with you." Ivy fled the house in her jeans and T-shirt despite the chilly morning.

I grabbed our windbreakers out of the coat closet and took off with the Coast Guard officer after her. Ivy, twenty feet in front of us, marched across the road to the yacht club and down the dock, boarding the Coast Guard boat without permission. One of the crew members started to object, but I warned him to save his breath as I joined my wife onboard.

The crewmen pushed off from the dock, and we traveled a half mile up the Cooper River to the place where they'd found the debris. For the rest of the morning and the first part of the afternoon, with the Coast Guard helicopter hovering over our heads, Ivy and I stood at the gunwale and stared down into the inky water, praying that we'd find Edward clinging to a section of the hull.

When we returned to the dock at three o'clock for a change

of crew, Ivy got off the boat and returned home, once again locking herself in Edward's room with her dog.

That evening, as the grandfather clock in the upstairs hall chimed six, a young police officer—a friend of the family who'd grown up in the neighborhood with Ivy—came to deliver the news that a body had washed up in the marsh over in Mount Pleasant.

I felt a sharp pain in my chest, and I worried I might be having a heart attack. Standing beside me with a death grip on my arm, Trudy muffled a sob.

"We need someone to identify the corpse," Stan said to me with a sympathetic smile. "It might be better if you do it. The body . . . well, it's not in great shape. Knowing how she feels about her father, I don't think Ivy can handle it."

Trudy called Alice while I was gone. She was waiting for me in the drawing room when I returned. My somber expression expressed what I lacked the words to say.

"We should tell Ivy together." Taking me by the hand, Alice led me up the stairs to the third floor and down the hall to Edward's room.

My wife accepted the news with a nod and a stiff upper lip. "Graham, if you don't mind, Bessie needs to go out, and it's time for her dinner."

My wife was dismissing me in order to be alone with Alice. I, too, had suffered a great loss. I was dying inside, and I needed to be with my wife. That my wife was choosing Alice over me felt like a knife stabbing my already broken heart. No matter what happened between Ivy and me, no matter how close we became or what we experienced in our marriage, Alice would always outrank me.

"Of course. Let me know if you need anything. Come on,

Bessie." I took the dog by the collar and dragged her out of the room.

That was the last I saw of Ivy or Alice until nine the following morning when Alice's mother, Evelyn, arrived with the first round of friends who'd come to pay their respects.

During the two days that followed, Evelyn and Alice rarely left the Stoney house. One or the other was always stationed at the door to accept the mass influx of food and flower deliveries. Ivy was stoic when meeting with the minister and funeral director and accepting condolences from her many visitors. But at night, she retreated with Alice to Edward's room.

On Monday afternoon, I came upon Alice in the butler's pantry silently weeping into a worn tissue. "It's so hard to see her like this," she said.

"She seems to be holding up quite well to me. Then again, I haven't had any time alone with her like you have."

"That's just an act. Ivy and I are proper Southerners. We were taught never to show emotion. Ivy loved her daddy dearly, and she will eventually crack."

And crack she did, but not until later. Ivy's eyes remained dry on Tuesday throughout the long service at St. Phillip's and the burial immediately following in Magnolia Cemetery at the family gravesite where her mother was buried. When I saw Edward's casket suspended above the dark hole where his body would rest for all eternity, I lost my composure and cried like a baby. But not Ivy. She held it together until long after the last person had left the reception and the house was empty except for the two of us and Bessie. Alice had gone home to check on Heath, and I'd given Trudy the long weekend off. At almost midnight, I was wandering around the empty mansion with Bessie at my side, when I heard the first loud and woeful sobs echoing throughout the vast hallways from the third floor.

Bessie looked up at me with those same concerned eyes. "I

know, girl." I sat down cross-legged on the floor, stroking her head between her ears. "All we can do is love her."

If only it were that simple. If only Ivy would let us.

I spent the remainder of that night in Edward's study with a bottle of his barrel-aged whiskey. I sat in the chair in front of the desk, the chair I usually sat in during my many talks with Edward. But on this night, my conversation was one-sided. I asked him repeatedly why he'd done such a foolish thing by going sailing in a hurricane, and how we were supposed to go on without him. When I was good and drunk, I moved behind the desk to his leather chair. I packed his pipe with tobacco and lit it, but when the smoke brought on a fit of coughing, I dumped the tobacco into the ashtray. I searched his drawers from top to bottom, searching for instructions on how best to take care of his daughter in the event of his demise. I came up empty. He'd died at fifty-nine years of age. He'd had so much life left to live. He hadn't been anticipating death. He'd been looking forward to spoiling his grandchildren. He was my mentor, the man I'd grown to love like a father. And I'd had the pleasure of knowing him for only fifteen short months.

I lay my head on the top of his desk and wept.

LILLIAN

I read well into the night. Sometime after three in the morning, I fall asleep with my head on Dad's desk, much like my father had done on Edward's desk the night of his funeral.

I wake to loud knocking on the front door. On unsteady feet, I make my way out of the office and down the hall. I'm surprised to find Marcus on the porch, his hair orange in the bright sunlight.

I lift my hand to shield my eyes. "What time is it?"

He checks his watch. "Ten fifteen. Did I wake you?"

"Yeah." I shake my head to clear it. "I was up late reading. I need coffee," I say and leave him standing in the doorway.

He follows me into the kitchen and watches as I pour the dregs of coffee from last night into the sink and set a new pot on to brew. "Did you find the truth you were looking for?"

I turn to face him. "I found Daddy's memoir. The chapters of his life with my mother. I'm only a third of the way through. So far, the *truth* remains a mystery." I cock my head to the side. "Why are you here?"

"I was worried about you, the way you left so abruptly

yesterday. When you didn't respond to my texts, I went to your house this morning to check on you. Trudy told me you were spending the weekend down here."

I pat the pockets of my shorts. "I have no idea where I left my phone. I'm sure the battery's dead by now."

When the coffee finishes brewing, I pour two mugs and hand one to him. "Do you still drink it black?"

"You remember."

"I remember a lot of things." An awkward silence settles over us, and I stare down at my bare feet. My pedicure is months old, what's left of the blue polish chipped and fading.

Leaning back against the counter, he crosses his long legs. "So, tell me about this memoir."

I take a minute to figure out how best to describe it. "It's the strangest thing. It's like reading fiction. My father is the protagonist and my mother the object of his desire. He was madly in love with Ivy. That was my mother's name."

"I know that," he says. "You used to talk about her a lot."

I scrunch up my face. "I guess I did." Was I obsessed with my dead mother? Probably. Another reason for him to break up with me. "You don't want to hear this?"

"Actually, I do. Have you learned anything about the day she died?"

"Not yet. I'm at the part where my grandfather dies. Ivy was close to him. She went off the deep end after his funeral."

"How did he die?"

"In a sailing accident. During a hurricane." I hold my hand up. "Don't say it. I know what you're thinking. Who—"

"Goes sailing in a hurricane?" he says, finishing my sentence.

"The storm came closer to Charleston than predicted." I stare down into my coffee. "I wish I'd had the chance to know my grandfather. He sounds like a true Southern gentleman. Ivy, on the other hand, was a complicated personality. She was fun to be around, even if she was childish at times. And she was athletic—a tennis player and adventure seeker. I get the impression she wasn't that into Dad. At least not like he was into her. Honestly, I can't see him with someone like Ivy. He was so stable, such a rock. And, from what I've read, she was impulsive and petulant. But he was determined to make her happy. I'm curious to find out if he ever did."

Marcus pushes off the counter. "I take that as my cue to leave. Now that I know you're okay, I'll let you get back to your reading."

I desperately want him to stay, even though I'm asking for the kind of trouble my heart can't take. "Actually, I need some time to reflect on what I've learned from the first chapters before moving on to the rest." I move to the window and stare out at the brilliant day. "I could use some fresh air and exercise. Isaac has already put the boats away for the winter, but if you want to hang around, we could get the kayaks out of the shed. I don't really want to be alone with all these ghosts, and while you're the last person I'd choose to be with, you're at least a warm body."

He laughs, spewing coffee. "I guess I deserve that."

"Yep. You do." I go to the refrigerator and look inside. "I don't have much to offer for lunch."

"Trudy sent a cooler."

"Of course she did." Closing the refrigerator door, I eye his faded jeans. "Did you bring shorts or a bathing suit?"

"I threw some clothes in a duffle, hoping you might ask me to stay."

My stomach does a somersault at the mischievous smile spreading across his lips. A voice inside my head warns, *Don't go there, Lillian.*

He slurps down the remainder of his coffee. "I'll get my things out of the car."

"And I'll go put on my bathing suit," I say, heading for the stairs. "You can change in the guest room. I'll meet you out back at the shed in ten."

Upstairs in my room, I put on my bikini from yesterday, look in the mirror, and quickly change into an old one-piece suit. I'd hate to give Marcus the wrong impression. I am not at all interested in rekindling our relationship. Period.

I slather on sunscreen and head out to the shed. I'm searching for life vests when Marcus emerges from the house, looking sexy in striped board shorts with his tight abs and broad shoulders. Obviously, he's been spending a lot of time in the gym. He's developed some serious muscles since I last saw him without a shirt on. Something deep inside of me stirs, and I avert my eyes.

We drag the kayaks down to the dock and paddle a half mile up Bohicket Creek. As I glide in silence across the calm waters, my mind drifts to Dad's memoir. I find it surreal to have this inside look at his love affair with my mother. I never gave his sexuality a moment's thought. If he ever took women on dates, I never knew about them. I was envious of my friends' happily married parents, most especially Marcus's devoted mother and father. I'd always assumed Dad stayed single because he preferred it that way. Based on what I've read so far, it was because he never got over losing my mother.

The sun is hot and the air humid, and by the time we get back to the dock, we're drenched in sweat. We hoist the kayaks onto the dock and dive back into the water. Marcus splashes me, and when I take off swimming, he comes after me.

Marcus and I had dated from our sophomore year in high school throughout college. He spent many weekends with my family at the cottage, and being here with him now feels like old times. We splash each other and fake like we're drowning and do cannonballs off the dock. When we finally get out of the water a half hour later, our muscles ache and our stomachs rumble. We spread our picnic out on a blanket on the dock and dig into the fried chicken, potato salad, and deviled eggs.

My eyes meet his as I bite into a fried chicken leg. "So . . . what've you been up to for the past ten years?"

"I've been living the good life, traveling the world and having wild adventures."

I imagine him in the Maldives, drinking tropical drinks with exotic women. "Have you really?"

"No," he says, shaking his head and laughing. "I've been working my butt off, first in school and then at a high-pressure firm in Manhattan. I've rarely seen the light of day, but I've learned so much. When our senior-most partner passed away two years ago, the younger associates began making changes I didn't approve of. And that's when I decided to move back. I always knew I would eventually come home to Charleston. It was only a matter of when."

I hate myself for bringing up his social life, but I have to know. "I bet you had plenty of girlfriends while you were in New York."

"Nope. No girlfriends. I wasn't celibate or anything like that. I went on some dates, had a few hookups." He tosses his chicken bone in the water. "I found the right girl for me once. But I let her go."

I manage an exaggerated eye roll despite my pounding heart. "Right."

"I'm serious, Lil. You're the only one for me. I've heard about you and what you were doing over the years through friends. I wouldn't have blamed you for moving on, for finding someone else. But I'm damn glad you didn't."

I pop a deviled egg into my mouth and lick my fingers. "If that's true, why didn't you call me when you moved back?"

"The timing was all wrong. I was about to reach out, when I heard about your father's diagnosis."

My expression turns serious. "The timing is still wrong, Marcus, with everything else going on in my life."

"I understand. I've waited this long. I can wait a while longer."

"There's the issue of faith. I don't know if I can ever trust you again."

"You will. One day. I'm committed to making that happen."

This man broke my heart once. I can't just let him swoop me off my feet again. "I'll be honest with you, Marcus. I don't see us ever getting back together. But I'd like for us to be friends."

"Friendship is as good a place to start as any." When I cut my eyes at him, he adds, "I mean it, Lil. I'm not giving up."

I notice dark clouds billowing in from the west. "Looks like a storm's brewing. You're welcome to stay. You could watch football while I read."

He grins, revealing perfectly straight pearly whites. "There are, in fact, several intriguing SEC games on this afternoon. And I brought some work with me, hoping you'd extend the offer."

"Great." I scramble to my feet. "But we should hurry before we get dumped on."

The first fat raindrops have begun to fall by the time we finish cleaning up our picnic and putting the kayaks away. I shower—fortunately there's no lightning, only heavy rain—and I'm seated at Dad's desk in front of his computer when Marcus comes to check on me.

"Can I get you anything? A cup of hot tea, maybe?"

"I'm fine for now. But thanks."

He stands behind me, looking over my shoulder. "Are you reading his memoir on that big screen?"

I crane my neck to look at him. "I have no choice. I didn't think to bring my laptop."

"Here, let me see that." He takes the keyboard from me, and

his fingers fly across the keys. "I'll email it to myself, and you can read it on my iPad."

"Are you sure? Don't you need your iPad to work?"

"I'll make do with my laptop." He goes into the other room and returns with his iPad. He taps on the screen and hands the iPad to me. "Now we need to get you comfortable." He pulls me to my feet and walks me over to Dad's Barcalounger. He switches on the floor lamp behind the chair, drapes a mohair throw across my legs, and pats me on the head. "I'll be in the other room if you need anything."

I offer him a smile of gratitude. After nursing Dad for three months, it's nice to have someone taking care of me for a change. Come to think of it, Marcus was always concerned about my well-being when we were together. My bitterness toward him has consumed me since our breakup, making it easy for me to forget his many positive attributes. In high school, he was always rescuing animals and helping friends in need. He was one of the good guys. Until he broke off our engagement.

I kick off my flip-flops and recline the chair. I smell the faint scent of Dad's woodsy cologne on the worn amber leather. He so loved this chair. Dad spent untold hours here, reading his favorite authors, and I feel as though his arms are around me as I slip back into his world.

GRAHAM

*I*vy holed up in Edward's room for the entire Thanksgiving weekend. I knocked on the door periodically, lightly at first to ask if she needed anything and then with more urgency, begging her to talk to me.

She answered with muffled pleas to leave her alone.

The trays of food I left in the hallway remained untouched, and she refused to see her beloved Bessie, who'd become a fixture on the floor outside Edward's door. Alice was the only one allowed entry into her sanctum, and she came to visit Ivy at least once a day, sometimes twice.

Late afternoon on Sunday, I stopped Alice in the upstairs hallway on her way out. "Have a glass of wine with me? I'd like to know how my wife is doing." I held up my glass, Edward's expensive cabernet sloshing over the rim. I'd already polished off one bottle and opened another.

She followed me into the drawing room. "But only for a few minutes. Heath's waiting dinner for me."

I poured her a glass of wine from the decanter and handed it to her. The afternoon sun streaming through the windows highlighted the bruises under Alice's eyes. She appeared pale and drawn, her brow pinched in concern.

"My wife won't talk to me," I said. "She won't even let me in the room. I have no clue how to reach her."

"She's having a tough time, Graham. She doesn't mean to shut you out. That's just how she is. She's always kept her emotions hidden. Even from her father. I'm the only person she really talks to."

"I understand that. And I'm glad she has you." I moved to the window. "This past week, our small world paused to honor a great man, but now, everyone is moving on with their lives as though nothing happened. When I've been out on walks with Bessie, I've seen the wreaths and Christmas trees going up in the houses around us. People are gearing up for the holidays, planning parties and shopping. I've never lost anyone close to me before. How am I supposed to move on with my life without Edward, with my wife in the depths of despair over the loss of her father? Do I go to work tomorrow? I honestly don't know."

She came to stand beside me, cupping my cheek in her hand. "Yes, Graham, you absolutely must go to work tomorrow. It will probably be one of the most difficult things you ever do, but we must set an example for Ivy. She needs to see that you and Trudy and I, all of the people she loves, are making an effort to move past Edward's death." Alice let out a sigh as she dropped her hand from my face. "I admit I'm worried about her, though. As you know, she's not eating. And I can't get her to bathe. She doesn't look good. If she's not better by week's end, I think we should call her doctor."

Alice promised to check in on Ivy frequently while I was at work, and we made a pact to communicate at least once a day. When Alice reported on Friday that Ivy had worsened instead of showing signs of improvement, I asked her doctor, an old family friend, to stop by on his way home from work.

"I gave her a sound lecture about not eating," Dr. Berry said when he came down from seeing Ivy. "While she's consumed by grief, I have no reason to fear she might try to hurt herself. At least not yet. We definitely need to watch her closely. I could prescribe antidepressants, but I'd rather hold off for now. I've seen patients affected by death this way. It just takes time."

"So, there's nothing we can do but give her space?" I asked the doctor as I showed him to the door.

Berry adjusted his fedora. "Get her to eat! She needs nourishment."

Closing the door behind him, I went straight to the kitchen in search of Trudy. "The doctor says we need to get Ivy to eat."

Trudy leaned back against the counter, arms crossed over her midsection. "Did he say how? I've been making her hearty dinners. Maybe I should try lighter foods, some of her favorites like yogurt and chocolate milkshakes and banana and mayonnaise sandwiches."

My lip curled. "I've never understood that particular fetish."

She laughed. "Because you're not a Southerner."

I gave her arm a squeeze. "Whatever it takes, Trudy. Cookies. Cakes. Pudding. I'm going out right now and get her some of that frozen strawberry yogurt she loves."

Our new strategy succeeded in getting Ivy to eat a little but not enough for my liking. For the next three weeks, as people around us carried on with their preparations for Christmas, she remained in her room, refusing to see anyone except Alice.

Early in the morning on Christmas Eve, I came upon Trudy in the kitchen preparing the rib roast for the following day. "There's no way Ivy's gonna eat that."

Trudy's shoulders sagged as her body deflated. "But it's Christmas. I make my rib roast every year." She rinsed her hands in the sink and dried them on her apron. "This house is so depressing. My Ivy won't let me put up a tree or even buy a poinsettia."

"You're right. We have to do something. We can't go on like

this." I stroked my chin as I thought out loud through our options. "Gift giving is out of the question. The only thing she wants is the one thing I can't give her—to bring her father back. We can't decorate the house with the old ornaments. They'll only remind Ivy of Edward and make her miss him even more." I flashed Trudy a smile. "But I have an idea that just might work. Can you put the rib roast on hold?"

"Yes, sir. Tell me what you want me to do."

"Go to the grocery store. Buy cranberries, popcorn, and plain white construction paper. I'm going to run a couple of errands, and I'll meet you back here later."

Planting her hands on her narrow hips, Trudy stared down her nose at me. "What are you up to, Graham?"

I grabbed Edward's car keys from the table beside the back door. "You'll see soon enough."

No one had driven Edward's Wagoneer since his death, but much to my relief, it started right up. Pickings were slim for trees and supplies. On the way to Walmart in North Charleston for colored lights, I stopped at three different lots until I found a tree that was fat and full and would've been perfect if not for the gaping hole on one side. Back at home, I positioned the tree between the windows in the drawing room with the hole facing the wall. I wound the colored lights around the tree while Trudy strung popcorn and cranberries and cut snowflakes out of the folded white paper.

When we finished, I stood back to assess our work. "It's the saddest tree I've ever seen. And that's saying a lot from a poor boy whose father believed Christmas was a waste of time and money."

Trudy shot me a sideways look. "You never talk about yourself. I always assumed you were rich like the Stoneys."

I trusted Trudy to keep my secret. "Does it surprise you that Edward let his daughter marry a man with no money?"

"Not at all. Mister Edward had a great deal of respect for you. He loved you like his own son."

This brought a smile to my face and a lump in my throat. "Thank you for saying that. It means a lot."

"I should've suspected about your upbringing. Your teeth give you away."

"Are they that bad?" I asked, bringing my lips together to hide my protruding canine teeth.

Trudy swatted me with the back of her hand. "Nobody's looking at your teeth, Mister Graham. People see your handsome face and those warm brown eyes. My granny used to call your kind of eyes soulful eyes." She touched the tip of her finger to her front teeth. "I have this gap between my teeth, but there was never enough money to send me to the orthodontist."

"I find your gap charming. It adds character to your face." I stared down at my feet. "Even if my parents could've afforded it, they never cared enough about me to have my teeth straightened."

A flash of anger lit up her brown eyes. "That's just a crying shame. I care about you, Mister Graham. And I'd like to get to know you better. I say we make a New Year's resolution to get better acquainted."

I smiled at her. "I'd like that."

She glanced toward the stairs. "How're you gonna get my Ivy down here to see the tree?"

"By doing what we should've done weeks ago. We're going to be firm, Trudy. We are going to stop pampering her and insist she come downstairs."

"I like your way of thinking. Let's do it," she said, and we hurried up the stairs to Edward's room.

I pounded on the door with my fist. "Open the door, Ivy. Trudy and I have a surprise for you downstairs." I winked at Trudy while we waited for an answer.

The door opened a crack and one of Ivy's navy eyes appeared. "I'm really not in the mood for surprises, Graham."

"Well, you'd better get in the mood." It dawned on me that she might not know the date. "It's Christmas Eve, in case you didn't know, and Trudy and I want to share it with you."

Trudy bobbed her head in agreement. "Come on out now, baby girl. Your husband has done something real special for you. The least you can do is come see it."

Much to my surprise, Ivy said, "Let me get my robe." When she opened the door wider to let us in, I was aghast at the sight of her emaciated frame through her flimsy nightgown.

Trudy helped Ivy into her robe, and with one of us on either side of her, we guided her down the stairs.

I wasn't sure how Ivy would react to my surprise, and I was thrilled when she burst out laughing at the tree. "That's a Charlie Brown tree if ever I saw one."

"Hey!" I say, my expression wounded. "Don't insult my tree. It's all I could manage on Christmas Eve."

As with a flip of a switch, her face fell, and she began to cry. "We can't celebrate Christmas. Not without Daddy."

I took her cold hand in mine. "Come over here and sit down." Trudy and I settled Ivy between us on the sofa. "I want you to close your eyes and think about how much your father loved Christmas."

"But—"

I touch my fingertip to her lips. "Please, Ivy. Listen to what Trudy and I have to say."

Trudy handed her a tissue. Wiping away her tears, Ivy squeezed her eyes shut. She was quiet for a moment and then a smile tugged at her lips. "He did love Christmas, didn't he? And last Christmas, he surprised me with Bessie."

Over the top of my wife's head, I gave Trudy the nod. She rose from the sofa, crossed the room, and opened the door to Edward's study. Bessie, a red velvet ribbon tied around her neck, spotted Ivy and made a flying leap onto the sofa, covering her mistress's face in licks.

Ivy collapsed under the dog's weight and fell back against the sofa cushions.

"She missed you," Trudy said.

"Bessie's not the only one," I added. "Your father would not want you wasting away in his room. His life was cut way too short, but you can make up for his loss by living every day to its fullest."

"I can't though, Graham. This sadness I feel is all I have left of him. If I let go of the pain, I'll be letting go of him. That sounds stupid, I know, but it's how I feel."

"You can't help how you feel, Ivy. And your feelings aren't stupid. Life will never be the same without your father. And we shouldn't try to replicate the Christmases you shared together. My tree, however pitiful it may be, is a symbolic gesture that's meant to represent our future holidays together. Next year, we'll adopt new traditions. We'll put our mark on the holidays. We'll do something outrageous like drive to the mountains and cut down our own tree."

Trudy shot me a knowing look. "We can change up the menu, if you'd like. Instead of the rib roast, I can make lasagna, or your favorite oyster stew and crab quiche."

I nodded. "Who knows? Maybe we'll have a baby by then. Or one on the way."

Ivy's smile didn't quite reach her eyes, but it was a smile, nonetheless.

"I'd like for tonight to be the first night of the rest of our lives together," I said. "You're not alone in this life, Ivy. You have me and Trudy and Bessie." I gave the dog's ears a rub.

"And Alice," Ivy said softly.

"And Alice," I repeated. What was it about the plain freckle-faced woman who was never far from my wife's mind? I smiled, more to myself than at Ivy, because even though I knew she'd

115

always love Alice more than me, I loved my wife enough for both of us. "We all miss him, Ivy. We might find it therapeutic if we tried missing him together."

Ivy was quiet for a long time before she said, "I promise to do better, if you promise not to push me to talk about my feelings." With a hint of her bubbly self that let me know my wife was still in there somewhere, she said, "I'm going a little stir-crazy in that room anyway."

GRAHAM

*I*vy slowly began to pick up the pieces of her life. Much to my dismay, she continued to sleep in Edward's room, and while she resumed her schedule, she did so without much enthusiasm. She was a shell of her former self. She walked and talked and ate like Ivy, but the part I loved most about her, her fun-loving spirit, had yet to resurface. I began to worry that it never would, that she was so profoundly affected by her father's death that she would forever be scarred. I sensed a baby would be the one thing that could lure her out of her depression, but when I asked her to move back into our room with me, she responded with an emphatic no and warned me not to pressure her.

Over coffee on the Monday of the second full week of January, Ivy announced that she would be traveling with a group of girlfriends to Alice's parents' house in Boca Grande, Florida, for the upcoming long holiday weekend.

I smiled at her across the table. "Good for you! Fresh air and sunshine are just what you need."

Uncertainty crossed her face. "Are you sure you don't mind?"

"I'm positive, sweetheart. Bessie and I will be just fine." At the sound of her name, the dog, at Ivy's feet, thumped her tail against the floor. "That's right, girl, it'll be just you and me. We may go down to Wadmalaw for the weekend. I've been wanting to polish up my stories from Africa. This will give me the perfect opportunity."

Ivy looked at me with a dazed expression. Her mind was a million miles away. She hadn't even heard what I'd said.

Glancing at the clock on the stove, I pushed back from the table. "I'd better get going. Today's the first day of classes."

The old Ivy would've wished me luck. This Ivy merely acknowledged my departure with a sad smile.

Relieved to have structure restored to my days, I immersed myself in my work. After my stellar performance in the fall, the department head entrusted me with my first upper level class, Advanced Fiction Writing, and I was excited for the opportunity to assess the talents of the juniors and seniors enrolled. I'd taught a few of these students before, but most were new to me.

I was in my office late Thursday afternoon when one of those newbies cracked my door and asked if she could have a word with me. I'd seen Melanie Hogan around campus. She possessed a rare beauty with alabaster skin, snow-white hair, the daintiest pert nose, and eyes as gray as a foggy morning.

And that body, the way she paraded through the halls in clothing that accentuated her feminine curves. On this particular day, she wore a tight-fitting gray wool skirt, black knee-high boots, and a cream-colored blouse sheer enough to see through to her lacy bra.

I wasn't completely immune to the beautiful coeds flocking our campus. While I was married to the love of my life, I was still a man. I could look at the menu without ordering.

I motioned her to the chair in front of my desk. "What can I do for you, Miss Hogan?"

Crossing her legs, she placed her leather satchel in her lap.

"I was wondering if you would be willing to read my manuscript." She removed a thick-bound sheaf of papers from her bag, plunking it on my desk. "I've been hard at work on this novel for the past three years. I'd like to use your class as an opportunity to polish the manuscript before submitting it to literary agents."

I rocked back in my chair. "Completing a novel is a great accomplishment. So many ambitious writers start novels, but so few actually finish. Tell me in one sentence what your story is about."

"It's a romantic comedy about a princess who has a steamy love affair with her chauffeur, set in London in modern times."

"The plot's not very original." I didn't bother hiding my skepticism. I had a reputation with my students for being up-front.

Melanie gave a nonchalant shrug. "Maybe not, but the writing is."

I chuckled. "Good comeback. I like your style, Miss Hogan. Yes, I'll read your manuscript. But you'll need to give me a couple of weeks."

She moved to the edge of her chair. "Really? That'd be awesome! Thanks, Professor Alexander. You're really gonna like it."

"Better let me be the judge of that."

When I got up to see her to the door, she surprised me by kicking the door closed. Spinning around to face me, she grabbed hold of my tie, pulling my face level to hers and pressing her luscious cupid's bow lips against mine. I'd had students flirt with me before, but none had been so bold as to make a pass at me. Hiking up her skirt, she placed my hand on her bare thigh, and whispered a husky, "I'm not wearing any panties."

The tension that had been building since Edward's death exploded inside of me, and a shudder of desire pulsed through my body. I flipped the switch, turning off the overhead light so as not to be seen through the window, and walked her backward, fumbling off our clothes and clearing my desk with one sweep of my arm. Pushing her down to the desk, I kneed her legs apart and drove deep inside of her. She responded by arching her back and wrapping her booted legs around my torso. When her moans escalated into cries of ecstasy, I covered her mouth with mine, crushing her lips. I came with the force of a volcano eruption, and collapsed on top of her, panting. Minutes passed, and I felt her skilled fingers on my manhood, coaxing me erect once again. Rolling on top of me, she rode me hard like a cowgirl on a bucking bronco in a rodeo.

When it was over, we lay entangled in each other's arms on the desk. "This is a fine time for me to be asking this, but are you . . . did you . . . protect yourself?" Everything had happened too fast for me to think about using a condom. Not that I had one stashed away in my wallet. I had no use for condoms. My wife and I were trying to start a family.

"I'm on the pill, silly." She ran her hand across my bare chest. "Take me to Wadmalaw with you this weekend."

In class earlier in the day, when one of my students inquired about my plans for the long weekend, I'd let slip that I was going to the island to do some writing, which had led to a lengthy discussion about the benefits of having a relaxing place that inspired creativity.

"I'm married, Melanie."

She snorted. "You're obviously not very happily married or what just happened would never have happened."

"It's complicated. My wife's father was killed in a boating accident right before Thanksgiving. She was extremely close to him, and . . . well, we've been going through a rough patch."

"It's not complicated. It's just sex."

Was it that simple? Fondling her breast, I pinched her nipple until she tossed her pretty head back and groaned in pleasure. I had my doubts as to whether sex-with-no-strings-attached relationships between two mutually consenting adults were even possible. But at that moment, I could've screwed her a thousand times, so blind was I with lust. I found myself telling her I'd pick her up the next afternoon at five o'clock at Porter's Lodge.

As I left Randolph Hall and set off on the twenty-minute walk to the Battery, the brisk January air sobered me and guilt set in. Aside from the fact that I loved my wife with all my heart, my contract with the college stated that relationships between teachers and students of any nonprofessional nature were strictly forbidden.

Ivy had flown off to Florida that morning, and Trudy had already left for the day by the time I arrived home. I lit a fire in the fireplace in Edward's study, poured a glass of red wine, and settled in for the evening with Bessie at my feet and Melanie's manuscript in my lap.

Any thoughts I had of canceling the weekend vanished when I read the first paragraph of her romantic comedy, *Crazy Love*, a novel about the escapades of a group of twenty-some-things living in a high-rise apartment building in Manhattan. Despite my initial speculation, her story line was quite original. She drew me into her setting with charming description, while her protagonist's unique sense of humor and knack for finding trouble held me captive.

I'd never before finished a book in one sitting, but despite the late hour, I read every last word. I was enamored of this budding young writer who'd waltzed into my office, had sex with me on top of my desk, and mesmerized me with her writing.

The next afternoon at precisely five o'clock, I pulled up in front of Porter's Lodge and Melanie climbed into the car. When she noticed Bessie in the back seat, she turned up her nose. "I'm a cat person."

I bit back laughter when Bessie growled at her. "Really? Because I despise cats. If this is a deal-breaker, I can let you off at the corner."

"No, it's fine. I'm not allergic or anything like that."

But Bessie didn't think it was fine. Whether or not she suspected I was being unfaithful to her beloved mistress, she knew something was up. She spent the weekend curled by the wood stove in the downstairs sitting room while Melanie and I engaged in a marathon of reckless sex in the queen-size bed in the guest bedroom upstairs.

We stayed tipsy on red wine and ate scrambled eggs and toast with orange marmalade when we got hungry. Melanie's appetite for sex was insatiable. I had my way with her in every position imaginable. I did things to her I'd dreamed of doing to my wife.

But my desire for Melanie dissipated once my sexual appetite was satiated. And by noon on Sunday, I was eager to take her back to campus where she belonged. It wasn't so much Melanie. She was damn near perfect and would make some lucky bastard happy. But she wasn't right for me. She wasn't Ivy. My experiment had yielded results. Sex-only relationships were possible. But once my body was satisfied, my sexual appetite quenched, the burden of my sins settled on me like a ten-ton gorilla. I was an adulterer. As a young boy, listening to my father's fists pound my mother's flesh late at night, I made a vow to myself to be not only a devoted and faithful husband to my wife but a loving father to my children. Ivy and I hadn't yet been married a year, and I'd betrayed her in the worst possible way.

My heart was heavy as Melanie and I started back toward Charleston in my car. We barely spoke a word during the drive.

On Montagu Street, she responded to my sullen mood as we neared the college. "This is it, isn't it? We're not going to see each other again outside of the classroom?"

I took my eyes off the road to look at her. "It has to be this way, Melanie. I love my wife very much. She's been through so much these past few months. I would never, ever want to hurt her."

The muscles in her pretty face tightened. "Whatever. It was fun while it lasted."

I returned my eyes to the road. "Can I count on you to keep this between us? It would cost me my job and my marriage if this got out."

"I don't kiss and tell, Graham," she snapped. "What about my novel?"

We'd been too busy doing unthinkable things to talk about her book. I had yet to even tell her I'd read the manuscript. "Your novel has enormous potential, Melanie. You're a brilliant storyteller. I read it Thursday night in one sitting."

Her pale eyes grew wide. "You think so, really?"

Despite everything, I couldn't help but smile at her enthusiasm. We were back to being professor and student. "I really think so."

"Yes!" She pounded the roof of my car with her fist, waking a sleeping Bessie in the back seat. Bessie let out a disgruntled snort and lay her head back down.

"Don't get ahead of yourself, now. It still needs some work, but we can address those issues in class."

GRAHAM

*T*rudy was at the stove, stirring lasagna noodles in a pot of boiling water, when I arrived home. Instead of her customary uniform, black dress and apron, she wore dark jeans and a red crew neck sweater with her hair held off her face with a plaid headband. I'd never seen her in plain clothes, aside from the black suit she'd worn to Edward's funeral, and her attire made her seem more real to me. She was more than the Stoney's maid. She was Isaac's wife and Ruthie's mother. She was my friend.

"I didn't expect to find you here today," I said, dropping my car keys in the pottery dish on the table beside the back door.

She twirled around, eyes wide with fear and wooden spoon raised to strike. Seeing me, she collapsed against the counter. "Jesus, Lord. You scared me. I didn't hear you come in."

"Sorry. I didn't mean to startle you. What're you doing here on a Sunday?"

"Isaac took Ruthie over to see his parents for the afternoon. I finished my chores at home, and I got lonesome, so I decided to come here to get ahead of my work for the week. I thought you'd still be down at the cottage."

"I finished my editing and decided to come on home." My face warmed as the lie slipped off my tongue. I'd done not a lick of work over the weekend.

Bessie scampered into the kitchen and made a beeline for Trudy, rubbing up against the backs of her legs.

Trudy looked down at the dog. "What's gotten into you, Bessie? Did something scare you?"

From behind Trudy's legs, the dog peeked out at me. Trudy looked from the dog to me. "What'd you do to upset this dog?"

I squirmed under her intense gaze. I couldn't lie. Not to Trudy. "I screwed up." I hung my head. "Oh, God, Trudy, I screwed up so badly."

"What'd you mean you screwed up? Did you wreck Mister Edward's Wagoneer or burn the cottage down?"

I shook my head. "Worse."

"A woman?"

I nodded, my eyes glued to the floor.

Trudy set her wooden spoon in the spoon rest and turned off the boiling pot. She came to stand in front of me. "Do you love her?"

"Not at all. I don't even really like her. I could blame any number of things—Edward's death, Ivy's despair—but there's no excuse for what I did." I dropped to a chair at the table, pushing my glasses to my head and burying my face in my hands to hide my shame.

Neither of us spoke, but I sensed her presence looming over me. After a few minutes, I heard her moving about the kitchen, filling the kettle with water, setting it on the stove, the whistling when it began to boil.

A few more minutes passed before she set a cup of Earl Gray tea in front of me and joined me at the table. "I ain't gonna lie, Mister Graham. There's something seriously wrong about taking your lover away for the weekend with your wife's dog in tow."

I forced myself to look up at her, to brave the disappointment on her face, but I had no words to defend myself. "I'm aware."

She locked her fingers together on the table in front of her. "When I was a girl of about thirteen, I heard my parents arguing late one night. As I listened at their bedroom door, it became clear to me that my father had been stepping out on my mother. Mama was heartbroken. She cried for weeks. I was furious at my father, but more than that, I was terrified they'd get divorced and split up our happy little family. By the grace of God, Mama found it in her heart to forgive him. My dad had been having some trouble at work, and the stress had driven him to make this horrible mistake."

Trudy wore a pained expression. All these years later, her father's betrayal still cut deep.

She continued, "I saw how hard it was for Mama to trust him again, and my father, who never dared do anything like that again, spent the rest of his life making it up to her. Whether for good reason or not, Mister Graham, people make mistakes. And these mistakes affect the whole family, even our loyal pets." She smiled over at Bessie, asleep on the floor in front of the stove. "I won't put any more stress on my Ivy by telling her this. I don't think her poor heart can take it. I've seen how much you've been suffering since Mister Edward's death, and I'm willing to turn a blind eye this once." She took my hands in hers and looked me square on. "But you can never let this happen again."

I tasted the salty tears as they streamed down my cheeks and into my mouth. "I won't, Trudy. I promise."

***

Even though I gave Bessie one of Trudy's soup bones for dinner and let her sleep in my bed that night, she nuzzled up against

Ivy, declaring her allegiance, the moment Ivy walked in the door the following afternoon.

I thought of Trudy's father, who'd had to work so hard to earn back his wife's trust. Perhaps my wife would be more inclined to forgive me if I told her the truth. Confessing my sins would alleviate my guilt. Never mind that it was the honest thing to do. It was what Edward would've done.

Ivy brushed her lips against my cheek. "How was your weekend on Wadmalaw?"

"Fine." Unable to meet her gaze, I took her two duffel bags and dropped them at the foot of the stairs. "Would you like to go down to the cottage with me for a weekend soon?"

Her face grew dark. "I can't, Graham. Not yet. There are too many memories of Daddy in that cottage."

"I understand." I helped her out of her lightweight jacket and hung it in the coat closet. "Are you hungry?"

"I'm starving," she said, her hand on her belly.

Her appetite hadn't fully recovered since Edward's death, and I took this as a sign her trip had gone well. "Trudy left us some chili. I'll heat it up, and we can eat on trays in front of the fire in the drawing room."

Fifteen minutes later, we were seated with our trays in our laps, backs against the sofa, and legs stretched out in front of us. "Tell me about your trip," I said.

"You're not gonna believe it, Graham. I finally beat Alice in tennis. I wish Daddy were here! He'd be so proud of me." I waited for the torrent of tears that usually followed mention of Edward, but none came.

I offered her a high five. "Your daddy *is* proud of you." I pointed heavenward. "And so am I."

While we ate, she spoke of the restaurants where they'd dined, the lazy afternoons lounging in the sun, and the shopping excursion to Naples. "It felt good to get away. I really needed a change of scenery."

"I can tell! I'm pleased to see you so happy."

"Alice and I had several late-night, heart-to-heart talks. She helped me realize how much I have to live for." Ivy set her tray on the floor and angled her body toward mine. "I know I've been difficult these past couple of months. I'd like to talk about our future. That is, if you still want a future with me."

I felt a stab of guilt. I didn't deserve a second chance. When a chill crossed my body, raising the hairs on my arms and neck, I convinced myself it was Edward, watching over us. At least that's what I needed to believe. "There's nothing I want more, my darling."

"I have an idea." Getting to her feet, she collected the trays and left the room, returning in a flash with a bottle of champagne and two flutes.

"What's all this?" I asked.

"I think we should toast our future." Popping the cork, she filled both glasses, handing one to me. She grabbed the cashmere throw off the back of the sofa and, sitting down close to me, tucked the blanket around our legs. "To us," she said, lifting her glass.

I touched my glass to hers. "To us."

She snuggled in closer. "I spoke with Henry Scott last week before I left for Florida. You may remember meeting him at the wedding. And the funeral. Daddy has several attorneys, but Henry is his most trusted."

"Right. Tall and skinny with gray hair. Loves Alabama football and playing golf."

"He's the one. Anyway, there are no surprises in Daddy's will. Everything passes to me." She sipped her champagne. "I don't know anything about money, Graham. I have no choice but to trust my father's financial advisers. But I'd like you to be included in the discussions. As my husband, you need to know what's going on."

"I'm flattered, sweetheart. And I'll help in any way possible.

But I'm an English professor. I know nothing about portfolio management."

"Then we'll figure it out together," Ivy said. "And Heath will help. I've been thinking we should move some money over to his firm."

"I don't know, Ivy. Mixing business with pleasure is never a good idea." When her face fell, I quickly added, "On the other hand, Heath seems like an intelligent guy."

"No, you're right. We should give him a little more time to prove himself." She nudged me. "See, you're providing sound advice already."

"That's just common sense." I guzzled down my champagne and refilled my glass.

"Daddy's untimely death taught me not to take tomorrow for granted." She took my glass of champagne from me and set it down alongside hers on the coffee table. She threw her leg across my lap, straddling me, and began unbuttoning my shirt.

"What're you doing," I asked with a smirk on my lips.

"What do you think?" she said, leaning down to kiss me.

I caught a whiff of flowers. "Since when do you wear perfume?"

"Do you like it? It's Gardenia Chanel. Alice bought it for me in Naples."

Alice? Wasn't it a husband's responsibility to buy perfume for his wife? Nevertheless, I was pleased Ivy was trying new things, and the fragrance smelled delicious on her. I buried my nose in her neck, sucking gently on her skin. "It's lovely."

We made love in the glow of the fire with the tenderness of two people who were finding their way back together again after having been separated. Our desire came from deep within, our passion mounting with an intensity that stemmed from the great loss we'd suffered. Our release was exquisite, wave after wave of ecstasy.

Afterward, she lay with one leg tossed over my body and

head nestled in my armpit. "That's an Ivy I've never seen before," I said. "Where have you been hiding her? I'd like to see more of her."

"I'm a new person, Graham. My grief has taken me to the depths of hell. There were times when I didn't think I'd survive. Not only did I survive, I emerged a changed person. More resilient and wise. Less naive and carefree. Although I miss that girl sometimes. I rather liked her."

"I liked her too. But she still resides inside you." I placed my hand over her heart. "The tougher, more astute version of that girl will serve you well as a mother."

"About that." She fingered the fringe on the blanket. "Alice and I have decided to stop obsessing about getting pregnant."

Alice appeared to be in full control of my wife's heartstrings. But who was I to argue if she got these kinds of results? "That's a smart decision. It'll happen whenever it happens."

She exhaled a gush of air. "I'm tired of feeling sad, Graham. Is it wrong of me to want to feel happy again?"

"Not at all. Your father would want you to be happy. He loved the way you lit up the room. The first time we had dinner together, after you'd run off to one of your meetings, he compared you to a hummingbird, dropping in for nectar at one party before moving on to the next."

"Did he really?"

I nodded. "He loved you dearly. But you don't need me to tell you that."

"I'm going to take advantage of every single day, to make up for the time Daddy lost. I want to make some changes to the house to suit our needs. I'm going to redecorate the master suite for us. Are you okay with that?"

I kissed her hair. "I'm fine with anything, as long as we get to sleep in the same bed again."

She smiled up at me. "I've missed having coffee with you in the mornings. The view of the river is much better from the master. I've been thinking about putting a desk and chaise lounge in the small sitting room off the bedroom. Wouldn't it make a cozy little hideaway for me to read and write letters?"

"I love that idea."

"And, whenever the time comes, we'll turn our old suite into a nursery. There's enough room in there to have a nanny, if we decide we want one." She paused to catch her breath. "You'll take over my father's study, of course. He would want you to use it. You can grade your papers in there at night. Maybe you'll write your first novel at his desk." She sat straight up, her small breasts exposed. "Never mind! You're going to write your first novel on Wadmalaw. I want you to hire a contractor and fix up the cottage. Lord knows it needs it. The place is falling down."

Propping myself on my elbows, I asked, "Are you sure that's what you want? You said yourself, the cottage is full of memories of Edward."

"Daddy's presence will always be there. By redoing the cottage, we'll be creating a clean slate for us to make new memories."

"All right, then. I'll get on it," I said, suddenly overcome with love for this incredible creature I was so fortunate to have as my wife. I made a silent vow, with only God as my witness, to never ever look at another woman as long as I lived.

GRAHAM

*I*vy's return from Florida marked the beginning of one of the happiest periods of my life. While I struggled constantly with telling Ivy the truth about Melanie, things were too good between us for me to risk ruining it. Our bond deepened and our relationship matured as we stepped into the roles of owners of one of the most prestigious homes on Charleston's elite Battery. For a man of my background, I found the sums of money that flew out of the house on a daily basis staggering. My salary alone would not even cover the basics. Ivy's insistence that I deposit my biweekly paychecks in a savings account for a rainy day served as a reminder that I'd married way out of my league.

In early February, we met for the first time with her financial advisers. Ivy was dressed to impress in a black pantsuit with white silk blouse, her golden hair pulled tight at the nape of her neck. She had her team of advisers, men in business suits gathered around a mahogany conference table, eating out of her hand.

On the walk home from their offices, I admitted, "I had no idea about the extent of your father's net worth."

The weather was unseasonably warm, one of those days that teased us into believing spring was right around the corner when we had at least another month of winter left.

"The Stoney family fortune has been handed down from generation to generation for two hundred years. The burden of responsibility to preserve it for our children and grandchildren has now fallen to us."

I looped my arm through hers. "I was impressed by the way you handled yourself in the meeting. You obviously have an intuitive understanding of portfolio management."

"Do I? I guess it comes from listening to my father all these years."

"I'll be honest, a lot of what they said was over my head. History and English were my best subjects at Harvard. I never studied business."

"Pay attention, Graham, and you'll learn. You need to know what's going on in case something happens to me."

As much as it pained me to even think about such a thing, Edward's premature death made me realize that, as adults, it was our responsibility to prepare for whatever the future might bring.

"Daddy, as you may have noticed, was a frugal old fuddy-duddy. He let the house deteriorate. You and I are gonna live a little."

And boy, did we ever live a little. While I was busy making arrangements to modernize the cottage on Wadmalaw, Ivy hired the South's most prestigious decorator, Courtney Adams, known to friends as Coco, to freshen up the house in Charleston. They went on a rampage, making small changes in nearly every room that rendered big results. They reupholstered the furniture in the drawing room with elegant fabrics in muted tones, while in the dining room, they installed Gracie wall covering—a garden design of birds and flowering trees on a pale blue background. In my study, they ripped out the dingy gray shag carpeting that reeked of pipe smoke and covered the hardwoods with a large zebra rug, a trophy from Edward's African safari decades ago. And they used a palette of greens and blues in the master suite to bring the outdoors inside.

When Ivy offered to renovate the kitchen, Trudy chased her out of her domain with a broom. "Don't you touch a thing in here. This is my room. I'm perfectly happy with the way these old appliances work."

Ivy relented, but the following Sunday, on Trudy's day off, she replaced the worn Oriental with an Aztec rug in vibrant reds and blues and yellows.

Ivy and I opted out of the hectic winter social season that year, choosing instead to have cozy red-wine dinners by the fire followed by intense lovemaking and soul-sharing talks that lasted well into the wee hours of the morning. Although she drifted in and out of her sullen mood, her father never far from her thoughts, for the most part, Ivy's grief appeared to have mellowed.

On a Wednesday afternoon in late February, I arrived home from work early evening to find Trudy and Ivy seated at the kitchen table with serious expressions and their heads close together. My stomach lurched. Had Trudy gone back on her word and told Ivy about my affair? Afraid to take off my coat or set down my briefcase, I asked, "What's wrong?"

"Nothing's wrong, Graham. In fact, everything's perfect. I should've waited until you got home, but Trudy's like my mama and I had to tell someone." She jumped to her feet and threw her arms around me. "Oh, Graham. It's the most wonderful news. I'm pregnant. We're going to have a baby."

I stared at her, slack jawed. "Are you sure?"

"I'm positive. The doctor confirmed it today. My due date is October thirteenth."

I wished I'd thought to take a photograph of her in the moment, in her pretty yellow sweater with her cheeks flushed pink, the happiest I'd ever seen her. I dropped my briefcase and lifted her off the floor. "That's fabulous, sweetheart."

She pushed away from me and sank back down to her chair. "How am I going to break the news to Alice? She called this morning, in hysterics because it didn't happen for them this month."

Trudy said, "Alice loves you, Miss Ivy. Whenever you decide to tell her, she'll be happy for you."

"That's right," I said. "Just be cognizant of her feelings until it does happen for her."

She smiled at me. "Let's not tell anyone just yet. With any luck, by the time I reach my second trimester, she'll be pregnant."

The first wave of morning sickness hit Ivy the very next day. She vomited up the oatmeal she'd eaten for breakfast and her skin turned a putrid shade of pea green. But she never complained. For the next six weeks, she went to bed early, took naps during the day, and existed on a diet of saltine crackers and ginger ale. Her morning sickness was so severe, she freaked out when she woke one day the second week in April to discover the nausea had subsided.

"Something's not right." Kicking back the covers, she swung her feet over the side of the bed. "I feel great. Better than I have in weeks. Better than a pregnant woman should feel. What if something's wrong with the baby, Graham?"

"I'm sure everything is fine, darling." Crawling across the mattress to her, I planted a trail of kisses in the crook of her neck. "What does your baby book say?" Since learning of her pregnancy, she'd been glued to the hottest new release for expectant parents. *What to Expect When You're Expecting.*

She gnawed on her thumbnail. "That morning sickness typically goes away around the beginning of the second trimester. But as bad as mine was, it can't be normal for it to go away overnight."

I slipped the spaghetti strap of her nightgown down her arm and continued my kisses along her collarbone. "Just ask the doctor the next time you go."

She stood abruptly, leaving me kissing the air. "But my next appointment isn't for two weeks. I'll go nuts if I have to wait that long."

"Then call his office when they open this morning. I'm sure if you tell them how worried you are, they'll fit you in today."

"I'll do that." She threw on her robe and headed for the door. "In the meantime, I'm going to get breakfast. I have a fierce craving for eggs and bacon and toast with fig preserves. And coffee, of course."

"Make sure it's decaf," I called after her.

When I left for campus forty-five minutes later, my wife was seated at the kitchen table, shoveling eggs into her mouth with the phone receiver tucked under her chin, her brows pinched together as she waited for the doctor's office to answer.

"Call me," I mouthed on my way out.

I was only mildly worried. But I was worried, nonetheless. And my concern escalated as the day wore on with no word from Ivy. I tried calling the house several times throughout the afternoon, but no one answered. Not even Trudy who was almost always around. By the time my last class ended, I was in a near-panic state and sped through the downtown streets on my way home.

Ivy and Trudy were deep in conversation at the kitchen table when I burst through the back door. "Is it bad?" I asked. "Is something wrong with our baby?"

Ivy appeared surprised to see me. "What're you talking about, Graham?"

"The baby. Did you get in to see the doctor? What'd he say?"

She smiled up at me. "Everything's fine, sweetheart. The doctor heard a strong heartbeat."

"Thank God." I braced myself against the table. When my breath had steadied, I said, "Then why the serious faces?"

"Because I don't like my doctor." Ivy pulled me down to the chair beside her. "Don't get me wrong. He's an excellent doctor. He delivered nearly all of my friends, including Alice. He's just so old."

"I don't necessarily view that as a bad thing." I couldn't keep the irritation out of my tone. I'd been worried sick all afternoon about our baby, and she was upset because her doctor was old? "Old means experienced where doctors are concerned."

"He's just so creepy." She jumped back up and began pacing. "Shame on me for talking about Dr. Horton like that. He's a fine doctor. It's not him. It's me. I want to deliver our baby here. Do you know how many generations of Stoney babies have been born in this house?"

I stared back and forth between Trudy and my wife. Trudy's expression was dreamlike, and Ivy's face was set in determination as she wore out her new Aztec rug. "Am I the only one here who remembers that the last home birth didn't go well?"

"That situation was entirely different. My mother originally planned to deliver me in the hospital. And yes, Dr. Horton was *her* obstetrician. When she developed complications from high blood pressure two weeks ahead of her due date, he ordered her to be admitted to the hospital. But she refused to go."

I looked to Trudy for confirmation. "It's true. Miss Virginia's labor came on hard and fast." Trudy hung her head. "There was so much blood. Praise Lord, my Aunt Dottie, who happened to be a midwife, had stopped in to visit my mama at the time. She delivered the baby. Miss Ivy is lucky to be alive. But Aunt Dottie couldn't save Miss Virginia."

I tried to imagine the horrible event that had taken place in the house I now thought of as home. "I've read many fictional accounts involving midwives, but I've never known anyone who actually used one. Is your aunt still practicing?"

"Nope. But she trained her daughter, my cousin, to take over her practice when she retired. Nita is an even better midwife than Dottie." Trudy chuckled. "But don't tell Dottie I said so. Nita lives in Beaufort, but she has so many patients in Charleston she rents an apartment here. It would be no problem for her to attend to my Ivy."

Ivy reclaimed her chair. "Please, Graham. I hope you'll go along with me on this."

I ran the back of my finger down her cheek. "Does it really matter what I think? You've already made up your mind."

She flashed me a devilish grin. "You know me too well. I promise. I'll do everything Nita tells me to do. If there is any sign of trouble, I'll go back to Dr. Horton. I won't risk our baby's life. Or my own," she added almost as an afterthought.

"I know you won't," I said, and kissed her forehead.

She glanced at her watch and pushed back from the table. "I'm late for my date with Alice. We're meeting for a drink. Obviously, I'll be having tea. I'll be home in time for dinner." She retrieved her down vest from the row of pegs on the wall. "I'm going to tell Alice about the baby. Wish me luck," she said, and was out the door in a flash.

Trudy and I exploded into laughter. "Miss Ivy is back. She can barely sit still."

"No more morning sickness for her," I added.

"Lord knows, I had so much energy during my second trimester. My Ivy won't know what to do with herself if the same happens to her."

Despite my excitement over the baby, I continued to experience severe guilt and anxiety over my affair with Melanie. I hated keeping the truth from Ivy. I felt like I was living a lie in my picture-perfect world with my wife whom I'd betrayed. I didn't deserve her. Yet I loved her too much to risk losing her.

Seeing Melanie in class on Tuesdays and Thursdays made matters worse. Much to her credit, Melanie conducted herself in a businesslike manner when she stopped by my office during open hours for feedback on her manuscript. She spoke often of moving to New York after graduation and living the bohemian lifestyle until she secured a literary agent and published her novel. Although I didn't consider her a serious threat, knowing she would soon be gone from Charleston made me feel more at ease.

With renovations on the Wadmalaw cottage nearing completion, Ivy was making preparations to spend the majority of her last summer of freedom basking in the sun and reading romance novels. I'd committed to teaching a full slate of classes during both sessions of summer school, and planned to drive down on Fridays for the weekends.

On the second Saturday in May, exhausted from exams and a hectic weekend of graduation festivities, I was reading in the drawing room with Ivy beside me on the sofa knitting a pair of yellow baby booties when the doorbell rang.

Ivy looked up from her knitting. "Who on earth is out in this weather?" she said of the rain that had been pouring in torrents for the past hour.

I was too engrossed in Ken Follet's current bestseller, *Lie Down with Lions*, to care who was at the door.

I heard the loud clanging of the brass door knocker followed by Trudy asking, "May I help you?"

The familiar voice that answered, "I'm here to see Graham," sent dread down my spine.

Trudy called up from downstairs, "Mister Graham, there's a young woman here to see you."

Ignoring my wife's curious stare, I got up and went to face my firing squad.

Melanie stood in the doorway, her hair and clothes dripping wet and mascara streaming in rivulets down her cheeks. "Melanie. This is a surprise. I would've thought you'd be on your way to New York by now."

She looked at me with pleading in her gray eyes. "Is there somewhere we can talk in private?"

From the top of the stairs, Ivy said, "Whatever you have to say to my husband, you can say in front of me."

Melanie hunched a shoulder in a what-the-hell gesture. "I'm pregnant, a party favor from our weekend together at your island cottage in January. Because it's too late to terminate the pregnancy, I'm going to put the baby up for adoption. My plan was to go home to Savannah after graduation. But when I told my parents about the baby, they freaked out and refused to help me. I was hoping I wouldn't have to involve you, but I have nowhere else to go."

I stared at her, not trusting my ears. Ivy and Trudy forgotten, I said, "You were going to give my child up for adoption without consulting me?"

Melanie stared past me at Ivy. "Well, yeah. You're married, remember?"

Ivy glided down the stairs. "Damn right he's married. How do we know you're not lying? You certainly don't look pregnant to me."

Pushing back her drenched raincoat, Melanie lifted her jersey top to reveal a mounded belly, almost identical in size and shape to Ivy's.

My wife's body went rigid. "You can spend the night tonight. We'll talk more in the morning." With eyes still on

Melanie, Ivy said, "Trudy, please take this young woman upstairs to the guest room and find her some dry clothes."

Trudy, with Melanie in tow, ascended the stairs ahead of us. I kept my head bowed as I followed my wife's feet to the drawing room.

Positioned by the fireplace, Ivy demanded, "Start talking."

I stood face-to-face with her at a total loss for words. "I don't know where to begin."

"Is there any chance the baby isn't yours?" she asked in a tight voice.

I thought back in disgust at the countless times in contorted positions we'd had sex that weekend. "I would insist on a paternity test. But there's a good chance it's mine."

Ivy's face was set in stone, her jaw tight and lips pursed. In the blink of an eye, the little bit of happiness we'd discovered had slipped away. "I can't believe you had the gall to take her to the island, to *my* sacred place. Tell me, my beloved husband, did you have sex in my bed?"

"Jeez, Ivy. Of course not. It didn't mean anything. I promise it was only one weekend. I'd been so worried about you and so sad about Edward. She made a pass at me. And I was weak. I'm not that kind of person."

"Oh?" She arched an eyebrow. "But clearly you are."

Ivy began pacing back and forth in short strides in front of the fireplace, twirling her hair and mumbling to herself. She was scheming, and I was terrified of what her unpredictable mind was plotting. But before I could ask, Trudy escorted Melanie into the room.

Trudy made a hasty exit, while Melanie, covered in a terry cloth robe I'd never seen before, approached us.

When Ivy failed to offer her a seat, I knew this meeting wouldn't last long.

"How did this happen?" I asked Melanie. "Did you lie to me when you told me you were using protection?"

"I was on an antibiotic for a sinus infection at the time," Melanie said. "My doctor neglected to tell me that antibiotics can interfere with birth control."

"When's your due date?" Ivy asked and grimaced when Melanie told her October eleventh, two days before *her* baby's due date.

"And you're absolutely certain you don't want to keep the baby?" Ivy asked.

"I'm positive. I'm not even sure I ever want children. But I definitely don't want one now. Not until I've established my writing career."

"If you want our help, you'll have to abide by our rules," Ivy said. "You can live here. But you have to stay inside the house at all times. I don't want anyone to see you. A midwife will deliver your baby. Afterward, you'll leave Charleston and never come back. Not even for your college reunions."

"What will happen to the baby?" Melanie asked.

"I will raise it as my own. I'm expecting as well, due around the same time. I'll tell everyone I had twins. No one will ever suspect a thing."

I stared at my wife in disbelief. "That's ludicrous."

"It's rather brilliant if you ask me." Ivy twirled a strand of her hair as if bored with the situation. "That's my offer. Take it or leave it."

"I need some time to think about it," Melanie said.

"You have until the morning. I'll have Trudy make up the guest room in case you decide to stay," Ivy said. With her head held high, she then left the room.

Melanie waited until we were alone. "What a cold bitch."

"That cold bitch just made you a very generous offer."

Melanie rolled her eyes. "It sounds like a jail sentence to me."

I stared down at her. "You're the one who came to us looking for help. You're not exactly in a position to refuse it.

The guest room is on the third floor. Take a right at the top of the stairs."

I left the room in search of my wife. I found her in her sitting room, stretched out on a chaise lounge with a wet washcloth on her head.

"Ivy, darling," I said, lowering myself to the edge of the chaise lounge. "Can we talk about this?"

She lifted the washcloth to look at me. "No, Graham. We will not talk about this. In fact, we will never mention this again. We had a real shot at happiness. I was beginning to feel things I never thought I'd feel for a . . . for you. But you ruined that. I'll never be able to trust you again. This is the last time I clean up your mess." She repositioned the washcloth on her eyes. "Now, please, leave me be."

GRAHAM

The following morning, Ivy and Bessie left in Edward's Wagoneer to spend the summer on Wadmalaw. She refused to let me go with her. She claimed she needed time alone to think. But she didn't need time alone. She needed time without me. I know this, because two weeks later, on the Friday afternoon of Memorial Day weekend, I saw Heath at the butcher's counter at Piggly Wiggly, and he told me Alice had been at the cottage with Ivy all week.

When I inquired about the length of her stay, Heath said, "I'm not sure when she's coming back. I know she's planning to stay through the weekend, at least. I suspect she'll come home when she ovulates." Heath smiled, although there was something sad in his eyes. "If this baby thing doesn't work out for us, we can always borrow one from y'all." He slapped me on the back. "Congratulations, buddy. I hear you're having twins."

I could hardly believe my ears. Was my wife seriously considering going through with her preposterous scheme? Melanie giving us her baby to raise was one thing. To pass them off as twins another thing entirely. The situation had the potential for disaster.

144

Trudy was at the stove in the kitchen when I got home. We'd been avoiding each other since Melanie's untimely arrival, and she refused to meet my gaze now when I asked, "Did you tell Ivy that you knew about Melanie and me?"

Trudy shook her head. "Lord knows, I feel bad about lying to her. The guilt is eating me up inside."

"If anyone should feel guilty, Trudy, it's me." Truth be told, now that the truth was out in the open, I felt relieved of my burden of guilt. "You didn't exactly lie to her. You just omitted the truth. You were protecting her from more pain and heartache."

She jabbed a wooden spoon at the vegetables in her skillet. "I know more than I want to about the goings-on in this family," she grumbled. "I wish Miss Ivy had fired me too."

Ivy had ordered Trudy to let the rest of the staff go to avoid having word leak out about the pregnant stranger living in the guest room.

She eyed the brown paper package in my hand. "Want me to cook that for you?"

"No thanks. I'll cook it later, if I cook it at all. I'm not really hungry." I tossed the steak in the refrigerator. "I ran into Alice's husband at the Piggly Wiggly. He congratulated me on having twins. I was hoping Ivy would give up on this harebrained idea."

"That's one thing we agree on. My Ivy's asking for trouble. It took some doing, but she managed to convince Nita to go along with her cockamamie idea."

I let out a sigh. "I'm sorry we're dragging the two of you into this mess."

"Me too, Mister Graham. I'd do just about anything for my Ivy. But this is stretching the limits of my loyalty. Mister Edward would not have approved of this one bit."

"But he would've gone along with it," I said.

She pointed her spoon at me. "You're exactly right. Because

he always let Ivy have her way. Just like we are now." She returns her attention to the stove. "Nita warned Ivy that she'll call for an ambulance at the first sign of trouble."

"Good." Removing my glasses, I wiped the sweat off my face with a paper towel. "I'm sorry the burden of the extra household duties has fallen on you. And having an extra person to take care of creates even more work for you. I'd like to share some of the responsibilities, if you'll let me."

"Oh, I'll let you, seeing how you're mostly to blame for the situation. Miss Melanie's no trouble, though. I feel sorry for her, being trapped in this house like a prisoner. Although she's a picky eater. Something's not right about a person who don't eat meat." Trudy scraped the vegetables onto a plate.

"Do you think Ivy will stay at the cottage all summer?"

Her brown eyes met mine for the first time since I entered the room. "She ain't planning to come back until the end of September. She's paying Nita extra to drive out to the cottage for her checkups."

"What about Melanie's checkups?"

"Nita will come here, to the house, for those."

I leaned back against the counter. "I want you to take off all the time you need this summer, Trudy. Paid, of course. You'll be working overtime when the babies come in October."

"Sweet innocent babies don't have a clue what they're getting themselves into."

I swore under my breath. There was nothing I could say to appease Trudy today. "You probably don't want to hear this Trudy, but there's nothing going on between Melanie and me. Our brief fling was meaningless for both of us. Things were different between Ivy and me when she came back from Florida. We'd finally begun to click. We were happy, and I aim to restore that happiness if it's the last thing I do."

"You're right. I don't want to hear it."

While I hadn't laid eyes on Melanie since she arrived, I'd heard her creeping around the house late at night. On Sunday of Memorial Day weekend, I ventured out onto the piazza with my first cup of coffee around nine o'clock and was greeted with the clicking and clacking sounds of a typewriter. To provide Melanie privacy, Trudy had placed a screen comprised of hinged wooden shutters at the corner of the porch. Craning my neck around the screen, I watched Melanie poking at the keys of an old-fashioned Underwood typewriter.

Unaware of my presence, she continued to type, pausing often to white out a mistake with Liquid Paper. My heart went out to her. She'd postponed her dream of publishing her book to see the pregnancy through, to give life to the baby she carried.

"Where'd you get that old clunker?" I asked, stepping around the screen.

"I found it in the attic," she said without looking up. "Beggars can't be choosers."

I stood behind her, staring over her shoulder as she typed. "Are you working on your manuscript?"

Her fingers came to a halt on the keyboard. "Clearly. What do you want, Graham? Can't you see I'm busy? Being held hostage in this house doesn't mean I have to defer my life. I've queried dozens of literary agents, and I've heard back from five, requesting the completed manuscript."

"That's wonderful news, Melanie. Congratulations. You're on your way to success."

She shoots me a glare. "That may be so, but being a prisoner presents certain challenges. Like how am I supposed to get bound copies made and mailed?"

"I can help with that. One of my students earns spending money by taking on typing projects. She's efficient and affordable."

"I can't afford her, even if she's willing to type it for free. My parents cut off my allowance, Graham. I scarcely have enough for the copies and postage."

"I'll pay for it, if you'll stop being so argumentative and let me help you." I sat down at the table beside her. "Your novel is quite good. In fact, I'd go so far as to say it's brilliant. But it needs polishing. I'm a decent line editor. We can work together. As we finish chapters, we'll pass them on to the typist. If we work hard, we'll have your manuscripts in the mail within a few weeks."

"I don't have weeks, Graham. I have to get these to New York immediately."

Crossing my arms over my midsection, I sipped my coffee. "Your prospective agents won't read past the first page if you submit erroneous work."

"What're you talking about? What errors?"

I nodded at the stack of pages on the table to her left, the ones she'd typed herself.

Her eyes scanned the top page until she arrived at the first of many typos. "I guess I'm not the greatest typist."

I gestured at the manuscript—the stack of lined pages with frayed edges torn from composition books that had been marked up and scratched through with red ink. "Now, the fourth paragraph reveals too much at this point. Consider moving it to the end of the chapter for a stronger impact."

She lifted the paper. "I see what you mean." She dropped the page on top of the stack and fell back in her chair. "I guess I do need your help. But we have to work quickly."

"As it happens, I have no plans for the day, and since we're on a time crunch, we might as well get started."

I was still wearing my pajamas and she the same terry cloth robe Trudy had loaned her the first night. To an outsider, we were a young married couple having a private discussion on our piazza. Fortunately, with the screen in place, we were completely secluded from the rest of the world. We could've had sex to our hearts' content, and no one would've ever known, but the chemistry that had drawn us together in January no longer existed.

Melanie notified her potential agents that she was completing her last round of revisions and would have the manuscript in their hands by the end of June. For the next few weeks, at night and on weekends, we worked tirelessly, meticulously combing through Melanie's chapters, making grammatical enhancements and tweaking the plotlines to heighten suspense.

At nearly midnight on a Thursday night of the last full week in June, we sat side by side at the kitchen table, an empty pizza box in front of us, addressing labels on the boxes of bound copies, readying them for me to drop off at Federal Express on my way to campus on Friday morning.

"Tell me the book is good, Graham."

I chuckled. "I've already told you a thousand times. Clearly, you need to hear it a thousand and one. Your novel is not just good. It's brilliant. I wouldn't be surprised if every one of these agents makes an offer to represent you." I sealed the last box and stacked it on top of the others. "I'm curious about something, though. How did you write a novel in such great detail about a city you've never visited?"

"From the time I was a child, beginning with Eloise's escapades at the Plaza, I've read everything I could get my hands on about New York. For as long as I can remember, I've fantasized about living in Manhattan."

"And now your dream is coming true. I admire the way you've remained committed to your goals."

"You know, Graham, I'm curious about something as well." A smirk played about her plump pink lips. "What did I ever see in you?"

"You mean aside from my rugged good looks and charming personality?"

"Ha. Your looks are bookish, and I'd characterize your personality as boring."

"Then it must be my extensive knowledge of American literature."

She considered this. "True, I found your intellect appealing. What I really wanted was to slide by in your class and still get a good grade."

"Well, your plan backfired. I gave you a B minus, because you earned a B minus. Not only did you fail to turn in numerous assignments, you exhibited complete disregard for my attendance policy."

Melanie inhaled a sudden breath as she placed a hand on her rounded belly. "The baby just kicked. I've felt flutters before, but that was a strong kick." Taking my hand, she placed it on her stomach.

Warmth spread throughout my body as the baby rolled beneath my palm. I found it strange to be experiencing these firsts with a woman who wasn't my wife. I wanted so much to be experiencing these firsts with the woman I love, but Ivy took that opportunity away by spending the summer on Wadmalaw.

"The miracle of having a living being growing inside of me is not lost on me, Graham. Do you think I'm a horrible person for not wanting to keep my baby?"

"On the contrary. I think you're showing a great act of courage by going through with the pregnancy and letting us adopt it. I, for one, am grateful for your sacrifice."

"Promise me you'll look out for the baby," Melanie said in a pleading tone. "Don't let your cold fish of a wife ruin him or her."

"Ivy's not as bad as you make her out to be. She's a good person, and she will be a devoted mother." Although I would never say as much to Melanie, I had my own reservations as to whether my wife could be impartial to another woman's baby when raising it alongside her own. Especially when I was the father of that baby.

While Melanie proved to be excellent company, I missed my wife terribly during those summer months. Ivy never returned any of the long-winded messages I left on the answering machine at the cottage. And, when I drove down to see her one scorching Saturday in July, Ivy hopped in the boat and took off, leaving me standing on the dock. I gave up after waiting two hours for her return.

Trudy advised me that I was only making matters worse by trying to contact her, and that I should give Ivy her space.

Melanie wore the healthy glow of a pregnant woman. Her skin glistened and her white hair shined from the vitamins and herbs Nita provided. Determined not to gain too much weight, she watched what she ate, her diet consisting mostly of fruits and vegetables, and got plenty of exercise by climbing stairs, circling the vast rooms, and walking the hallways at a fast pace. Once the manuscripts had been submitted to the prospective agents, with little to occupy her time, she soon became antsy. She awaited my return home from campus every evening with great anticipation. We ate dinner together in the kitchen, and afterward, Melanie helped me grade papers. We spent weekend afternoons on the piazza, drinking iced tea and watching sailing regattas on the harbor, the overhead fans offering little relief from the southern heat. When the weather was too hot to even be on the porch, we camped out in drawing room with the drapes drawn. We organized the books in my library according to author and title, and we schemed plot ideas for her next novel, which she was eager to get started on. We watched old movies and played countless games of gin rummy. But our favorite pastime that summer was reading. We devoured classics and current bestsellers, often the same books at the same time, sharing lengthy and in-depth discussions about them after we'd finished.

I'd never had a friend like Melanie. During those seemingly endless summer days, we shared our souls by confiding our deepest secrets. She told me about her idyllic childhood—being from a family of wealth and privilege with two loving parents— and how hurt she'd been when those loving parents turned their backs on her in her time of need. She lent a sympathetic ear when I confessed that I was the son of a poor lobsterman and described in detail the beatings I'd received at my father's hand. Melanie accepted me for who I was. She made me feel whole, in a way I'd never felt before, and I would miss her when she left.

I told her as much on our last night together in late September. We were eating dinner together on the piazza and Trudy had just informed us that Ivy would be returning to Charleston the next day, on Wednesday, October 1, ten days before Melanie's due date and twelve until Ivy's.

"I'm going to miss you too, Graham," Melanie said, picking at her salad without taking a bite. "I have a confession to make."

"What's that?" I stared at her over the top of my forkful of macaroni and cheese.

"I realized within a few weeks of my first missed period that I was pregnant. I didn't tell you, because I was afraid you'd force me into having an abortion. Even though I didn't want to keep the baby, I couldn't bring myself to terminate the pregnancy. I kept thinking about our genes and wondering what kind of special gifts our baby might have. He or she deserves a chance to live." She set down her fork and leaned back in her chair, both hands massaging her swollen midsection. "I've grown quite attached to this little bugger."

I shoveled in the macaroni and wiped my lips. "Are you having doubts about giving it up for adoption?"

"Not at all. But I will rest easier knowing our baby will be raised by the more principled of its biological parents." She pinched off a morsel of buttermilk biscuit and pointed it at me. "You know, you're not at all the man I thought you were when I made a pass at you in your office that night in January."

"How so?"

"I thought you'd be a pompous ass, typical Harvard grad from a wealthy family. But you're so much more. You care deeply about things. About people. You're gentle and kind. You're a rare breed, Graham. You deserve to be loved, if not by your wife then by our child."

"That means a lot, Melanie," I said past the lump in my throat.

"What do you think of me?" she asked as she slathered butter on another piece of biscuit. "As a person, I mean."

I chose my words carefully, because I knew my opinion was important to her. "I've watched you grow up these past few months. You're talented and driven. You know exactly what you want out of life, and you have the courage to go after it. What you're doing for our baby is selfless and honorable. Our relationship has evolved from lovers to student and professor to close friends. Which, I feel, makes me qualified to say you're one of the finest women I've ever met."

Her face flushed. "I'm flattered, Graham. You're more than a friend to me. You're my mentor. Not only do you understand my writing, you know how to make it stronger. I hope we can work together on future manuscripts."

"I'd like that."

"But we have to agree to never talk about the baby. Things will need to be strictly business between us."

My brow shot up. "Do you honestly think you can do that?"

Melanie rose from her chair and walked over to the railing. With her back to me, she said, "I'm gonna try. For my sake and yours and the baby's. I don't even want to know if it's a boy or a girl."

I couldn't see her face, but I heard her sniffling. I went to stand beside her, handing her my linen handkerchief. "I've given this a lot of thought, Melanie, and I want to give you some money. It's the least I can do after the sacrifice you've made for our . . . for my child."

Dabbing at her eyes with the handkerchief, she said, "I can't take your money, Graham. It wouldn't be right."

"I'm giving you money, Melanie, whether you like it or not. You'll need train or plane fare to New York and a nest egg to help you get settled. If, for some insane reason you fail to strike it rich as a published author and ever find yourself in need, don't hesitate to call me."

She leaned into me and I wrapped my arms around her. A tremble passed through her body as she unleashed a torrent of tears.

I never knew the reason for her breakdown that night. She cried for hours, but she never talked about her feelings. It could've been uncertainty of the future or fear of failure. But I suspected that giving her baby away was more difficult than she cared to admit, even to herself.

GRAHAM

J arrived home from campus midafternoon the following day to find my wife and Coco overseeing the transformation of our old suite of rooms into a nursery for the babies. I watched, unobserved, from the doorway as deliverymen brought in matching cribs, a rocking chair, changing table, two chests of drawers, and a daybed for the baby nurse Ivy had hired.

My wife carried every ounce of pregnancy weight in her belly, which was the size and roundness of a small basketball, not what one would expect from a woman having twins. On the surface, Ivy appeared the picture of health—her skin bronzed and hair bleached from the sun—but as I studied her, I noticed the telltale signs of the stress from the past year. Her smile no longer twinkled, snuffed out like an extinguished candle, and she stood with a rigid stance that dared anyone get too close.

When Ivy finally spotted me in the doorway, she told Coco she needed a word with her husband and stalked out of the nursery and down the hall to our room with me trailing her like a disobedient child about to receive punishment for a naughty exploit.

Closing the door behind us, she turned to face me. The sun streamed through the windows, casting a halo over her golden hair. She was a Madonna, the woman whose virginity I'd stolen and whose womb I'd implanted with my seed. I wanted to take her in my arms, to place my hands on her abdomen and feel our baby move inside of her. I wanted to read bedtime stories and sing lullabies to our baby. But Ivy's blue eyes, dark with contempt, signified the opportunity to bond with our child in utero, as I'd done with Melanie's baby, would not be forthcoming.

Ivy gave me a quick once-over. "You're looking well, Graham. I can't help but wonder what happened between you and Melanie in my absence."

Everything suddenly made sense to me, and I palmed my forehead. "So that's why you left Melanie and me here alone all summer. And why you insisted Melanie sleep in the guest room in the main part of the house closer to our bedroom. You were testing us. Well, something did happen between Melanie and me while you were gone. We became friends. Nothing more."

She stared down her nose at me. "You may find it difficult to continue your newfound little friendship going forward. In addition to the standard adoption papers, I've asked Henry Scott to draw up an agreement stating Melanie will leave Charleston and have no further contact with the child."

I figured this was a bad time to tell my wife I'd agreed to work with Melanie on future manuscripts. "That shouldn't be a problem, since Melanie wants nothing to do with the child."

A look of relief crossed Ivy's face. "Fine. Then we need to talk about our marriage." She motioned me to sit down on the bed.

Her suitcases were spread open on the mattress, her clothes strewn across the chairs and floor. As I cleared a spot to sit, I wondered if we were to share the room or if she planned to kick me out. I would go along with whatever she wanted. She was in the driver's seat, and I was along for the ride.

"Although I'm not sure it's possible, I'd like to try and salvage what's left of our marriage. I can't make any promises to you, Graham. You hurt me deeply. I may never be able to trust you or feel close to you again. However, I know what it's like to be raised without a mother, and I wouldn't wish that on anyone. Our babies deserve to have two parents, Graham, a mother and a father."

"I agree, but I have to ask. Knowing how you feel about Melanie, are you sure you'll be able to raise her child without animosity?"

Her face registered surprise and then offense. "That should be the least of your concerns, Graham."

For the next ten days, I left for campus early in the morning and returned home late at night, avoiding the misery that came with having two full-term hormonal pregnant women who disliked each other immensely under the same roof. While their paths rarely crossed, each was acutely aware of the other and complained excessively to Trudy, Nita, and me.

On the second Sunday morning in October, Nita had just arrived for her daily visit and we were drinking coffee in the kitchen when Trudy bustled into the room. "Thank goodness, you're here," she said when she saw Nita. "I was just about to call you. Melanie started having labor pains about an hour ago."

Fingers splayed, Nita braced herself against the table. "Here we go! I imagine we're in for a long day. Tell Melanie to start walking, and I'll be up to check on her in a minute."

I'd grown fond of our midwife. She'd allowed me to be in the room when she examined both mothers-to-be, and I had the utmost faith in her ability to safely deliver my babies into the world.

By the time Nita and I arrived on the third floor, Trudy had already converted the guest bedroom into a birthing suite, her standards of cleanliness rivaling those of any hospital. I spent the rest of the morning and most of the afternoon running back and forth between the guest bedroom and master suite, coaching Melanie through her contractions and reassuring a distraught Ivy that her time would come soon.

Melanie had previously declined my invitation to be in the room when the baby was born, but when it came time to push, she begged me to stay. "Please, don't leave me, Graham!" she cried with pale face and trembling lower lip. "I'm terrified. I can't do this alone."

"Then I'll stay. I'd be honored to witness the birth of my child."

During the next ninety minutes, a panting Melanie, her face covered in sweat, screamed a litany of obscenities at me. I was beginning to worry she might need a cesarean section when Nita announced she could see the baby's head. "One final push should do it."

Trudy stood behind her with a clean towel ready to catch the baby. "Come on, Melanie. You're strong. You can do it."

Melanie scrunched up her face and groaned as she bore down one last time. When the baby emerged, pink skinned and wailing, Trudy scooped it up and swaddled it before anyone could get a good look at it.

Walking the baby to Melanie's side, Trudy moved to place the bundle in her arms. "It's a beautiful baby—"

"Stop!" Melanie hollered, squeezing her eyes shut and placing her hands over her ears. "I don't want to know what it is! Get it out of here."

Nita said, "Are you sure, Melanie? This may be your only chance to see your child."

Melanie shot daggers at Nita. "I realize that. And I'm fine with it. I've signed the papers. Graham and Ivy will raise the baby, and I will move on with my life."

Trudy's eyes traveled to Nita who nodded her approval to take the baby to the nursery. I yearned to follow her, to meet my son or daughter, but I didn't dare leave Melanie at such a traumatic time.

I sat down on the edge of the bed, and while Nita delivered the afterbirth and cleaned her up, I talked to Melanie about her future. "Just think, in a matter of days, you'll be in New York, starting a brand-new life."

Melanie stared up at the ceiling, refusing to meet my gaze. "I wanted to wait until now to tell you. Last week, I received an advance, a very sizable one, from Leslie Harmon at Harmon and Associates."

"Are you kidding me? Leslie Harmon? She's your top choice for agents. Why didn't you tell me sooner?"

"Because I knew this moment would be difficult, and I wanted to have something exciting to talk about. Tomorrow, or the day after, as soon as Nita gives me clearance, I'm outta here." Her eyes glistened with tears when they finally met mine. "Take care of him or her, Graham. That baby will forever remain in my heart, but in order to survive, I need to erase it from my mind."

A woman's scream resounded through the hallway outside our door. Footfalls followed and Trudy burst into the room. "My Ivy's water broke. Her contractions are close together. She says she needs to push."

"Goodness!" Nita said, stuffing an armload of soiled linens in a pillowcase. "I've delivered two babies in the same night before, but never in the same house. And certainly not under these conditions."

Trudy and Nita hurried from the room, and Melanie waved me on. "Go! Be with your wife. She needs you."

"Are you sure?"

She swiped at her tears. "I'm sure, Graham. I really need to be alone right now."

"All right, then." I tucked the blankets around her and exited the room, leaving the door cracked in case she needed to call for help.

Ivy was already in the throes of delivering our baby when I reached our bedroom. I leaned down and whispered in Nita's ear. "Why is this happening so fast? Is something wrong with the baby? Melanie's delivery lasted for hours."

"Every woman's different, Graham. Every *baby's* different. This little one is suddenly in a hurry to make an appearance."

I moved to my wife's side, taking hold of her hand.

Through gritted teeth, as she pushed through another contraction, Ivy asked, "Melanie's baby? Boy or girl?"

"I don't know," I said.

"What do you mean, you don't know?" Ivy snapped.

"Melanie sent the baby away. She thinks it'll be less painful if she doesn't know the sex."

When another contraction ripped through her body, Ivy brought my hand to her mouth and sank her teeth into my knuckles. I forced myself to keep a straight face. My pain was nothing compared to hers.

When the contraction subsided, Ivy pushed herself up on her elbows. "Do you know, Nita? Is Melanie's baby a girl or boy?"

Nita looked up from between her legs. "Melanie had a healthy baby girl."

"Perfect. Now it's up to me to give her a sister," Ivy said, and let out a bloodcurdling scream at the onset of another contraction. As I watched my wife suffer through the delivery of our baby, my thoughts drifted multiple times to the mother of my firstborn in the room down the hall. I prayed Melanie's pain had subsided and that she was resting peacefully. I hoped that one day my wife would see what a selfless gift Melanie had given us.

"You have a beautiful, healthy baby girl," Nita said, as she wrapped the crying baby in a blanket.

Ivy folded her hands over her heart. "A girl, Graham. We have another girl."

Nita held the baby out to Ivy. "Are you ready to meet your daughter?"

"No!" Ivy vehemently shook her head. "Take her to the nursery. Clean her up, and then bring both babies back to me. I want to meet both my daughters at once."

I stared at my wife. "Are you sure about this?"

She nodded. "I've thought about this long and hard, Graham. If I don't know which baby is my flesh and blood, I won't be able to show preferential treatment. We were blessed with the perfect scenario by having the babies, both girls, born within hours of each other. They'll carry my name. Lillian Stoney Alexander and Layla Stoney Alexander. As far as the world's concerned, they're fraternal twins. If, for some reason, one looks exactly like Melanie or me, then . . . Then, I don't know what we'll do. Hopefully, by that time, I'll love them both so much it won't matter."

I stared openmouthed at my wife, unable to wrap my tongue around any of the words that came to mind in that moment. Her act of selflessness was as great as, if not greater than, Melanie's. "You're remarkable. And you're going to make an incredible mother. Our daughters, Lillian and Layla, are fortunate to have you." I leaned over and hugged her as gently as I could. When I pulled away, I saw tears welling in Nita's eyes.

I smiled at Nita. "You heard the lady. Let's get these babies cleaned up so we can meet our daughters and bestow upon them their names."

Nita scurried from the room with the baby, returning an hour later with Trudy and both babies wrapped in different colored blankets—one pink and one yellow. They placed a baby in each of Ivy's arms. With tears streaming down her cheeks, Ivy studied their little faces, fingers, and toes. "They're beautiful."

I ease myself down on the bed beside her. "How will you decide who is Layla and who is Lillian?

"I will name them alphabetically from right to left. This one's Layla." She kissed the baby's head in her right arm. And this one's Lillian." She kissed the other baby's head.

"You're not going to give the naming any more thought than that?"

"Why make it difficult? Look at them. They're nearly identical, little clones of you. I can't even tell them apart. Until they start to develop personalities, Layla will wear pink and Lillian yellow."

LILLIAN

*D*usk has fallen and the room is dark, but I make no move to turn on the floor lamp beside Dad's chair. I struggle to understand how any of this could be true. Yet I know it is. Everything makes more sense now. My *life* makes more sense. Most especially my relationship with my sister.

"Why are you sitting in the dark?" Marcus asks from the doorway.

I don't answer him. I don't know how long I've been sitting in the dark, any more than I know how long he's been standing there watching me. "Did Trudy send any wine with you?" I ask instead.

He flips the wall switch and a dim glow from the overhead light fixture fills the room. "No, but I stopped at the wine shop in John's Island on my way here. Do you want red or white? I bought both."

"Either. I'd drink lighter fluid right now if it'd take the edge off my frayed nerves."

His ginger eyebrows become one. "That bad?"

"Pretty shocking."

"I'll get the wine."

163

While he's gone, I google Melanie Hogan on his iPad. Images of the famous romance author fill the screen. There's no question she's the attractive mystery woman I saw at the cemetery the day of Dad's funeral.

"Who's that?" Marcus asks when he returns with the wine.

"There's a fifty percent chance she's my mother."

"Your mother? Are you kidding me?" Still holding the stemless wine glasses, Marcus lowers himself to the arm of the chair. "How is that even possible?"

"My father had an affair with this woman. She was his student at the time." I jab my finger at the iPad screen. "She's a bestselling romance author now. Her name is Melanie Hogan. You may have heard of her." I snatch one of the glasses from him and gulp down the wine. "Layla's not my twin, Marcus. We're only half sisters. We've never shared that special connectivity most twins have, and now I know why."

He leans closer, studying Melanie's picture. "You don't look like her."

I snap the iPad cover shut. "Of course I don't look like her. I look like Layla. And we both look like Dad. It's a long story." When I move to the sofa, he follows me. We sit close together, sipping the smooth red wine while I tell him about Ivy's depression and Dad's brief affair with Melanie and the irony of our births.

"The convenience of Layla and me being born the same day made the lie of us being twins more plausible."

Marcus shakes his head, as if he's having trouble believing any of what I've told him. "That's some serious shit, Lil."

He pulls me close, and I don't push away. His embrace is familiar and comforting, and I need him right now. I am not thinking about the future. Or even tomorrow. I can't get past this minute. "Tell me about it."

"I spent a lot of time with your dad when we were dating,

and I thought I knew him pretty well. I can't believe he'd agree to such an outrageous scheme."

"Dad was desperate to get Ivy back after she found out about his affair. He would've done anything she asked of him."

"Maybe," Marcus says. "But this is extreme. In my book, what Ivy and Graham did is unethical. Not as much Melanie because she was so young, and they offered her an easy way out of a difficult situation."

We drink our wine in silence, each of us lost in thought. "Did you learn anything about Ivy's death?" Marcus asks finally.

I'm grateful to him for not saying *your mother's* death. "Not yet. I still have more to read. I can't imagine what other surprises Dad has in store for me."

"Do you want to finish it now?"

"Not tonight. I can't take any more right now."

"Then let's fix dinner. I'm starving." He stands and pulls me to my feet. "Trudy sent steaks. It's stopped raining, so we can cook them on the grill."

I hand him his iPad. "As long as we don't have to talk anymore about any of this."

"Deal," he says with a definitive nod that assures me he won't bring it up again.

But even though we agree not to talk about it, I can't stop thinking about it during dinner. How hurt Ivy must have been when she learned of Dad's affair, especially when she'd finally allowed herself to open up to him. Did Melanie have regrets about giving up her child? Did she ever have children of her own? Did Dad continue his friendship with Melanie?

The steaks are tasty. I'm not surprised Marcus has become something of a chef in the past ten years. He never does anything halfway. But I don't have much of an appetite and leave most of my dinner unfinished on my plate. After we've cleaned up, we find an old scary movie to watch on Netflix. I'm grateful for the distraction, and I fall sleep halfway through. We spend the night cuddled together on the sofa.

I wake before Marcus and slip from his hold without disturbing him. The rain from the previous day left cooler temperatures in its wake, and I wrap a blanket around me when I take my coffee outside to the porch.

I stare up at the clear blue sky. I've often wondered over the years if Ivy was looking down on me from heaven. Is she looking down on me now? What if she's not my mother? Being a Stoney means everything to me. My whole life is a lie.

I'm so lost in thought, I don't hear Marcus until he says in a soft voice near my ear, "Can I interest you in an omelet?"

I place my hand against my pounding heart. "Jeez, you scared me." The thought of eggs makes me nauseous. "I'm not really that hungry. I think maybe I'll take a walk before I eat."

"I'll come with you. Let me grab my running shoes."

I cock an eyebrow. "You brought your running shoes too? Were you that confident I'd ask you to stay?"

"I'm an Eagle Scout, remember? I'm always prepared for anything."

I laugh. "I remember."

My shoes are just inside the front door, and I'm sitting on the steps, tying the laces, when he returns. The brisk autumn air is invigorating, and we walk at a fast pace for nearly an hour. We don't talk except to make general observations about our surroundings—the wildlife coming alive, the leaves beginning to change color, and the marsh grass starting its transition from the green of summer to the yellow of autumn. Our companionable silence is a reminder of how easy our relationship had once been. When we broke up, I not only lost my fiancé, I lost my best friend. And I desperately need that friendship right now.

We are on the last stretch of road toward home when he says, "Are you planning to keep reading today? Because I can stay. I don't think you should be alone."

I kick at a rock on the road. "Surely you have better things to do."

"I brought plenty of work to keep me occupied."

"Right. The always-prepared Eagle Scout," I say with a smile. "I appreciate the offer, but I've decided to go back to Charleston after breakfast. I really want to talk to Trudy before I read any more of the memoir. She was there the night I was born. I'm curious what she has to say."

"That makes sense. Keep my iPad. It'll make for easier reading."

"Don't you need it for work?"

"I can make do without it for a few days," he says. "I'll check in with you this afternoon. In the meantime, promise you'll call me if you need me."

"I promise." Looping my arm through his, I lean into him as we walk up our driveway. "Thank you for coming, Marcus. I don't know what I'd done if you hadn't been here."

I've been to Trudy's house only once, when her car broke down and my father had to give her a ride home from work. I was in middle school at the time, but oddly enough, I remember exactly how to get there. She lives near the medical university on a street lined on both sides with tidy homes and well-tended yards. Trudy's Cape Cod-style house has cheerful yellow siding, dormer windows, and a row of white rockers on the front porch. She's on her knees in the grass, planting pansies in the bed bordering her brick sidewalk. She's wearing her straw hat, a yellow-and-white striped housedress, and her bedroom slippers.

She sees me pull up and lumbers to the end of the walk to greet me. She only has to look at my face to know I've found out something about my past. "Bless your heart," is all she says.

"Tell me the truth, Trudy. Who's my mother? Ivy or Melanie?"

She opens the wooden gate for me. "You'd better come up to the house. I'll fix us something cold to drink."

I follow her to the porch and wait in one of the rockers while she goes inside. She returns minutes later with two large glasses of freshly squeezed lemonade. Handing me a lemonade, she lowers herself into the chair next to mine. "How on earth did you find out?"

I pat the thumb drive and folded note in my pocket. I need to store them in a safe place. I don't want Layla getting her hands on them until I'm ready to give it to her. "Dad left me his 'memoir,'" I say, using air quotes. "The chapters from his life with Ivy."

"Why do you keep calling your mama Ivy?"

I've been asking myself the same question, but I haven't been able to answer it until now. "It's hard to explain. Despite Dad's efforts to keep her memory alive, Ivy's never been anything more to me than a woman in a portrait hanging above our sideboard. But his memoir brought her to life. I see her now through a young man's eyes. She's Ivy, the woman my father was passionately in love with. Not the mother I barely remember. If she is even my mother."

"I reckon that makes sense. Do you know how she died?"

"Not yet. I haven't reached the end of the memoir."

She stares out into the front yard with a look in her eyes that tells me she's thinking of the past. "My Ivy was as headstrong as the day is long. There was no stopping her once she got it in her mind to adopt Melanie's baby and raise the two of you as twins. But I was against her cockamamie scheme from the beginning. I've wanted to tell you the truth so many times."

"Dad's the one who should've told us. Why didn't he?"

Trudy presses the sweating glass against her cheek. "Your father was a man of his word. He swore to Ivy he'd never tell.

Just as he vowed never to cheat on her again. He kept both promises till his grave."

For the first time, I'm angry at my father. "I'm sorry, Trudy, but I can't commend his honor when he lied to us all these years. Layla and I are his daughters. He had a responsibility to us too." I bang my fist on the arm of the chair. "This is absurd. We're not twins. We don't even share the same mother."

I force myself to calm down. Trudy didn't do this. This is all on Dad. While she may have been a part of everything that happened, she didn't cause any of it. And it wasn't her place to tell us. "I've always felt pressured to be more like Layla, and guilty because we weren't closer. Do you know how much that has torn me up inside over the years?"

"Hmm-mm. I saw it with my own eyes. I tried to tell Mister Graham, but in his mind, he was doing the right thing."

I take a gulp of my drink, the tart lemonade burning my parched throat. "You haven't answered my question. Who is my mother, Trudy? I know you know. You were there that night."

"But I don't know. I promise you, cross my heart." Trudy fingers an x over her heart.

"How is that possible? Weren't you alone with Melanie's baby when Nita brought Ivy's baby to the nursery?"

"Yes, but then Nita sent me on an errand, to the kitchen to fix her some tea. When I returned with the tea, she'd stripped you babies down to your naked little bodies." Trudy smiles. "I can still see you now, lying side by side on the bed. Practically identical, neither of you with a single birthmark or feature that set you apart from the other. Nita had mixed you babies up on purpose. She was granting my Ivy her wish."

"So, everyone was in on the conspiracy."

Trudy ignores my sarcasm. "Your mama . . . Ivy insisted we dress you girls in different colors to keep from mixing you up. Layla in pink and you in yellow." She chuckles. "Funny thing how Layla turned out to be the prissy one and you mellow yellow."

"Is that what you think of me, mellow yellow?"

"It's true, ain't it? You're even-keeled while Layla is prone to drama."

"In other words, I'm boring."

"You are anything but boring, sweet girl." Trudy strokes my arm.

I exhale a deep breath, releasing some of my tension. "I have no idea what I'm supposed to do. Should I tell Layla?"

Trudy doesn't hesitate. "I don't know how you can *not* tell your sister."

"I guess you're right." My voice is tight as I fight back tears. "She'll be furious Dad imparted this information to me instead of her. Then again, she'll be as relieved as I am to know we're not twins." I stare down into my glass. "You lied to me, Trudy, when I asked you about the beautiful blonde at Daddy's funeral. That was Melanie at the cemetery. You saw her. I know you did."

Trudy grimaces. "I didn't mean to lie to you. Seeing her after all these years caught me off guard. I didn't know what to say."

"What was Melanie like?"

Trudy rested her head against the back of the chair. "Oh gosh. That was so long ago. She was young back then, barely out of college." Trudy laughs. "She's the first person I ever knew who doesn't eat meat. I never trusted her, though. I always thought she carried a torch for your daddy. I saw the pain in Miss Melanie's face when she refused to hold her baby. She was too young to raise it on her own, but that didn't mean she loved it any less. She sacrificed a lot to follow her dreams."

I run my finger along the rim of the glass. "Even though I don't approve of what Ivy did, I give her credit for her determination not to show favoritism."

"I thought my Ivy had lost her mind, wanting to raise

another woman's child. Her *husband's* baby by another woman, no less. When she insisted on meeting both babies at the same time, well that's the single most selfless act I witnessed in all my many days. She loved you and Layla so much. She never played favorites. She had a great big heart. But she wasn't perfect. My poor Ivy was troubled."

I furrow my brow. "Emotionally troubled?"

"I'll let you figure that out on your own. Finish your Daddy's memoir. If you still have questions, I'll give you all the answers."

"I'll hold you to it." I angle my body toward hers. "You knew Ivy and Melanie. And you raised Layla and me. If you had to guess, which one of us belongs to which mother?"

"Lord, child, I gave up trying to figure that out years ago. After my Ivy died, I missed her so much I nearly drove myself nuts looking for signs of her in you girls. You're more reserved like your father. And you share your love of books with him. But Layla, she ain't like none of them."

"Do you think I should tell Layla now or wait until I finish Dad's memoir?"

"I think you should wait until you finish, until you've completed the puzzle."

As she walks me to my car, Trudy implores me to call her anytime if I need her. I drive away from her house feeling less alone but not yet ready to face the truth about my mother's death. On the way home, I make a sudden detour, turning left instead of right onto East Bay. I drive over the Cooper River Bridge through Mount Pleasant and onto Sullivan's Island, parking at a friend's cottage near Station 21. Making my way down the boardwalk to the beach, I kick off my shoes and trudge down the beach past Fort Moultrie.

So many changes have taken place in my life since my father died a week ago today. I don't know who my mother is. My sister's not my twin. Our family is in financial crisis, and we may lose the house. I stop in my tracks. *Did I just consider putting the house on the market?* On the bright side, if I am forced to sell, I'd be able to afford a condo or small house in Mount Pleasant or North Charleston with the proceeds. *What am I thinking? It's not just the house. My soul resides on the Battery. I can't give up without a fight.* I start walking again, picking up my pace, my arms swinging.

When I return to the car, I brush the sand off my feet, put on my shoes, and drive back to Shem Creek in Mount Pleasant. Seated at the waterfront bar at Tavern & Table, I order a flat-bread pizza and a black and blue mule. I watch the Sunday afternoon boat activity on the creek while I eat. When I can no longer delay the inevitable, I pay the check and tip the bartender. As I cross back over the Cooper River, the sun is beginning to set—earlier every day now with the onset of autumn. At home, I'm surprised to see a Cadillac in the court-yard, the front license plate identifying it as a Hertz Rental Car. I let out a groan. So, Layla is planning to stay indefinitely. And while I'm fighting to save my home, she's blowing money on an expensive luxury rental car.

I'm relieved when I don't encounter Layla on my way through the house to Dad's study. Even though I asked her not to, Trudy has returned all the books to the shelves. Stretching out on the sofa, I drape the cotton throw over my body and open Marcus's iPad.

GRAHAM

During the thirty-six hours following the births, I never mentioned the babies to Melanie, and she never asked about them. I last saw her when I stopped in to check on her around eleven o'clock on Monday night. She was gone on Tuesday morning when Trudy delivered her breakfast tray. Even though Ivy and I had been awake with the babies during the night, neither of us heard her leave.

Later that morning, when I got a moment's reprieve from nursery duty, I took my coffee out to the piazza. Staring out over the Cooper River, as Melanie and I had done so many times that summer, I bid her a silent farewell, wishing her great success in the Big Apple and vowing to forever cherish the friendship we'd forged and the child she'd entrusted to me.

A young mother, with her two little girls skipping along beside her, passed by on the promenade. I wondered if I would be able to tell my children apart as they grew. Would one exhibit Melanie's creative genius? Would one find it difficult to sit still like Ivy? Lifting my face to the sky, I prayed to Edward and God and whoever would listen to let my children become their own persons separate from any of their three biological parents.

With the exception of the yellow fuzz on their perfectly-shaped heads, Lillian and Layla were the spitting images of me. Both had my chocolate eyes and pointy chin. They could've easily passed for identical twins. Everyone fell in love with the little darlings, including Bessie who took up residence outside the nursery door, standing guard over the newest members of the family.

I was amazed at the capacity two seven-pound infants had for turning our household upside down. Ivy ordered Trudy to rehire staff to assist with the growing household duties. Mary, the baby nurse, arrived from Savannah at lunchtime on Tuesday. Ivy initially hired Mary for three weeks, but she ended up being with us for six months. Every time she'd try to leave, I'd give her more money and beg her to stay. The twins weren't the problem. They were easy babies, and Ivy was delighted with them, overly attentive to them even. But Ivy, prone to severe mood swings, would frequently lock herself in her sitting room with the drapes drawn and the lights out.

When I asked Trudy about it, she shot me a quizzical look. "Ain't nothing new. My Ivy's always been like that—on top of the clouds one minute and down in the dumps the next. You were just too taken with her to notice."

Was that true? Was it possible I'd been too in love with my wife to see her obvious flaws? "Are you talking about clinical depression?"

Trudy hesitated, as though she hadn't considered it but that it was a possibility. "We never thought to send her to a head doctor or anything."

"I saw how down in the dumps she was after Edward died, but that was understandable considering how much she loved him. Do you think this could be postpartum depression?"

Trudy shook her head. "According to Nita, Ivy wouldn't be

bonding with the babies if it were postpartum depression. She'll snap out of it. She always does."

Much to everyone's relief, Ivy's lows became fewer and further between as the girls transitioned from babies to toddlers to children. Appearancewise, Lillian and Layla remained mini versions of me. While outsiders often had a difficult time telling them apart, try as I might, I could never bring myself to think of them as twins. They shared similarities—a love of reading and creating things with their hands—but, while Lillian was reserved, to the point of shyness, Layla was more outspoken and prone to temper tantrums. Ivy and I jokingly remarked that we had his and her children. When I was at home, Lillian could be found at my feet, in the cavity of my desk with her books and crayons, hiding from her overbearing sister, while Layla spent most of her time with Ivy in her sitting room, stretched out on the floor with her paper dolls.

A month prior to the girls' third birthday, on a Sunday afternoon in mid-September of 1989, we were in our respective locations when Melanie called from New York to warn us of the threat of Hurricane Hugo.

Melanie's career had taken off eighteen months ago with the release of *Crazy Love*. Renowned reviewers referred to the romantic comedy as edgy, fresh, and bold. Six months later, when Universal Pictures purchased the movie rights, she'd aided in the screen adaptation and flown out to Hollywood for filming. She was in the final stages of editing for her second novel, which was scheduled for release in the Spring of 1991. We'd been mailing the manuscript back and forth and speaking on the phone several times a day. While I didn't flaunt our business relationship with Ivy, I never tried to hide it from her either. Ivy was fine with it as long as Melanie continued to keep her distance.

"I hope you're watching this storm," she blurted when I answered her call.

"What storm, Mel?"

"The one currently pummeling Guadeloupe with 140 mile-per-hour winds. Don't you watch television, Graham?"

"Not if I can help it."

"I have a bad feeling about this hurricane. I'd hate for anything to happen to my editor in the midst of these crucial revisions."

While Melanie and I talked at length about her work, I never asked about her personal life, and she never inquired about mine. In all this time, she had raised not one single question about her child.

I craned my neck to look under the desk at my daughter who'd fallen asleep with her cheek stuck to one of her cardboard books. I straightened. "So, if I understand you correctly, you're saying it's okay if I drown in a hurricane as long as I wait until after we finish these edits."

"Shut up, Graham! You know what I mean."

Phone in hand, I swiveled around in my chair and rolled over to the window. "You have nothing to worry about. I'm looking out at a clear September sky."

"The hurricane is still days away. Tune into the Weather Channel, Graham. Pay attention to this storm. They're predicting an East Coast landfall by the end of the week."

Her serious tone got my attention. "Okay. I'm on it."

I left Lillian sleeping peacefully under my desk and moved to the drawing room, tuning the television to the Weather Channel. When Ivy, who considered herself something of an expert on tropical storms and hurricanes, entered the room some thirty minutes later, I asked, "Should we be worried about this hurricane?"

Ivy barely glanced at the television. "It's too early to worry from what I've seen so far, but we definitely need to keep a watch on it."

As the days wore on, I noticed her paying closer attention to

John Hope, the Weather Channel's hurricane expert. By lunchtime on Wednesday, when there was little doubt the South Carolina coast would experience a direct hit from the category four hurricane, we began making preparations. Isaac took me down to Wadmalaw and showed me how to properly board up the windows at the cottage, while Trudy and Ivy shopped for supplies at the hardware and grocery stores. They stocked up on enough batteries, candles, jugs of water, and food to survive Armageddon.

Late Wednesday afternoon, President Lightsey ordered any College of Charleston students who could feasibly travel home to do so. All others were to be bussed inland to Winthrop College in Rock Hill and the University of South Carolina in Columbia. Ivy and I were eating pancakes in the kitchen with the girls on Thursday morning when Governor Carroll Campbell ordered a mandatory evacuation of all South Carolina beaches. The wall phone rang before the governor's press conference ended.

"I've got it," Ivy said to Trudy as she reached over her head for the receiver. She answered hello and listened for a minute. "Yes, Alice. I told you that last night. We're staying." She held the phone away from her ear so I could hear Alice.

"I thought maybe you'd changed your minds. My parents just left for Columbia. They booked an extra room at their hotel for Heath and me. What should I do, Ivy? I'd hate to get stuck in Columbia. You know how the National Guard won't let folks back into town after a storm until they deem it safe. Depending on the severity of the damage, that could mean weeks. And Heath's no help. He doesn't know anything about hurricanes. We've lived through many a storm, but none of this magnitude."

"Why don't you and Heath come stay with us?" Ivy suggested. "We have plenty of room. Safety in numbers and all that."

"Really? Do you mean it, Ivy? I know it's silly, since you're a block closer to the water, but I'd feel better being with you."

"Sure! It'll be fun. We'll have a hurricane party."

At the mention of a party, the girls jumped to their feet and began dancing around in a circle, chanting, "Party! Party!"

Ivy, too, got to her feet and began pacing, the phone receiver now close to her ear. "We need to get our butts in gear, though. We have a lot to accomplish in a short amount of time. Bring over whatever food, clothes, and valuables you want. I'll have Graham call Heath. They can work together to secure the outsides of our homes."

Alice was still talking when Ivy hung up.

From the sink where she was washing dishes, Trudy said in a voice loud enough to be heard over the girls, "Miss Ivy, if you need the apartment for your friends, Isaac and I can take Ruthie down to my family in Beaufort."

"Nonsense, Trudy," Ivy said. "I promised you the apartment, and we have plenty of room in the main house. However, if you feel safer going to Beaufort, by all means go. I can't make that decision for you. You have to do what's best for your family."

Trudy dried her hands on her apron. "I'm with Miss Alice on this one. I feel better staying close by. Our neighborhood's on such low ground, it's sure to flood. The sooner we can start cleanup the better."

"End of discussion, then. We're all staying." Ivy clapped her hands. "Okay! Everyone listen up for your marching orders. Graham, you'll need to close all the hurricane shutters and go to the hardware store for sandbags. Be sure to fill the car with gas on the way. Get Heath to help you, and then you help him. Put everything in the garage that has the potential to become a projectile in heavy winds, like benches and planters and swings." She turned away from me. "Trudy, I want you to cook that turkey breast we bought yesterday and bake some of your delicious homemade goodies for us to snack on in the days ahead. After we make up the guest room for Alice and Heath, the girls and I will go buy ice for the coolers and put fresh batteries in all our flashlights and transistor radios."

Despite the seriousness of the situation, I grinned at my wife. She was in her element bossing everyone around.

Heath and I worked straight through the day without stopping for lunch. By the time we finished, the first outer bands of wind and rain from Hurricane Hugo were making landfall. The city was battened down, every window on every house on the Battery boarded up. The streets were eerily quiet, even though I knew many of our neighbors had chosen to stay in town and brave the storm.

The darkness inside the house felt confining with the hurricane shutters in place. I found it disconcerting to enter a room expecting to be greeted with a view of the harbor through our home's many windows only to have my eyes meet with black holes.

Alice had lined the upstairs hallway with stacks of boxes containing her valuables, things she could never replace like wedding albums and antique sterling candelabras that had been in her family since the beginning of time.

I showered and dressed in khaki pants and a short-sleeved striped polo. Following Ivy's instructions, I cleaned the tub with the supplies she'd left and filled it with water to use for washing, bathing, and flushing the toilet after the storm.

The hurricane party was already in full swing when I joined the others in the drawing room. The twins, high on sugar and caffeine, shrieked at the top of their lungs as they chased each other in and around in matching pink footed pajamas. The grownups, cocktails in hand, helped themselves to a platter of cheeses.

"I'm famished. What's for dinner?" I asked, giving my wife a peck on the cheek.

"Trudy left a lasagna warming in the oven. We'll serve ourselves later, once we get the girls situated."

I raised an eyebrow in the direction of my daughters. "That could be awhile. I'm not sure I can make it long on cheese and crackers."

"Don't be such a grouch," Ivy said with a slur that made me wonder just how much wine she'd already drunk. "We've been working hard all day. Let's relax a little."

"I'm not gonna lie," Heath chimed in. "I'm pretty hungry myself."

Alice cut her hazel eyes at her husband. "We're guests here, Heath. You'll eat when you're fed."

Ouch, I thought, and then remembered Ivy telling me that the hormones Alice was taking for fertility treatments were making her irritable.

"All right, then." Heath drained the rest of his bourbon and rattled his ice cubes. "I guess I'll have another drink."

"I'll get that for you." Stuffing several slices of cheese in my mouth at once, I took his glass from him and crossed the room to the bar. I refilled his bourbon and mixed myself a vodka tonic, returning his drink to him.

Alice stood beside him, watching the twins with such raw emotion exposed on her face, such anguish and longing. My heart went out to her. It didn't seem right that a woman who desperately wanted a baby should be deprived one.

When Layla yanked a handful of Lillian's hair, Lil let out a yelp that could be heard all the way in Columbia. Alice called, "Hey, girls! I've got a great idea. Why don't we build a hurricane fort?"

When the girls squealed in delight, she corralled them into the corner of the room.

Ivy plopped herself down on the sofa with the bottle of wine. "Turn on the TV, Graham. Let's get the latest update."

I clicked the power button on the remote, and for the next hour, we switched back and forth between the Weather Channel and the local stations as we watched the cyclone spin its way toward us.

Around eight o'clock, when Bessie began growling at the wind rattling the hurricane shutters, I suggested to Heath that we go to the kitchen for lasagna. "We're liable to lose power soon, and I need to let Bessie out. We'll bring our wives plates, although neither appears to be interested in food at the moment."

Ivy's eyelids were fluttering as she fought off sleep, and Alice was reading *Charlotte's Web* to mesmerized twins in their blanket fort.

"Sounds good to me," Heath said, already on his feet.

Heath and I huddled on the back stoop while Bessie did her business, the shed's roof protecting us from the driving rain.

"It's getting bad!" I hollered over the roar of the wind. For the first time since learning of the hurricane threat, I felt genuine fear.

Heath, as though sensing my unease, said, "Don't worry, buddy. This house is built like a fortress."

"I hope you're right." I held the door open for Heath and Bessie who scampered into the kitchen with tail between her legs.

I removed the warm casserole dish from the oven and handed Heath a fork from the silverware drawer. We stood at the stove, eating lasagna straight out of the dish.

"I'm curious, Graham. Do you like living in Charleston?"

I stared at him over a forkful of noodles and stringy cheese. "I do. Quite a lot, actually. Don't you?"

He shook his head. "Not so much. The heat and humidity really drag me down. I've been offered a job in Raleigh."

"Good for you. Congratulations, man." I retrieved the large bowl of salad from the refrigerator and tore off the plastic wrap. I held the bowl out to him. "Salad?"

"No thanks." When he chuckled, his double chin wobbled. He'd gained weight since his wedding, and I thought maybe he would benefit from eating more salad and less lasagna.

"So? Are you gonna take the job?"

"I'm not sure. I just got the offer on Monday. I've been too distracted by this damn storm to give it much thought."

I jabbed a forkful of lettuce. "Needs dressing." I got the bottle of homemade Italian dressing from the refrigerator door and poured a healthy amount over the salad. "What does Alice think about moving to North Carolina? Ivy would be devastated if she left Charleston."

"Alice feels the same way. She won't even talk about the offer. Truthfully, I think it'd be good for my wife to get away from her parents." Under his breath, he added, "And Ivy."

While I agreed the separation would be a good thing, having her best friend move away would be a blow from which Ivy might never recover.

When the lights flickered, I said, "We should feed our wives and get the girls in bed while we still have power."

We prepared two plates and took them to the drawing room. Everyone in the room had fallen asleep, Ivy on the sofa with her mouth wide open and the girls with their tiny limbs thrown across a softly snoring Alice.

I nudged Alice awake. "I'll relieve you of your duty. I need to get these two in bed."

I made three trips to the third floor, carrying first my limp daughters one at a time and then my wife. When I went back down to say goodnight to our guests, Alice was alone on the sofa, staring at an untouched plate of food in her lap.

"Where's Heath?" I asked.

She smiled up at me. "He went to bed."

182

Eyeing her plate, I asked, "Aren't you hungry?"

She set the plate on the coffee table. "I filled up on cheese and crackers earlier."

The lights blinked off but came back on within a few seconds. "How about a night cap? I have an excellent bottle of port that is perfect for the occasion."

"That sounds nice."

Uncorking the bottle, I filled two glasses and joined her on the sofa. With the television on mute, we could hear the wind howling and the waves crashing angrily against the seawall.

"Have you ever questioned your purpose in life, Graham?"

"Every single day of my youth. I feel blessed to have found my calling in teaching. I'm making my mark on the world, however small that mark may be."

"All I've ever wanted was to be a mother, but the odds of that happening aren't in my favor. What am I supposed to do with my time? I can't just play tennis every day. I'll have to determine a new focus for my life."

"Back up a minute, Alice. Forgive me for being so personal, but it seems like you're giving up on having a child without much of a fight. Have you run out of options for fertility treatments?"

Her chin dropped to her chest in a sad nod. "Unfortunately. Our last shot at in vitro fertilization failed."

"I'm so sorry, Alice. Have you considered adoption?"

"Of course. I'm all for it, but Heath refuses to even discuss it. He wants a baby as much as I do, but only if the child is of his own flesh and blood." A single tear spilled over her right eyelid and rolled down her cheek. "I'm the problem. I'm the one who is flawed. I'm preventing him from being a father. And now that this job opportunity has come up in Raleigh . . ." She raised her right hand and let it drop back in her lap. "I'm not moving to North Carolina. Period."

The power flickered again. This time it stayed out.

"With no air conditioning and the windows closed, it's gonna get hot in here in a hurry," Alice said.

I lit the pillar candle Ivy had placed on the coffee table, and then went around the room lighting others. I refilled my glass— Alice had barely taken a sip of hers—and rejoined her on the sofa.

"Why does everything come so easily for some people?" Alice asked, tucking one foot beneath her. "I call them the beautiful people, the ones with all the looks, athletic ability, and intelligence."

"You mean people like Ivy?"

"Ivy doesn't have it so easy," Alice snapped.

"I was thinking more in terms of her natural talents. She's pretty, athletic, and smart. But she's definitely had her share of disappointments."

Alice shot me a hard look I couldn't decipher. "You don't understand your wife at all."

My skin bristled. "On the contrary, I know her better than anyone. She's my wife. I agree, she's complicated."

"She's actually not complicated at all," she said in that same snippy tone.

This discussion was getting us nowhere fast. I directed her attention to the television. "Look! The storm is making landfall."

GRAHAM

During the overnight hours, Hugo pounded the coast with a twenty-foot storm surge in some places and wind speeds of up to 135 mph. McClellanville suffered the worst with neighborhoods completely destroyed and shrimp boats grounded in people's yards. After making landfall at Sullivan's Island, the storm diminished in strength as it traveled inland but still packed a considerable blow when it hit Charlotte, North Carolina.

The knee-deep water we discovered outside our door when we opened our shutters on Friday morning slowly receded, leaving thick mud and debris covering the downtown streets. Our drinking water was declared safe within forty-eight hours, but we lived without power for twelve days.

During the days following the storm, I experienced the remarkable resilience of the strong-minded Southerners as neighbors and strangers came together to rebuild our beloved city. While the hurricane brought out the best in most people, it brought out the worst in a few, one of them being Heath. He complained incessantly, but he never lifted a finger to help, as though he was somehow exempt from the cleanup. To no one's surprise and everyone's relief, he left for Raleigh as soon as the roads were cleared to drive on Sunday. Even though their house was in no worse shape than ours, Alice continued to live with us for the next six weeks.

The aftermath of the hurricane was the closest I would ever come to a war zone. The mayor issued a curfew, and the National Guard positioned their armored vehicles about the city to protect merchants from looters. Restaurants gave away free meals and donations flooded in from around the world. The sound of chainsaws filled the air as men worked from dawn until dusk, hauling away fallen trees and rubble from collapsed buildings. Women stood in long lines for bags of ice to preserve our dwindling supply of food.

The college suffered considerable damage to buildings and grounds, the worst being the loss of four majestic live oaks in Cistern Yard. When my colleagues returned to town and discovered their homes damaged or destroyed, Ivy and I opened our doors to them, offering them the seldom-used guest wing on the back of the house. First to move in was Bethany and Roger, a young married couple from Mobile, Alabama. Roger was an associate of mine in the English department and Bethany a campus librarian. Next came Kent, Lewis, and Steve, a trio of young bachelors from the marine biology department.

We soon began to think of ourselves as one big extended family. We gathered around the dining room table every night for dinner served on paper plates. Trudy was in charge of the cooking, but everyone pitched in. She often joined us for dinner and sometimes Isaac and Ruthie as well. We drank wine and told stories and sang songs. Even old Bessie enjoyed herself, devouring the extra table scraps.

The twins thrived on the additional attention. Bethany read to Lillian and Layla every night at bedtime and the marine biologists, in three-year-old jargon, taught them about sea life.

Kent, in particular, appeared to enjoy spending time with the girls, and took them for exploratory walks along the waterfront.

I accompanied them on such a walk on a brisk Saturday the second week in October. We were on the seawall when Kent pointed at a pelican flying overhead. "Look! He has a fish in his bill!"

The pelican was close and the fish big, but the girls didn't appear to see it. Their eyes traveled from Kent to the bird and back to Kent. "What fish?" Layla asked.

"Do you see it, Lil?" I asked.

She shook her head, the corner of her lip tucked under her teeth.

The next week, Ivy took the girls for a checkup with our optometrist who diagnosed both with near-sightedness and fitted them for glasses. Lillian chose wire-rimmed glasses like mine while Layla insisted on the more fashionable aqua-colored plastic frames.

We were all sad when our time together came to an end the first short week of November. We planned a going away celebration for that Thursday night, before our six guests would move out after work the following day.

I arrived home Thursday afternoon to find Ivy in her sitting room with the door closed. Assuming she was alone, I tapped lightly and then let myself in. I was surprised to find Ivy and Alice crying and comforting each other.

They didn't hear me come in, and I startled them apart when I asked, "What's going on? Has something happened?"

"Heath's divorcing me," Alice said, snatching a tissue from the box on a nearby table. "I don't know why I'm so emotional. I'm honestly relieved. Heath turned out to be a huge disappointment."

"I'm sorry to hear that, Alice." I asked my wife, "But why are you crying?"

"Obviously not about the divorce," Ivy said. "I say good

riddance to Heath. I'm sad because Alice is going back to school. She's going to be a lawyer."

I remembered my conversation with Alice the night of the hurricane. So, law school is her new purpose in life. I offered Alice a high five. "Good for you! That's great news." I turned to Ivy. "But that still doesn't explain why you're crying." And back to Alice. "Where are you applying to law school?"

"At the University of South Carolina. I have to take the LSAT, but Daddy has connections. He's optimistic about getting me in."

Placing my hands on my wife's face, I thumbed away her tears. "Columbia is less than two hours away. You'll still see each other all the time."

"No, we won't," she sobbed. "Alice is my best friend. Our lives are taking different paths. We've always dreamed of raising our children together. And now that's never going to happen."

Dropping to the loveseat, I pulled Ivy and Alice down on either side of me. "Not all dreams come true. When they don't, we need to reassess our lives and make new dreams. Alice's dream of a happy family with Heath didn't work out. And I'm sure she's disappointed, but she's found new direction for her life. We should be happy for her."

Ivy looked around me and smiled sweetly at Alice. "Of course, I'm happy for you. I'm being selfish. It's just . . . we've been so close these past two months with all of us living here together. I'm going to miss you."

"And I'm going to miss you as well," Alice said. "A lot of good things happened as a result of the hurricane. I'll never forget the time I spent here with you and the girls and the new friendships I made with Roger and Bethany and the marine biologists. But it's time to move on. You'll be happy to have your house back."

Ivy sucked air into her lungs as she steadied her breath.

"You're right. I'm being silly. I'm exhausted. It's been a hectic couple of months. It'll be good to get my life back on track." She stood and ushered us to the door. "Y'all run along downstairs. I'm going to fix my makeup, and I'll be down in a minute."

When Ivy finally joined us thirty minutes later, she was the same gracious hostess she'd been the past two months, although a tightness in her face hinted at trouble ahead.

After she moved out of the house, Alice dropped off our radar screen like a plane disappearing over the Bermuda Triangle. Not only was she studying to take the LSAT in January, she'd begun working as a receptionist in her father's law firm.

In the days leading up to the holidays, Ivy spoke often about finding new direction in her own life. While I understood she was trying to prove something to someone, I wasn't sure if that someone was herself or Alice or me.

After Christmas, Ivy hired a live-in nanny—Nanny Watson, a Mrs. Doubtfire type with coiffed hair and a British accent—to take care of the girls while she looked for a job. During the spring months, she worked in a few of the popular boutiques on King Street— Bob Ellis's shoe store, M. Dumas men's shop, and Croghan's Jewel Box. But she bored easily and spent every dime she made. By the time summer rolled around, deciding she was a better shopper than salesclerk, she packed up the kids, the dog, and the nanny and moved to Wadmalaw for the summer.

I drove down every weekend, and we enjoyed some happy times with our little family. But when she returned to Charleston after Labor Day, Ivy seemed more restless than ever.

One Sunday afternoon in late October, we were on the way home from visiting a friend with a new baby in the hospital when Ivy blurted, "Let's have another baby."

"Yes!" I said, pounding the roof of the car. I'd been trying for years to convince her to have more children. "Can we start trying tonight?"

"Fine by me." She walked her fingers up my arm and then leaned over in her seat to kiss my cheek. "Maybe this time we'll have a boy."

Ivy approached our sex life with renewed vigor, but her interest in having a baby waned when she failed to get pregnant the first few months. After Christmas of that year, she bought a new Labrador puppy and returned to volunteer work, which occupied her time but failed to provide much meaning or happiness to her life.

GRAHAM

$\mathcal{I}$n October of 1992, on the occasion of Lillian's and Layla's sixth birthday, Alice reappeared in our lives as suddenly and unexpectedly as she'd disappeared. That's not to say we hadn't seen Alice at all since the hurricane. But her visits to our house had been few and far between, mostly during the holidays when she was home from law school on break.

We hosted a party for the girls in our courtyard on a warm Saturday afternoon of their birthday week. Lillian and Layla had started kindergarten at Ashley Hall in September, and Ivy had insisted on inviting every girl in their class. She'd ordered an enormous ice cream cake and hired a magician who was currently entertaining his audience by making animals out of long skinny balloons.

When I heard my wife calling my name, I searched the crowd until I spotted her dragging Alice toward me. "Look who's here."

I kissed both Alice's cheeks. "It's nice to see you. Have you graduated from law school yet?"

"I finished in August. I'm currently interviewing for a

number of jobs. I'll wait and see where I land before taking the bar."

"Are these jobs in Charleston?" I asked.

"Mostly," she said, her smile lighting up her face. She'd cut her auburn hair to her shoulders and wore a long black cable knit sweater over faded jeans with ballet flats on her feet. There was something else different about her, an inner glow that had nothing to do with her attire or physical appearance.

"You're radiant, Alice," I said.

"Thank you for saying that, Graham. It's been a long journey, school and the divorce, but I've learned a lot about myself in the process."

"Alice and I are playing tennis in the morning," Ivy volunteered, bouncing from foot to foot.

Alice rolled her eyes. "She'll beat me for sure. I can't remember the last time I played."

"How're your parents?" I asked.

"My parents are great, although I hardly ever see them. They're spending more and more time at the condo in Florida." Alice stood on her tiptoes, peering over the tops of the children's heads. "I see Layla on the front row. Where's Lillian?"

"She supposed to be watching the show," Ivy said, searching the crowd. When she didn't see Lillian, first panic and then irritation crossed her face. "That child is always running off, hiding somewhere."

I pointed at the linen-draped table we were standing next to. "She's under here," I mouthed. I'd known all along where my shy child was hiding.

Ivy leaned over and lifted the hem of the tablecloth. "What're you doing under there, goose? It's your birthday party. All your friends are here to help you celebrate."

While we couldn't see Lillian, Alice and I exchanged a look when we heard her say, "They're not my friends. They're Layla's friends."

"Well, Alice is your friend. Come say hello to her."

"Alice is here!" Lillian crawled from under the table on all fours, dirtying the knees of her jeans. Layla loved the pink frilly matching dresses Ivy had bought the girls for the party, but Lillian had refused to wear hers.

Still clutching her *Dick and Jane* reading primer, Lillian wrapped her arms around Alice's legs, hugging them tight. "You haven't come to see me in a really long time."

Alice knelt down, eye-to-eye with the child. "I know, sweetheart, and I'm sorry." She brushed a wisp of hair out of the way and kissed Lillian's forehead. "I promise to make it up to you now that I've finished law school."

"Did you bring me a present?" Lillian asked, her rosebud lips turning up in a mischievous smile.

"Lil!" Ivy cried. "It's rude to ask such questions."

Alice touched the tip of Lillian's button nose. "You know I brought you a present, silly. But it's in my car. You'll have to wait until your other guests leave to get it."

"Okay," Lillian said, her lips turning downward.

Cheers erupted from the crowd of children. The magician had ended his show with the magic appearance of a fluffy white bunny. Placing a hand on our daughter's back, Ivy gave Lillian a gentle push in the direction of the kitchen. "Lil, be a dear and go tell Trudy we're ready to cut the cake."

The three of us watched her skip off, braided pigtails dancing along her shoulders.

"I can't wait to give them their presents," Alice said. "I got them wooden easels. Two of them because I know they don't like to share. Are they getting along any better now that they're in kindergarten?"

"Sadly, I don't think they'll ever be close," Ivy said. "Their personalities are too different."

"I find that strange for twins," Alice said. "Are you worried that Layla is bullying Lillian. Little Lil is just so timid."

I tensed. "Timid implies a lack of courage or confidence, but my daughter has both traits in abundance, I might add. Layla is overbearing. She dishes out to Lillian more than any sister should have to take. But Lillian is not timid. Sure, she goes off by herself with her books. But that doesn't concern me at all. She needs her alone time. I know, because I was exactly like that as a child."

Alice placed a hand on my arm. "I'm sorry, Graham. I didn't mean to ruffle your feathers."

"In the future, I'd appreciate you keeping your opinions to yourself. Because, godmother or not, Alice, you haven't been around my daughters enough recently to understand their personalities." As I stalked off, I felt two sets of eyes staring daggers at my back.

Alice had been back in our lives for less than an hour and she was already stirring up trouble. I feared what was in store for us now that she'd finished with school and had time on her hands until she secured a job. She'd said she was mostly looking for a job in Charleston. *Mostly* implied that she was also looking elsewhere. I could only hope that elsewhere included Siberia.

As predicted, much to my dismay, Alice insinuated herself into our lives as though the past three years had never happened. But something in Alice and Ivy's relationship had shifted during their time apart. The new Alice was no longer the calming influenced she'd been to Ivy after Edward died. This Alice set my wife on edge. Her newfound confidence and independence made Ivy more unsure of herself. And Ivy's childish nature appeared to irritate Alice when once she'd been humored by it.

When I mentioned the friction between Ivy and Alice, Trudy admitted that she'd noticed it as well. "Reminds me of their younger days," Trudy said, "Every so often, Alice would get it in her head that she wanted a new best friend. She'd disappear for weeks on end. Alice always came running back, and Miss Ivy always forgave her."

"Alice needs a good dose of her own medicine," I said.

"Don't count on my Ivy being the one to give it to her. It's shameful the way Ivy lets that girl walk all over her."

That night, I tried to talk to Ivy about Alice, but she shut me down. "Don't interfere, Graham. Our relationship is complicated. We're working through some issues."

The next day, I came home one day from work and found Ivy sitting in a chair in the upstairs hall with one hand resting on the telephone receiver on the console table beside her.

"What're you doing?" I asked.

"Waiting for Alice to call," Ivy said, crossing and uncrossing her legs.

"Are you *expecting* Alice to call?

Eyes glued to the phone, she said, "No, but I'm hoping she will."

A week later, I happened upon Ivy sitting cross-legged on the floor in the drawing room, surrounded by old photo albums with a box of tissues in her lap and tears streaming down her face. I assumed she was looking at pictures of her father, but as I drew closer, I could see the books were full of photographs of Alice and Ivy through the years.

Ivy exhibited other signs that she was coming unglued. She stopped sleeping. I often heard her pacing the floors of the third-floor hall at night. And she was irritable, snapping at anyone who crossed her in the slightest way, most especially her daughters.

We all walked on eggshells around her, until things finally came to a head on Halloween.

Nanny Watson, who'd been feeling poorly in recent weeks, had asked for the weekend off to visit her sister in Mount Pleasant. We'd been invited to a neighborhood Halloween party, and naturally, Ivy had asked Alice to accompany us. Layla and Lillian were dressed as the Little Mermaid and Minnie Mouse, respectively, their costumes fashioned by Nanny on her ancient Singer machine. The scene was mayhem with adults socializing over cocktails while their little ghosts and goblins ran about at will. The children were getting along beautifully. Even Layla was being nice to Lillian for a change. Until Lillian won first prize in the costume contest, and Layla came in second.

I watched the scene unfold as I assisted some of the younger kids at the apple bobbing barrel. Layla had gathered a group of the older neighborhood children in the corner of the backyard. While I wasn't privy to what she was telling them, I had no doubt that they were whispering about Lillian. When one of them called her Minnie Rat, they rest of them began chanting the same. Lillian took off, darting around the corner of the house and shimmying up the trunk of a live oak tree.

Before I could break away from the apple bobbers, Ivy, with Alice on her heels, beat me to Lillian's rescue. Much to my surprise, my wife didn't try to gently coax our daughter down from the tree, but reprimanded her in a stern voice I could hear across the yard.

"Lillian Alexander, you come down outta that tree this instant. What is wrong with you? Why can't you get along with the other children like your sister? Don't be a coward. If those kids are picking on you, stand up to them."

Racing across the yard, I took Ivy by the arm and dragged her away from the tree. "What're you doing? You can't talk to her like that. She's a sensitive six-year-old child."

Ivy's face turned beet red. She knew she'd done wrong. "But Alice said I needed to be firm with her, to toughen her up."

I glared at Alice. "Since when does having a law degree make one an authority on parenting?" What I didn't say hung in the air between the three of us. Alice lacked parenting skills because she wasn't a parent.

Alice glared back at me. "I was just trying to help."

Turning my back on Alice, I spoke to my wife in a low voice. "You take Layla home. We'll discuss her punishment later. I'll stay here and do damage control with Lillian."

The old Ivy would've apologized to Lillian and to me. But this new Ivy, this under-the-influence-of-Alice Ivy, stomped away without a backward glance.

For the remainder of the party, I kept an eye on my daughter while I busied myself with the games and festivities. Lillian waited until the last guest had left to come out of the tree.

"Are you ready to go?" I asked, holding my hand out to her.

She placed her tiny hand in mine. "I'm sorry, Daddy."

"What do you have to be sorry for, Minnie Mouse?" I covered my mouth in mock surprise. "I mean, Lillian Mouse."

"Dad-dy." She tugged on my hand. "You know what?"

"I know some other children who should be sorry, but you're not one of them."

This seemed to satisfy her, and we walked in silence for several blocks. On the way home, I escorted my daughter on a detour through Battery Park. When we came to a bench, I sat down and pulled her onto my lap.

"You know, kiddo, you remind me a lot of myself when I was your age."

"Really, Daddy? How?"

"Well . . ." I kissed the top of her head. "For starters, I loved to read as much as you. The downside to reading is that it's something you do alone. But there's nothing wrong with being alone if you don't mind being by yourself."

Lillian chewed on her lower lip. "But I'm not really alone when I'm reading. I'm with the people in the books."

My throat swelled. At that moment, I knew we were kindred spirits. That the person I would be the closest to in my life was my daughter. When I trusted my voice again, I said,

"That's very intuitive of you, Mouse. We meet all kinds of fascinating people in the stories we read." I shifted her little body on my lap so I could see her face. "You know, Lil, not everyone enjoys being alone. Some people have a need to be around others. Some even have to be the center of attention."

"You mean like Layla."

"Exactly. And that's okay, because that's who she is."

"But why is she so mean, Daddy?"

This was the confirmation I needed that Layla was bullying her sister. "The same reason you're nice, honey. Layla has niceness in her heart too, we just have to work harder to find it. Everyone is different."

"But we're twins. We're supposed to be the same."

"Not necessarily. You may look a lot alike on the outside, but your personalities are very different on the inside." I straightened the mouse ears on her head. "When people call you names that hurt your feelings, try to ignore them because they don't know any better."

"Like Mommy when she called me a cow-yard. What's a cow-yard, Daddy?"

"The word is coward, sweetheart. It's when a person is afraid of something. Your mommy was trying to get you to stand up to those big kids who were teasing you. But that's a scary thing to do, isn't it?"

She nodded as tears welled in her eyes. "Because they're so mean."

"What if I helped you? What if, together, you and I practiced what you will say to them the next time they're being mean? Would that help?"

"Yes, but . . . "She hid her face in my chest. "Mommy's right. I am a cow-yard, because I am afraid."

"I don't want you to be afraid." I held her back so I could look into her eyes. "Why don't we take it one day at a time? If someone is being mean, you need to tell me about it. I can't help you unless I know what's going on at home and school. Okay, sweetheart?"

"Okay, Daddy."

"When I was your age, I used to hide with my books like you do. But I made certain my mother always knew where to find me."

I could see the wheels turning in her head as she thought about what I was telling her. "In case of an emergency," she said.

"That's part of it. Parents get scared when we don't know where our children are. Promise me, you'll always let someone know where you are, either Mommy or Trudy or Nanny or me."

Her brown eyes stared at me from behind her glasses. "I promise, Daddy."

We walked home together hand in hand and went straight to my study, closing the door against the rest of the world. While I graded papers at my desk, Lillian curled up on the sofa with a blanket and stack of books. Not long after, she nodded off. I thought back to my childhood as I watched her sleep. I never had anyone take up for me, certainly not my older brothers who bullied me as much as the neighborhood kids. I would not fight my child's battles for her, but I would not tolerate the bullying in my home.

I slipped out of the study and went upstairs to the girls' room where I found Layla playing quietly on the floor with the new Plantation Belle Barbie she got for her birthday.

I sat down on Layla's bed and patted the mattress beside me. "Come sit with me, sweetheart. I want to talk to you about something important."

Ignoring me, Layla combed through the Barbie outfits and accessories on the floor around her until she found a matching pair of tiny pink-plastic heels.

I slid to the floor beside her. "Put the Barbie down, Layla. I need to talk to you." When my daughter still refused to acknowledge me, I took the Barbie from her.

"Stop, Daddy. I'm playing." When she tried to snatch the doll away, I tucked it beneath my leg. "You can have it back in a minute. After we have a little chat about what happened at the party today. I'm disappointed in you, Layla. I don't expect you to be best friends with your sister, but you will treat her with kindness. If you pick on her again, you'll face serious consequences."

Crossing her arms, she huffed, "What does that mean, con-se-quences?"

"That means you're gonna be in big trouble with me."

We glared at each other with the same brown eyes. My two little girls were so vastly different — one so headstrong and independent and one so . . . so, me.

I saved my lecture for Ivy until later that night, after the girls were tucked into bed and all the ghost and goblins had tricked and treated their way through the neighborhood. I asked her to join me for a night cap in my study, the room where all her serious conversations with her father had taken place.

"I don't know what's going on with you, Ivy, but, for our daughters' sake, you need to pull yourself together. You were way out of line today. That woman I saw at the party is not the real Ivy. You called Lillian a coward, but you're the one acting like one. You're letting Alice control you. You're totally under her spell. But you need to stand up to her."

She stared at the amber liquid in her glass. "You don't know what you're talking about, Graham."

"I know what I saw today. Something is different between you and Alice. I sense tension in your relationship. Where's it coming from?"

"Alice has changed. She acts so high and mighty now that she's a lawyer. She only cares about herself." Her eyes shifting,

Ivy looked past me to the moonlit window. "Is our life enough for you, Graham?"

The bottom dropped out of my stomach. "Our life is a dream come true for me, Ivy. We have a lovely home and beautiful children, and I have a career I'm passionate about. Are you not happy?"

"I wish Daddy were still alive. He'd know how to help me."

I left my chair and rounded the desk, kneeling down beside her. "Talk to me, Ivy. If something's bothering you, I want to know about it."

She turned her head away, staring at the bookcases. "You wouldn't understand."

I stroked her arm. "I might if you tried me."

She jerked her arm away. "I'm not talking to you about this. It's none of your business."

"Then maybe you should talk to an unbiased party, a professional."

Ivy jumped to her feet. "I don't need a shrink, Graham. I'm not crazy." She nearly knocked me down as she brushed past me.

"Then stop acting like it," I called after her.

GRAHAM

*A*fter church the following day, I took Ivy and the girls to brunch at the Variety Store, the cozy restaurant at the city marina. Ivy and Lillian sat in silence while Layla prattled on about her friends at school. I retreated to my study as soon as I returned home. Lillian came looking for me an hour later.

"I have to tell you something, Daddy."

"What's that, sweetheart?" I set down my pen and leaned over in my chair, eye level with her.

"I have a secret hiding place. I wanted you to know where to find me. It's in one of the bedrooms in the back wing."

While I was thrilled she'd listened to me, I was concerned about how long she'd been hiding out in the back wing of the house and why none of the adults in her life knew about it. "I appreciate you telling me this, Mouse. But you know you're not supposed to be back there."

She nodded, her chin trembling.

"Why don't you show me this hiding place?"

"Okay! Let's go." She took me by the hand and led me up the stairs and down to the end of the guest bedroom wing. Each room was known by its color scheme—the aqua room and rose room and lavender room. Lillian had chosen the yellow room with yellow roses on the drapery fabric that matched the walls, and lush green shag carpet.

"Why the yellow room?" I asked her.

"Because the walls are the color of the sun and the carpet is like summer grass between my toes. It's like being outside in the garden."

"But doesn't it make you afraid to be so far away from the main house?"

She shook her head. "It's quiet here. I can read my books. And Layla won't bother me."

The windows stretched from floor to ceiling, but the bedroom wing had no access to the piazzas. Lillian had dragged a green velvet swivel chair over to one of the windows and brought some of her stuffed animals and books from her room. I went to stand by the window. From this angle I could see the brick courtyard and all the way down the driveway to the street.

Lillian came to stand beside me, and I knelt down in front of her. "I'll let you keep your secret garden, but you may only come here when I'm at home. And you have to always let me know you're here. Deal?"

She flashed a snaggletooth grin. "Deal."

We walked to the door together. "I'll be in my study. Let me know when you come back to the main part of the house."

For the next few hours, I engrossed myself in lecture planning for the upcoming week. When the phone rang late afternoon, I was surprised to hear Melanie's frazzled voice. "Graham, thank God I caught you. I'm in town, and I need to see you right away."

"We had an agreement, Melanie. Charleston is off limits for you."

"I'm here on business, Graham. This is an emergency. I have

a manuscript due to my publisher a week from tomorrow. I feel it's my best work yet, but my agent disagrees. She won't turn it in to the publisher until I make *her* suggested changes."

On average, Melanie released a book a year, each with more fanfare than the one before it. "I've worked with you on all your other books. Why is this the first I'm hearing about this one?"

Melanie let out a sigh. "Because my agent says you have too much influence over my work, that she hears your voice in my characters."

"Sounds to me like you need a new agent."

"I'm considering it. But before I go firing my agent, I'd like for you to read the manuscript. I believe in this novel. I think it has enormous potential. But I need your opinion. I trust you to tell me the truth, Graham. You know me, and you know my work."

"All right," I said with a sigh. "Where are you staying?"

"I have a suite at the Charleston Place," she said and gave me the room number. "I'll see you in a few."

I grabbed my briefcase as a prop. If I ran into Ivy, I would tell her I was going to my office at the college. I was on my way out of the house when I remembered that Lillian was in her secret garden. Climbing the stairs to the third floor, I found her tucked in a ball, sound asleep, in the green velvet chair. "Your mommy's taking a nap, and I have to leave for a little while. I need you to go back to your room."

Lillian pushed herself to a sitting position. Rubbing her eyes with balled fists, she said, "Please, Daddy, can't I stay here?"

"Tell you what. Nanny is due back soon. I want you to watch for her out of the window." I tapped on the glass pane. "When you see her car in the driveway, go downstairs and ask her to help you with your bath. Okay?"

"Okay," she repeated with an affirmative nod.

I patted her head and exited the room, hurrying out of the house before Ivy spotted me. I drove to the hotel instead of walking, despite the pleasant autumn weather. I don't know why I felt guilty. I was meeting a work colleague, not a mistress. But Ivy would freak out if she discovered Melanie had broken our agreement by coming to Charleston.

I entered the grand lobby of the Charleston Place with my head bowed and eyes glued to the marble floor, and rode the elevator to the sixth floor. I'd seen Melanie's photograph plenty of times over the years in magazines and on the dust jackets of her books, but I was in no way prepared for the sophisticated woman who greeted me at the door of her suite. In the six years since I'd last seen her in person, she'd transitioned from bubbly blonde to regal beauty. She wore a red cashmere turtleneck, her lips painted the same shade, and her hair fastened at the nape of her neck with a tortoiseshell barrette.

She stepped into my outstretched arms. "It's so good to see you, Graham."

"Success agrees with you. You look stunning," I said, inhaling her intoxicating perfume. The spark I'd once felt for her threatened to reignite, and I quickly pushed away from her.

"That's nice of you to say. Teaching agrees with you."

I entered the suite and took a look around. The living area was furnished with a sofa, two comfortable chairs, and a desk, arranged so the occupant could appreciate the view of the city market through the bank of windows. "Not too shabby."

"I figured we'd need room to work. That is, if you agree to help me." She lifted a glass pitcher of clear liquid off the granite-topped wet bar. "Care for a martini?"

"Sure. Why not?" I needed something to calm my frazzled nerves.

She poured two glasses, handing one to me. We clinked glasses and, in unison, said, "Cheers."

Melanie took a dainty sip of her martini. "As I said on the phone, I'm having a bit of a disagreement with my agent.

Although I trust my gut instincts, I'd feel better having your feedback before I make any drastic decisions."

"I'll need to read it first, obviously."

"And I have a copy all ready for you." She swept her hand at the bound sheaf of papers on the desk. "I understand this is an imposition for you, Graham. But time is of the essence. Am I out of line in asking you to read it tonight?"

"Out of line? No. That's the nature of the publishing business. I'll warn you, though, I've had a bit of a trying weekend. I may not be able to stay awake long enough to finish." Realizing I'd crossed the boundary by mentioning my personal life, I quickly changed the subject. "Can you give me a brief synopsis?"

We moved to the sofa, and while we sipped our martinis, she told me about her latest project. The story was more character-driven, the plot of a more serious nature, than her other books, and by the time she'd finished talking, I was eager to start reading.

"You're a good sport to do this for me." She moved closer to me. Side by side with our legs pressed together, her gray flannel against my worn corduroy, I was all too aware of the heat radiating from her thigh. I jumped up, stuffing the manuscript in my briefcase.

"I didn't mean to scare you off, Graham," she said following me to the door. "I'm not planning to seduce you. This is a strictly professional arrangement. I booked a suite, so you'll feel comfortable working here with me, if you decide to take the job."

I burst out laughing. "Does that mean I'm getting paid this time?"

Placing a manicured hand on her boyish hip, she stared up at the ceiling while she thought about it. "We can work something out. I should've been paying you all along, truthfully."

"Keep your money, Mel. It's my pleasure to work on a manuscript with my most famous former student."

"I thought I was your only famous former student."

I smiled down at her. "There have been a few others."

Melanie hooked me from the very first word. The emotions were raw, and I had tears in my eyes when I finished the last chapter at nearly three in the morning. Too enthusiastic to sleep, I stayed up another hour making notes on ways she could enhance her story. Her agent's criticism of the novel made no sense to me. Aside from some additional character development and general polishing, in my opinion, she was well on her way to another blockbuster bestseller.

"I see no major obstacles," I told her when I called her hotel room from my campus office prior to my first class. "You can easily have this manuscript ready for your publisher in a week's time. We'll talk about how to handle your agent when I see you. I have all-morning classes this semester. I can be there around one. In the meantime, you can start by identifying areas where you can flesh out your characters." After a brief discussion of the characters that needed more attention, I added "They don't need much. But they need some."

"Perfect," she said. "I'll have room service bring lunch up, and we can get right to work."

As I hung up the phone, I could almost see her radiant smile. I'd forgotten how much I enjoyed her company, and as the week wore on, we easily settled into our roles as author and editor. We'd spent untold hours on the phone discussing her work over the past six years, but our creative juices flowed more fluidly in person. I'd missed the human connection, the face-to-face conversation, her quirky expressions.

We revised her manuscript chapter by chapter, and by late

Thursday afternoon, I deemed it nearly ready for her publisher. "Make those last few changes we talked about in the morning, and you should be good to go."

"Let's have some champagne to celebrate." Melanie pushed back from the small round table, its surface covered with messy stacks of marked-up pages, and crossed the room to the bar. She removed a small bottle of Dom Perignon from the minifridge and popped the cork.

"You're bringing out the good stuff," I said, coming to stand beside her.

"This is the only brand they offered. And it can't cost but so much. There's hardly any in the bottle," she said, filling two flutes halfway.

She handed me a glass, and we toasted to her newly titled, nearly complete novel, *Sunrise Over the Mountain.*

"What're you going to do about your agent?" I asked. During the week, we'd discussed her options for handling the situation at length.

"I'm going to fire her. But not before I secure a new agent. I've already put in calls to my top two choices. I hope to hear back from them tomorrow."

"Good for you," I said, clinking her glass.

"I'd love it if you'd stay for dinner."

I felt longing deep within my groin and not for the first time that week. I sensed Melanie wouldn't turn me down if I made a pass at her. She was so damn beautiful and witty and intelligent and talented. But she wasn't Ivy. When I married Ivy, I pledged to love her for better or worse, in sickness and in health. With each passing day, she was becoming more and more distant. She was slipping away from me, from our family She needed psychiatric help. And I intended to get it for her.

"I'm sorry, Mel. Ivy's expecting me at home." I drained the rest of my champagne. "Are you planning to stay through the weekend?" I asked, hoping she'd remain in Charleston but knowing it was best for both of us if she went back to New York.

"I'm flying standby for a flight out late tomorrow afternoon."

My heart shrank three sizes. How would I ever live without this woman in my life? But having her around was too tempting. If I traveled down that path again, I would risk losing my wife and my family. "Hopefully you will have heard from one of your agents by then."

She walked me to the door. "It tears me apart to think I may never see you again. Have lunch with me one last time tomorrow?"

Say no, the voice inside my head shouted but the words, "It would be my pleasure," rolled off my tongue.

Angry and disappointed with myself, I purchased a bouquet of autumn lilies, the color of the yellow leaves on the gingko trees bordering our courtyard, for Ivy from a flower vendor on Broad Street on my way home. But when I arrived at the house, Trudy reported that Ivy, who claimed to have a migraine headache, had locked herself in her sitting room where she remained throughout the evening.

After a pleasant dinner with Layla and Lillian, I turned them over to Nanny and retired to my study. In working with Melanie on her manuscript, I'd gotten behind on my class work. At almost midnight, I was still grading papers when I heard footsteps on the stairs followed by the opening and closing of the front door.

I passed through the drawing room to the piazza and peered over the railing at Ivy who was hurrying down the driveway on foot. I called down to her. "Where are you going at this hour? I thought you had a headache."

"I do," she said, lifting the back of her hand to her forehead. "But Alice is having a crisis and needs to see me."

That was a first. I'd never known Alice to need anyone. She

barely broke a sweat when Heath divorced her. "What sort of crisis?"

"That's none of your business, Graham."

"If it's important enough to drag my wife out at midnight, I think I have a right to know."

Either not hearing me or choosing to ignore me, she said, "I won't be gone long," and left without further explanation.

GRAHAM

*I*vy had still not returned by the time I fell asleep around two o'clock. The following morning, I woke up in an empty bed to the sound of heavy rain pinging the gutters. I shaved and dressed and went down to breakfast. To my surprise, Ivy was seated at the kitchen table with Nanny and the girls. Nanny was explaining to Ivy that she had a doctor's appointment scheduled for that afternoon, while Trudy, at the stove, poured melted butter and warmed maple syrup over the tops of five stacks of pancakes.

"My doctor is sending me to a cardiologist to rule out the possibility of a serious problem." Nanny had finally confessed that, along with fatigue, she'd been experiencing a fluttering in her chest. "The girls have a half day of school today, but Sally Simmons has invited them for lunch and a playdate. Her mother will bring them home around four o'clock. I'll be back way before then."

Ivy, with her hands around her coffee mug and her mind a million miles away, stared at Nanny with a dazed expression.

I wedged myself into the empty chair between my daughters. "Who is Sally Simmons? Is she a new friend at school?"

"Her father is a surgeon," Nanny answered in a tone that expressed her approval of the father's occupation. "Lillian and Layla have been to their house before. They live nearby." She paused. "I can see the house, although the name of the street escapes me."

"That sounds like a fun afternoon for you girls," I said, patting both of them on the heads.

The girls chatted on about their playdate while they gobbled up their pancakes. Layla did most of the talking, but I could see the excitement in Lillian's face as well.

Desperate for a word alone with my wife, I waited at the table until Nanny took the girls to school and Trudy disappeared into the laundry room.

"Where'd you sleep last night?" I asked in a concerned tone.

When she didn't respond, I waved my hand in front of her face, drawing her out of her trance.

"Huh? What?" she asked as though surprised to see me sitting across from her.

"I asked where you slept last night."

"On the sofa in the drawing room."

I reached for her hand. "Talk to me, Ivy. Tell me what's troubling you."

Elbows on table, she planted her face in her hands. "You wouldn't understand."

"You keep saying that, but how do you know if you won't give me a chance? Believe it or not, I'm a good listener." It dawned on me, and saddened me, that she didn't already know this after seven years of marriage. We'd never fully opened up to one another. While we'd come close a time or two, I'd always felt like she was holding a part of herself back. And that would have to change in order for our marriage to work. "Why don't we leave the girls with Nanny this weekend and sneak away to Wadmalaw by ourselves. Assuming, of course, that everything goes okay at Nanny's doctor's appointment."

Ivy stared at me as if the sight of me disgusted her. "I don't want to be alone with *you*, Graham. I just want to be alone. Maybe I'll go by myself to the cottage."

I banged my fist on the table so hard Ivy's coffee cup bounced in her saucer. "Then go to the cottage by yourself. Spend a week. A month. A year. Whatever it takes to draw you out of this funk you're in." I shot to my feet, snatched my rain-coat off the wall hook, and stormed out of the house through the back door.

Dread settled over me as I backed out of the driveway. I'd never spoken to my wife in such a harsh manner. And while she needed to know I was nearing the end of my patience, I had a nagging feeling that something was desperately wrong in Ivy's world.

Unfortunately, a classroom of students awaited me, and I couldn't afford to be late to campus.

I moved through the morning like a zombie, and my students yawned and nodded off to let me know they found my lectures uninspiring. I couldn't wait to see Melanie. I wanted to beg her not to go. Even more so, I wanted to go with her. The idea of escaping to New York with Melanie thrilled me. I was treading on dangerous ground, but I no longer cared. I wanted to be with a woman who wanted to be with me. But I would never leave my children.

Melanie greeted me at the door of her suite when I arrived a few minutes after one. "Guess what? I have a new agent. My top choice took me on without hesitation."

"That's fabulous news, Mel." I gave her a bear hug, lifting her off her feet.

"I've ordered a special lunch to celebrate."

"I hope that order includes champagne."

"You know it!"

The room service attendant arrived with the lunch cart, and while Melanie signed the bill, I went over to the window. As I was staring down at the wet streets of Charleston, I noticed a woman exit the front entrance of the hotel with head ducked against the rain. I recognized my wife's long graceful limbs. Ivy tied the sash of her London Fog tighter and increased her pace to a jog. When she reached the corner, without pausing to check for oncoming traffic, she stepped off the curb into the intersection. The driver of the beer truck barreling down the road laid on the horn and swerved to the right, missing her by inches. I gasped, my hand flying to my throat. But Ivy, with barely a glance at the truck, kept running.

Why had Ivy been at the hotel in the first place? Did she somehow find out Melanie was in town? Did she know we'd been working together? Was it possible she'd seen me enter the hotel? Who was I fooling? In her current state of distraction, I doubt she'd even care. Whatever had made Ivy so upset as to step out in front of a speeding beer truck had nothing to do with me. But, in order to save Ivy from herself, I needed to find out what was so terribly wrong in her life.

I barely tasted the mushroom bisque and autumn chicken salad. When I begged off the creme brûlée for dessert, I explained, "I have things I need to attend to at home."

Melanie glanced at her Cartier watch. "And I should be leaving for the airport soon. Thank you, Graham." Standing on her tiptoes, she brushed her lips against mine. Her breath was a whisper when she said, "For everything."

Aching with desire for her, I took her in my arms and kissed her with every ounce of passion I'd been feeling those past few days. When the kiss ended, I said, "I'm sorry, Melanie, but we can't see each other again. I can no longer deny my attraction to you. The temptation is too great."

"But I need you, Graham. I promise we'll keep it strictly professional from now on."

"You don't need me, Mel. Your work is getting stronger. You have your new agent to provide feedback." Her lower lip trembled, and I kissed it one last time. "You'll find the right man. But that man will never be me."

I left Melanie standing in the doorway with tears streaming down her cheeks.

As I retrieved my car from the deck, I experienced a sense of urgency to get home. Something was wrong. I felt it deep in my core. I considered abandoning my car when an accident at the intersection of Broad and Meeting caused traffic to come to a complete standstill for thirty minutes. My panic mounted, and by the time I arrived home, I was sweating profusely, and my heart was hammering against my rib cage.

"Where's Ivy?" I asked Trudy, who was unloading groceries in the kitchen.

"I'm not sure. I've been gone a good while. I had a parent-teacher conference at Ruthie's school. I stopped in at the Piggly Wiggly on my way here."

I charged past her on my way to the front of the house. As I rounded the corner from the dining room into the hallway, I saw a stream of water pouring from the ceiling and puddling on the hardwood floors. I stopped abruptly, and Trudy, who was right behind me, collided into me.

"What on earth? Where's that coming from?" she asked.

Calculating the distance, I said, "The master bath."

We raced up the stairs to my bedroom. The bathroom door was cracked, and the scene I spied within stole my breath.

I shouted at Trudy, "Go call nine-one-one and wait outside for the ambulance."

"Yes, sir," she said, and scurried from the room.

Careful not to slip on the slick floor, I wrestled Ivy's limp body out of the tub to the floor. I yanked bath towels from the chrome bar and tied them around her wrists, but the blood had ceased to flow when her heart stopped. Ivy's lips were blue. She'd been gone for some time. I gripped the lapels of her trench coat and shook her, letting out a bellow of sorrow and rage. "Why, Ivy? Why?"

The metallic taste of blood was on my tongue and the sickly sweet scent of gardenias from the shattered Chanel perfume bottle on the floor assaulted my nose. I crawled to the toilet and vomited my lunch. The EMTs found me hugging the porcelain bowl when they arrived a few minutes later. When they realized there was nothing to be done to save Ivy, they turned to me. "Sir, do you need medical attention?"

"I'm fine. Just take care of my wife." Wiping my mouth on my sleeve, I scrambled to my feet and stumbled out of the bathroom, collapsing onto Trudy who was waiting outside the door. "Oh, Trudy. Why would she do such a thing?"

Trudy held me tight, cooing, "Hush now, Mister Graham. My Ivy was a restless soul. She's never been truly happy. And she hasn't been the same since her daddy died. We need to think about Lillian and Layla now. This will tear those little girls up."

I'd been in too much of a state of shock to think about the girls. "Where are Lillian and Layla?" Then I remembered. "Right, the playdate. Nanny said they would be home around four. What time is it?"

Our eyes traveled together to the alarm clock on the bedside table, its red numbers displaying 3:58. Seconds later, I heard one of the girls calling for me downstairs.

With Trudy matching my pace, I hurried down the stairs to the foyer. "Layla, sweetheart."

My daughter ran into my arms. "What happened, Daddy? Why are all these people in our house?"

"Mommy had an accident." When I picked her up, Layla wrapped her legs tight around my waist.

I noticed an attractive woman standing awkwardly by the front door. The playdate's mom. I remembered the child's name was Sally, but for the life of me, I couldn't recall her last name.

"Why are you all wet, Daddy? And what's that red stuff on your shirt?"

I glanced down. The front and sleeves of my white button-down were drenched in blood.

Layla persisted, "Is Mommy okay?"

The woman caught my eye, and I shook my head, letting her know that Layla's mommy was not okay. "Where's your sister?" I asked, holding the woman's gaze. "Is she still in the car?"

Sally's mother fiddled with the string of pearls at her neck. "Isn't she with you? She wasn't feeling well when I picked them up from school. She had a tummy ache. I dropped her off here hours ago. Layla came inside with her to make sure someone was home."

I set Layla on the floor and knelt in front of her. "And was someone home, Layla? Did you see Mommy?"

Toying with the zipper of her raincoat, Layla shook her head. "I didn't see anyone."

"You mean you left your sister here alone?"

She nodded. "I thought Trudy was here. Or Nanny."

"But you didn't check to make sure?"

"No, sir," she said, biting down on her quivering lower lip.

I pinned Sally's mom against the wall with my glare. Who trusts a six-year-old to make certain an adult is home? "If you don't mind, my family needs to be alone right now."

A look of relief swept over Sally's mom's face as she slipped out the door.

"Trudy, please take Layla to her room while I look for Lillian. I'm pretty sure I know where to find her."

Please, God, let her be there, I prayed as I took the stairs two at a time to the third floor.

At the end of the back wing, I burst into the yellow room. Flashing blue-and-red lights from the rescue vehicles in the driveway below filled the dark room, bouncing off the walls and ceiling. My legs gave way at the sight of my daughter cowering in the green velvet chair. "There you are, Mouse. You scared me." Dropping to my knees, I crawled across the shag carpet to her. "Are you okay?"

"Tell them to turn them off," Lillian said through chattering teeth.

"Turn what off, sweetheart?"

"The lights. They're hurting my eyes."

I pulled her out of the chair onto my lap. "They'll be gone soon." The smell of urine burned my nose. Lillian had wet her pants. *What could've possibly happened to my child to cause her to lose control of her bladder? Did she happen upon Ivy in the bathtub? Oh, dear God. Please tell me she didn't witness her slitting her wrists.*

LILLIAN

I need air. The imagined scent of gardenias is powerful, and I fear I might suffocate. I leave Dad's study, staggering through the drawing room and out onto the piazza. Gripping the railing, I gulp in deep breaths of salt air, and squeezing my eyes tight, I tilt my face toward the sky. Events from the day my mother died stream across the backs of my eyelids like a rerun of an old black-and-white movie.

I'm in the back seat of the car with Layla and Sally. Layla is in the middle with Sally and me buckled in on either side. The rain pounds the windshield as the wipers beat back and forth. Sally's mother's dark hair is tied up in rollers with a pink kerchief.

With an evil glint in her eyes, Layla says to Sally's mother, "Mrs. Simmons, my sister has a tummy ache. Can we please take my sister home on the way to your house?"

"But my stomach doesn't hurt," I whisper to Layla, and she digs her elbow into my side.

Sally's mother shot me a frantic look in the rearview mirror. "Do you need to throw up, sweetheart? I can pull over."

"She doesn't have to puke," Layla says with mean snicker. "She has to poop."

My face burns, but I don't defend myself. Mrs. Simmons will believe Layla over me. Everyone always believes Layla over me. Except Daddy.

Sally's mom takes a sharp right into our driveway and screeches to a halt in front of the door. She wants me out of her car before I soil her upholstered back seat. "Layla, dear, please walk your sister inside," she says, patting her kerchief. She doesn't want anyone to see her with curlers in her hair.

"Yes ma'am," Layla says all sugary sweet, and reaches across me for the door handle and shoves me out of the car.

"Make certain someone's home," Mrs. Simmons calls after us, her voice barely audible over the sound of the rain.

We make a dash for the front door with the hoods of our yellow slickers drawn over our heads and red rain boots on our feet. I stand to the side while Layla struggles with the heavy brass door handle. "Why can't I go with you?"

"Because Sally doesn't like you. Her mother made her invite you." Layla jostles the door open and pushes me inside.

The house feels empty, and I sense that nobody is home. "Please don't make me stay here alone."

"I'm sure Trudy's here somewhere. Go find her," Layla says and slams the door on her way out.

I search every room in the house, but there is no sign of anyone. I go to the yellow room, my safe haven. I like it that Daddy calls it my secret garden. I've been spending more and more time here away from my overbearing sister. I even moved some of my clothes into the drawers of the big brown chest. I hate changing in front of Layla. Her critical eyes on my naked body gives me the creeps.

I change out of my wet dress into dry clothes—jeans, a plain gray sweatshirt, and pink sneakers—and stand at the window waiting for someone to come home. My tummy growls several times, and then it begins to rumble with that empty feeling that makes me nauseous.

I'm relieved to see Mama running down the sidewalk, her head ducked against the driving rain, and I hurry out of the room to greet her. When I enter the main part of the house, I spot her at the end of the hallway near her bedroom. I call her name, and she turns to me. Are those tears on her face or rain drops?

"I'm hungry, Mama. Can I have a sandwich?"

Her arm shoots out, her finger pointed at my bedroom door. "Go to your room, Layla."

Tears spring to my eyes and a lump develops in my throat. "But I'm—"

"I said. Go to. Your room." Her face is red with anger. She's never spoken to me in such a cross tone. As I back down the hallway, she jabs her finger at me. "And don't come out until someone comes for you," she says and slams her bedroom door on me.

"I'm not Layla," I say in a tiny voice. I stand rooted to my spot in the center of the hallway, mustering the courage to return to the yellow room. I'm making a run for it when the muffled sound of Mama crying stops me in my tracks. I tiptoe back down the hall, and turning the knob slowly, I push open her bedroom door. Through the empty bedroom, I see the bathroom door is closed. I pad in bare feet across the carpet and press my ear against the door. She's sobbing louder. My heart races. I should go for help, but there's no one home. I should call Daddy at work, but I don't know his number. I'll ask Mama to give me the number. She would want me to call him. I crack the door. There is red everywhere. Blood. Pooling on the floor. Smeared on the side of the tub. Soaking the bathmat and the sleeves of the trench coat she's still wearing. The smell of

Mama's perfume is strong, and I notice a jagged piece of glass in her fingertips from the shattered bottle on the floor beside the tub.

Mama sees me and smiles. And then she closes her blue eyes and a peaceful expression falls over her face. I'm paralyzed, too terrified to move. I lose control of my bladder and warmth spreads down my legs.

I'm back in the secret garden. I have no memory of how I got there. I wrap myself up in a blanket and curl into a ball in the green velvet chair. I hear a car in the driveway, and then another, followed by hurried footsteps on the hardwood floors downstairs. There are sirens, so loud they hurt my ears. Flashing lights fill the room from the driveway below. Blue and red. So much red. So much blood.

My father finally comes for me, but he waits until much later, until he tucks me into bed that night, to ask what I know about my mother's accident.

I shake my head and mumble, "Nothing," because I can't bear to think about it.

He kisses my forehead and turns out the light. In the darkness, from the matching twin bed beside mine, Layla says, "This is all your fault, Lillian. You pushed Mama down the stairs. Thanks to you, she's never coming back."

I'm too young to comprehend death. For all I know, it is my fault. "I didn't mean to," I say. "I just wanted a sandwich."

My sleep is plagued with nightmares, and when I wake the following morning, I remember nothing about the events of the previous day.

I open my eyes wide to the starry night sky.

Layla used the situation to torment me every single day for the remainder of my childhood. She wasn't in the house that day. She doesn't know what happened. But that didn't stop her from speculating. *It's your fault, Lil. You were the only one here with Mama when it happened. What'd you do to her? Why'd you make her angry? Did you push her down the stairs?*

Did I make Ivy angry enough to kill herself? Heck no. I asked her for a sandwich. Even if I'd gone for help, she'd already lost too much blood. I was traumatized. I was a six-year-old child who'd discovered her mother bleeding to death in a bathtub. No one in their right mind would ever blame me.

An anger like I've never experienced before pulses through my body. Spinning on my heels, I turn away from the dark night. I go inside to the bar and pour myself a shot of Dad's whiskey, downing it in one gulp.

If anyone's to blame it's Layla for leaving me at home alone. I march across the hall and up the stairs to the room I once shared with my sister, bursting through the door without knocking. In a menacing tone, I yell, "You're a straight-up bitch, and I hate your guts."

I realize too late that Layla's on the phone. She's not crying but her eyes are swollen as though she has been. She says, "Roger, I need to call you back," and hangs up on him. "What the heck, Lil?"

I don't even know where to start, and she won't believe me anyway. I remove the thumb drive and note from my pocket and drop them on the bed. "Read these. Then we'll talk."

I slam her door so hard an old black-and-white photograph of us as children falls off the wall to the floor, the frame's glass cracking down the middle, a jagged line separating two smiling little girls who look so much alike.

I fly down the stairs, out the front door, and across the street. Despite the late hour, the promenade is crowded with locals out walking their dogs. I start off at a jog and quickly increase my pace to a run. By the time I reach Battery Park, I'm out of breath.

At the gazebo, a black Labrador retriever wiggles her way over to me, dropping her tennis ball at my feet. I give her a good scratching behind her ears and toss the ball back toward her owner. The dog reminds me of Bessie. We had so many pets throughout the years. A succession of black Labs and a horde of fat cats. But old Bessie was my mother's favorite, her constant companion. Where had Bessie been that day? Why wasn't she at Mama's side?

I drop to a nearby bench as the good memories come flooding back. Happy times spent on Wadmalaw. My mama thrived in the summertime. We spent whole days on the water, tubing and swimming and sailing. We pitched our tent in the front yard and slept under the stars. We went on nature hikes with my mother pointing out various species of plants and animals. Until that fated day, I'd never seen my mother angry. Distant at times, maybe. And absent a lot, for sure. We were often left in Nanny's care while she was out volunteering or shopping or playing tennis. But she loved us. Of that much I'm certain.

My phone vibrates with a call from Marcus. I've been avoiding his texts all afternoon and evening, but I can no longer put him off. Accepting the call, I tell him everything I've learned.

"Are you all right, Lil? I can come over if you need me."

"I'm not at home. I walked down to the park to cool off. But I'm fine, aside from being mad as hell at my evil sister. I finally understand the guilt that has plagued me all these years. It's such a relief to know I wasn't responsible for my mother's death."

"I'm so sorry you're having to go through this, but at least you can begin the healing process now that you know everything."

"But I don't know everything yet. I don't know why Ivy

killed herself. I was so furious with Layla, I had to take a break from reading."

I get up from the park bench, and as I retrace my steps toward home, Marcus and I speculate about what could've driven her to commit suicide. "Whatever it was, I'd be willing to bet it had something to do with Alice," I say when I reach the end of our driveway.

"Are you sure you don't want me to come over?" he asks.

I yearn to see him. Marcus always makes everything better. But we are no longer a couple. I am single, all on my own. And I need to figure this thing out for myself. "No, but thanks. I'm going inside to finish Dad's memoir. I'll talk to you tomorrow, Marcus."

The house is eerily quiet, and even though she's nowhere in sight, I'm acutely aware of my sister's presence. The house has harbored so many secrets for so many years. While I once felt safe here, I now feel vulnerable.

I make my way through the rooms and hallways, turning off lights and locking doors. I retrieve Marcus's iPad from Dad's study before heading up to the third floor. I pause, listening, outside of Layla's room. Light seeps from the crack under her door, but only silence comes from within. I imagine her reading Dad's words, and I fear how she'll react when she discovers all that I now know.

I bypass my room and continue to the end of the back wing of the house. A layer of dust covers the furniture and the room smells musty from being closed up, but everything in my secret garden is just as I left it. How ironic that out of all the color-themed rooms in the guest wing, I picked the yellow one. Mellow Yellow Lillian.

I continued to come here after my mother died. In fact, Dad and I would often spend time here together. He read to me the children's classic, *The Secret Garden*, by Frances Hodgson Burnett. I fancied myself Mary Lennox, looking for adventure in *my* secret garden. I found that adventure in the novels I read and in my art.

I curl up with a blanket in the green velvet chair and open Marcus's iPad. I feel protected here. I know I can handle whatever Dad has in store for me next.

GRAHAM

I remembered little about the days that followed Ivy's suicide. The guilt consumed me. I nearly drove myself mad contemplating the *what ifs*. What if I'd been at home instead of in a hotel room kissing Melanie? What if I'd gotten Ivy professional help sooner? The pain itself, the agony over losing my wife, was intolerable. And the girls . . . no six-year-old should ever lose a parent, least of all her mother. Telling Layla and Lillian that Ivy had gone to live with Jesus in heaven was one of the hardest things I ever had to do. But they were too young to comprehend she was never coming back. When they took their fighting to a new level—clawing and biting and hair pulling—Nanny divided their bedroom down the middle with a strip of duct tape, forbidding either to cross the line into the other's space.

When Lillian begged me to let her return to the yellow room, her secret garden, as much as I hated denying her her quiet space, I declared the back wing off limits until further notice.

Using a tactic from Ivy's playbook, I put on my game face, shelved my emotions to sort out at a later time, and moved through the process of burying my wife. I would never have made it through those three days without Trudy. She picked out the mahogany coffin and worked with the minister to select the appropriate hymns and readings. She even chose the yellow tweed summer suit Ivy had worn as her going away outfit from our wedding reception and would now wear to meet her maker. The girls, of course, were too young to attend the funeral, and with no other family, I insisted Trudy, Isaac, and Ruthie sit with me in church and at the cemetery.

Hundreds attended the catered lunch following the services, the same friends and colleagues who'd been in and out of our house during the days prior. It was all over by late afternoon. The servers had finished cleaning up, Trudy had gone home, and the girls had gone out for pizza with Nanny. The house felt unbearably empty. I had no clue how I would survive.

I retreated to my study and was filling a highball glass with straight bourbon when Alice knocked on the door. I was surprised and dismayed to see her. I thought everyone had gone home, and I'd been avoiding her for days. I did not offer her a drink now, this woman who'd been my wife's best friend and who, I believed, was somehow responsible for my wife's suicide.

"We need to talk, Graham."

I screwed the lid back on the Maker's Mark bottle. "It's been a long few days, Alice. Can't it wait?"

"No. It can't. I've waited long enough as it is." Her eyelids were puffy and red-rimmed, and she wore her auburn hair pulled tight off her freckled face in an unflattering bun.

I motioned her to the drawing room. "Let's go out to the porch."

The day was mild, and we'd opened all the exterior doors to allow fresh air to circulate during the reception. As the sun began to set, we sat down side by side in the wicker lounge chairs.

With shoulders hunched, Alice stared down at the wad of

tissues in her hand. "I would've handled the situation differently if I'd known she'd take it so hard. I never thought she'd . . ."

"Just tell me what happened, Alice."

"I invited Ivy for lunch at the Charleston Place Hotel."

So that explains why she was at the hotel. This information only offers the slightest relief. I'd never really thought Ivy's suicide had anything to do with me.

Alice continued, "Ivy would never cause a scene. That's why I decided to break the news to her in public." Alice's voice remained steady despite the tears streaming down her cheeks. "I told her I'd accepted a job in San Francisco with a law firm specializing in women's rights. I ended our relationship, Graham. Ivy and I were more than best friends. We were lovers."

I surprised us both when I burst out laughing. "I'm sorry. Did you just say you were lovers? As in you're gay?"

"Bisexual, technically, since both of us were married. We knew we could never tell our parents. They would never understand. And we wanted so much to have normal lives. To have husbands and children."

"How long did this affair go on?"

"From the time we were old enough to experience sexual desire." Alice's face turned scarlet. "We never stopped after we got married. We couldn't. We loved each other too much."

A fog lifted as everything became crystal clear. "My wife used me as a pawn. Our marriage was a farce to hide her lesbian affair. And I was nothing more than a sperm donor to father her children."

"That's not true, Graham. Ivy loved you. As much as she . . ."

"Could ever love a man." I finished her sentence. Ivy had said something similar to me once, on the night she found out Melanie was pregnant with my child. *I was beginning to feel things*

I never thought I'd feel for a . . . for you. I understood now what'd she'd been trying to tell me.

Alice smoothed out one of her tissues and blew her nose. "Ivy was content with our relationship the way it was. She liked being a wife and mother and seeing me on the side. I was the one who was unhappy. I'm tired of living a lie. Which is why I'm taking this job in San Francisco."

So many missing pieces fell into place, making the puzzle whole. "So that's why she's been so sullen these past few weeks?"

She nodded. "She knew I was interviewing in California. You know how much I love Charleston. Moving to the West Coast was not an easy decision for me. I begged her to go with me. But she worried she'd lose the girls in a custody battle."

I sprang to my feet. "So you forced her hand." My voice was raised and angry, but I didn't care if the neighbors heard. "You gave her an ultimatum. She couldn't live without you, and she couldn't live without her daughters, so she decided not to live at all."

Alice stood to face me. "You've gotta believe me, Graham. I never wanted this to happen. I loved Ivy more than anything."

"You have a funny way of showing it." My ears roared, and my heart pounded against my rib cage. "Get out of my house," I shouted, pointing at the open doorway. "I never want to see you again. As far as I'm concerned, you are no longer my children's godmother. Have a nice life in California."

In the days, weeks, and months that followed, my guilt was replaced by anger, an emotion I could at least relate to having been raised by an abusive father. I thought a lot about Alice and Ivy, wondering what their love must have been like. Forbidden love. Having to hide behind their friendship. If they'd been born a decade later, a whole world of opportunity would've opened up for them. Although I never forgave Alice, I eventually softened toward Ivy's memory. I know in my heart that she had loved me in her own way. If not for Alice, Ivy and I would've grown old together. But she had been vulnerable, a child in so many ways. Instead of protecting her, Alice preyed on that vulnerability. In retrospect, Ivy's mood swings had all been a direct result of Alice's actions. Alice got married. Ivy wanted to get married as well. Alice went to law school, Ivy hired a nanny and looked for a job. When Alice was around, Ivy was happy. When Alice decided to move to California, Ivy opted out of her life.

I never found a suicide note from Ivy, but I did find her day planner, which was full of engagements for the months ahead. In my heart, I don't believe Ivy ever intended to kill herself. Her suicide was yet another one of my wife's impulsive acts.

During my loneliest hours, Melanie was the one I missed the most. And I allowed myself to mourn the loss of our friendship without feeling guilty. I was able to finally admit to myself that I'd always been a little in love with Melanie, sometimes more than others. Ours was a love based on friendship and our shared appreciation for literature. We could sit in the same room for hours, never saying a word but knowing what each other was thinking. But there was a fundamental difference between us. Over the past six years, in all the time we'd spent on the phone together and during the week we'd worked on her manuscript in Charleston, she'd never once asked about the girls. I knew she thought about them, and I understood how difficult it had been for her to give up her baby. But she'd chosen career over family. She would always choose career over family. And that was the one thing keeping us apart.

While Layla grew from a headstrong child into an independent adolescent, Lillian struggled with more dark days than bright. She refused to talk about the day Ivy died, and I feared her mind had blocked out the painful memories. About six months after Ivy's death, I took her to see a child psychiatrist. After years of therapy, Dr. Hudson gave up. During our final consultation, she said to me, "We have to accept that we may never know what happened to Lillian the day her mother died."

The summer before the girls' twelfth birthday, Lillian moved out of the bedroom she shared with Layla and into the guest room. While the room was considerably smaller, she immediately seemed less anxious. That same year, on the day before school started, she pleaded with me to transfer her to a school for gifted students. I readily agreed, and Lillian blossomed at her new school—academically, socially, and artistically.

Immersing myself in my work prevented me from going insane during the loneliest times, and I thrived professionally over the next two decades. Increasingly more opportunities became available to me at the college. I taught top-level writing classes that yielded many published authors over the years. In 2010, I was awarded the most coveted position as head of the English department.

Friends badgered me constantly about going on blind dates, but I ignored them. I devoted my life to my work and my family. Trudy is my best friend and my daughters fill my heart with joy. I have no regrets. I've long since forgiven myself for betraying my wife. If not for my affair with Melanie, I would be one daughter short. I've led a good life. While I'm disappointed my time on earth has come to an end, I pray my beloved Ivy will be waiting for me in heaven.

LILLIAN

I finally have closure. My mind is free of the memories that have held it hostage for twenty-seven years. Knowing I had nothing to do with my mother's death is liberating. I can finally move on with my life. Marcus's words from the day by the fountain in Waterfront Park come back to me. *I wanted you to find yourself . . . I wanted you to get out from underneath the hold your sister had over you.* I can do that now. I still don't know whether Ivy or Melanie is my mother. I'm no longer sure I want to find out.

The urge to paint hits me the following morning, and I set up my easel beside the little girl statue in the hidden garden behind the carriage house. I've painted this scene many times, and now I understand the importance of the garden. It reminds me of the yellow room. Today, I see it through a fresh set of eyes. The whole world looks different to me. The colors of the earth, sea, and sky are more vibrant, the smell of the marsh more pungent.

I've been painting for hours when I sense Trudy's presence behind me, watching me from a distance. "It does my heart good to see you painting again," she says.

"My strokes are a little rusty, but I'm tapping into new inspiration."

I dip my brush in gray paint and shade the base of the stone statue. When I'm finished, I turn to face her. "I'm curious, Trudy. Where was Bessie the day Ivy died?"

"At the vet's, getting her annual shots. I didn't know this at the time. Your mama had taken her in without telling me. I was frantic with worry about that dog. I looked everywhere for her. I thought she'd run off, and I feared we'd never see her again when the vet called the day after the funeral and told me to come and pick her up." Trudy studies me closely. "You had a breakthrough, didn't you?"

Setting my brush down on my easel, I wipe my hands on my smock. "I remember everything."

Trudy lowers herself to a nearby stone bench and pats the empty space beside her. "Sit. Tell me."

As I walk her through the events of the day Ivy died, her eyes darken and the creases in her brow deepen. She's thinking bad thoughts about my sister, even though I know she would never repeat them to me.

She places an arm around me, giving me a half hug. "You, poor child. It's worse than I suspected. No wonder your little mind kept you from remembering what happened. If only I'd been here, I could've spared you so much heartache."

"Don't be ridiculous. You were at your daughter's teacher's conference." I rest my head against her breast. "If it's any conciliation, Trudy, you've brought so much joy into my life. I don't know what I would've done if not for you. You were the best stand-in mother a girl could ever ask for."

She strokes my leg beneath my smock. "You were a good girl, Lillian. You deserved to have your own mama."

We sit in silence for a few minutes. "Did Dad tell you about Alice and Ivy?" I ask. "About them being gay?"

She nods. "But I don't believe it. Ivy wasn't gay. At least not in her heart. I don't have anything against gay people, mind you. One of my great nephews is gay, and I love him dearly. I'm not questioning Ivy's love for Alice either. I just don't think it was that kind of love. I believe Ivy was confused about her feelings. Since they were wee little girls, I fretted about the hold Alice Browder had over Ivy. It got worse after Mister Edward died."

I pick at a fleck of gray paint on my smock. "Alice claims she sent Layla and me cards for our birthdays and Christmases. But Dad never gave them to us, and I didn't find them when I was searching through his things. Do you know anything about them?"

"I took those cards. Stole them out of the mail when the mailman dropped them off. They're in a box at my house if you'd like to see them. Your daddy never knew anything about the cards. I've never trusted Alice, and I wasn't about to let her anywhere near you girls."

I laugh out loud. "Trudy! You have a naughty streak in you after all."

"There's a lot you don't know about me." Trudy waves her hand in front of her face, fanning herself, and I can see the beads of perspiration on her forehead.

I angle my body toward her. "Are you okay, Trudy?"

"I'm fine. Just a tad warm." She wipes the sweat off her face with her apron. "What're you planning, now that you know everything?"

"I'm waiting for Layla's next move. I took your advice and gave her Dad's memoir. She has a right to know everything, but there are some chapters she's not gonna like. I'm anticipating an explosion of nuclear proportions any minute."

"Layla ain't here. Her fancy rental car was in the driveway when I got here this morning, but it's gone now. She snuck out of the house without me seeing her."

"With any luck, she won't come back."

Trudy has always reprimanded me for such comments in the past. But today, she lets it slide. "Do you want to find out who your mother is?"

"I'm not sure. But I don't think so. Melanie made it clear she wants nothing to do with her child. And I respect that. Biologically or not, Ivy was my mother." I say that, but in my mind, I still think of her as Ivy. "I was robbed of her at an early age, but you and Dad helped make up for that loss. I feel at peace now that I know everything. My life has been on hold far too long. I'm ready to move on. Who knows? I may even call Dr. Hudson, to help me sort through my memories."

"I think that's a grand idea."

My phone vibrates in my pocket with a text from Bert. *Call me or come by the gallery asap. I may have a buyer for some of your paintings.*

"Bert says he may have a buyer for my paintings." I give Trudy a wet smack on the cheek. "Who knows? Maybe this is a sign my luck is changing."

A wide grin spreads across her face. "Lord knows you're way overdue a bit of good luck."

⸻

"I have the most fabulous news," Bert says, holding the door open for me when I arrive at the gallery. "My client loves your work. He purchased all three of your paintings at a remarkable price."

His hands me a check and my eyes grow wide when I see the amount. After I deduct Bert's commission, I'll have enough for a down payment on a house. Suddenly, the idea of owning my very own home, one I don't have to share with my sister, appeals to me a great deal.

Bert claps his hands like a delighted child. "*And* he wants to see more. How's your website coming?"

My smile fades. "I'm an artist, Bert. Not a web designer."

"There's more than one way to express creativity, Lil. I've seen your website. You're off to a good start. You can bring it to life with a few small changes. But be sure to add some more photographs from your stash of paintings in your storage room. This is a serious and motivated buyer, Lil. I told him I would have you post some of your other work right away. He's from the North but loves the South. He has big connections. His endorsement could mean instant success for you."

"Whoo-hoo!" I do a little victory dance in the center of the gallery. "Okay," I say smoothing out my blouse. "I'm on it. I've already taken the photographs and uploaded them to my site's library. I'll post them to my main page when I get home."

He whips out his phone and his fingers fly across the screen. "I just texted you links to websites of some of the other artists I represent. Check them out. With a few simple changes, you can make your site more current."

I pucker my lips, blowing him a kiss. "You're the best. I'll let you know as soon as the website is ready."

I'm walking on air toward home, relishing the notion of soon having money in the bank, when Marcus calls. "We have a big problem. I need to see you right away. How soon can you get to my office?"

I can see his building from where I stand. "Five minutes tops. I'm on Broad Street, less than a block away from your office."

"Perfect," Marcus says. "I'll wait for you in our lobby."

When I exit the elevator on the third floor, Marcus sweeps me down the hall, jerking me along when I pause to say hello to Messrs Ball and Cross.

"Jeez, Marcus," I say once we're in his office. "What's the big deal?"

"I just had a little visit from your sister. Most of what she told me I'd already heard from you. Big shocker about Ivy and Alice, by the way. Layla wants to contest your father's will."

My neck snaps as I jerk my head back. "I'm sorry, what? On what grounds?"

"She claims she's the only Stoney heir, which makes her the sole beneficiary."

I gawk at him. "Am I missing something here? How does she know she's Ivy's daughter?"

Marcus shakes his head. "She doesn't. She's speculating."

I collapse in a nearby chair. "What did you tell her?"

"That her claim is preposterous, even if a DNA test proves she's Ivy's daughter. Any judge in his right mind will laugh her out of court. Ivy bequeathed the entirety of her estate to your father. Graham could have gifted it to the dog if he'd wanted."

I'm back on my feet, standing at the window and staring down at the traffic congestion on Broad Street. "But I've decided I don't want to know who my mother is."

Marcus joins me at the window. "Unfortunately, that decision isn't yours alone to make. Your sister is a woman on a mission." He turns me toward him. "I know Layla. She's normally so controlled, but she was hysterical, like she's going off the deep end. Is something else bothering her?"

"She's having some problems in her marriage. I wouldn't wish that on anyone, but I don't blame her husband if he divorces her. She's always been self-centered, but her narcissism has reached a new all-time high."

"I noticed that myself the last few times I've been around her. I told Layla, if she decides to proceed, she'll need to find a different attorney, because our firm will be representing you."

"Isn't that a conflict of interest considering you're Dad's attorneys?"

He flashes a mischievous grin. "She doesn't know that. If she finds an attorney foolish enough to file this lawsuit, I'll find a way to represent you."

"Find me a criminal attorney, Marcus. I'm gonna need one when I murder my sister." I spin on my heels, away from the window, and storm toward the door.

"Don't do it," Marcus yells after me. "She's not worth it."

I make it home in record time. Heat radiates through my body when I see Bennett Calhoun exiting our front door. His expensive sports car is parked in the driveway, and he's about to get in it when I approach him. "I don't know what my sister told you, Mr. Calhoun, but this house is not for sale."

"According to Layla, her attorney discovered a discrepancy in your father's will, and the house belongs to her."

My armpits are soaked and beads of sweat trickle down my back. "You can better bet there's a discrepancy. And I plan to hire a team of attorneys to lock his estate up so tight in litigation it will never be settled."

Calhoun raises his hands in surrender. "I'm a man of peace, Miss Alexander. Keep me out of your family feud. You know where to find me if and when you decide to sell." He slides in behind the wheel and speeds out of the driveway.

When I enter the house, my sister's loud voice booms throughout the halls from upstairs. I find her in the drawing room talking to someone on the phone about cleaning out the house in preparation for putting it on the market.

"What the hell do you think you're doing? You have no right to sell this house without my approval."

"I'll call you back." Layla ends the call and pockets her phone. "Like hell I don't. This house belongs to *me*." She jabs a thumb at her chest. "I'm the Stoney heir. You're the red-headed step-sister."

"You can't possibly know that without a DNA test."

"I don't need any damn DNA test." Like a cat bearing its claws, Layla pounces on me, ripping a hank of hair from my scalp near my hairline.

I let out a bloodcurdling scream that brings Trudy running.

I tackle my sister onto the sofa. It tips over and we roll off the other side. Legs and arms entwined, we tumble across the floor and crash into an eighteenth-century Pembroke table. A heavy brass candlestick falls off the table, missing my head by inches as it clatters to the floor. We are kicking and screaming, scratching and biting. When Trudy tries to break us apart, Layla shoves her hard, sending her stumbling backward.

Trudy screams at us. "Stop it this instant, or I'm calling the po-lice!" She has the receiver in her hand and she's pushing buttons on the phone. I attempt to crawl away from my sister, to stop Trudy from placing the call, but Layla grabs hold of my foot, pulling me back to her. She straddles my torso, slapping my face over and over with her palm and the back of her hand, in one direction and then the other. Wrapping my legs around her torso, I wrestle her off of me and scramble to my feet.

She's on my heels as I dart out of the room and race up the stairs. She grabs at me, but she can't catch me as I sprint down the back wing to the yellow bedroom. This time, the secret garden can't protect me.

"I read all about your little secret garden." She yanks the drapes from the rods and overturns the green velvet chair. She grabs a porcelain lamp from the bedside table and smashes it against the wall. "You were such a loser, always alone with your books. None of our friends wanted to play with you."

"Because you turned them all against me."

Layla picks up a brass floor lamp and comes after me. I clamber over the top of the mattress and crouch down behind the bed.

"Our mother was right about you when she called you a coward. A cow-yard," Layla says in a mocking tone. "You were afraid of your own shadow."

"Because you made me that way. You tortured me at every turn."

She swings the lamp at me, cracking me in the side of the

head. The pain is excruciating, and I'm seriously pissed now. When the stars clear, I jump on her, and we tumble to the ground. We roll around a few times and then we're back on our feet, standing breathless and face-to-face in the center of the room.

"I'm glad we're not twins," Layla says. "As far as I'm concerned, we're not even sisters. I was supposed to be an only child. But then your slut mother came along and seduced our father."

I get up in her face. "If you *are* Ivy's daughter, you're certainly nothing like her."

Layla balls her fists at her sides. "What do you know? You don't even remember her."

"I know she loved this house and her family and Charleston. Why, if she was your mother and her heritage meant everything to her, are you so eager to sell it to the highest bidder?"

Layla rears her arm back and lands a blow with her fist in my left eye socket.

Through clenched teeth, I say, "I'll fight to my death to keep you from getting your hands on this house." Brushing past her, I take off toward the main house. Layla chases me down the stairs to the drawing room. I make a beeline for the piazza, closing the door on her. But she's stronger than me. She forces the door open and propels me backward to the railing. Her hands are on my throat, and I'm teetering over the edge when a large man in a navy uniform pulls my sister off of me.

Gripping us by our necks, the policeman marches us back inside to the safety of the drawing room. Despite his firm grip, we're still trying to get at each other. "Break it up, you two! Either calm down so we can work this out here, or I'll arrest you for domestic violence and we'll talk it through at the station."

I struggle free of him. "Keep her away from me! She's a

raving lunatic! She scalped me!" I touch my fingers to the bald spot, and the tips come away bloody.

The officer rights the sofa, forcing Layla to sit down, and points me to the chair opposite her. Noticing Trudy hovering near the doorway, I collapse in the chair. "I'm so sorry, Trudy," I say. "I guess we got a little carried away."

She's too angry to look at me. "Mmm-hm. Your behavior is disgraceful. Your daddy would've been ashamed of you."

The policeman sits down next to Layla on the sofa with his iPad in hand. "Who wants to go first?"

I read the nameplate on his uniform shirt. Officer Delgado is tall, dark, and not particularly handsome, although his brown eyes are sympathetic. I imagine he witnesses a lot of domestic disturbances in his job.

Layla crosses her arms, refusing to speak.

"Fine." I explain about our father's death, our family's financial problems, and the discovery that we're not twins as we've been raised to believe but that we have two different biological mothers.

Delgado listens with earnest attention until I finish talking. "You have some serious issues at hand. Don't you think it'd be easier to sort through them if you worked together instead of fighting?" When neither of us answered, he says, "What's it gonna take to make peace between you two?"

Again, we don't respond.

"I would suggest you start with the facts," Delgado says. "Which means getting a DNA test."

"Fine," Layla says.

"Whatever." After what just happened in this house, I'm all for it. Identifying our biological mothers will either widen the rift between Layla and me or bring us closer together. Either way, we can't go on like this.

"I take that as a yes," Delgado says. "Now you just need the DNA. Since only one of the mothers is still alive, I suggest you reach out to her. If need be, I can assist in locating her contact information."

I want this man out of my house so I can crawl off somewhere and lick my wounds. Resigning myself to the DNA test, I say, "I'll try contacting her through her website. If that doesn't work, is there a number where I can reach you?"

Delgado stands to leave. "My cell is your best option." He hands me his business card. "I don't want to be called back here. Can I trust you to take care of this?" His eyes are on me, not Layla.

I salute him. "Yes, sir."

"I'll show you out, officer," Trudy says, motioning Delgado ahead of her to the hallway. Layla and I are left alone in the room. She looks at me with pure hatred in her eyes, and I stick out my tongue at her. I go into Dad's study and close the door behind me.

LILLIAN

I'm sitting in Dad's chair, staring blindly out the window and wondering how Layla and I could possibly move past what happened today, when Trudy enters the room with a first aid kit in one hand, a sandwich on a china plate in the other, and a bag of frozen peas tucked under her armpit.

"I'm so sorry about earlier, Trudy. I know you're ashamed of us. I'm ashamed of us."

She sets the plate on Dad's desk and hands me the bag of peas. "That's for your eye." She opens the first aid kit in my lap and comes at my bald spot with a tube of antibiotic ointment.

The ointment stings my scalp, and I shy away from her. "Ouch. That hurts."

"You don't want it to get infected." When she finishes with the bald spot, she dabs ointment on the scratches on my face.

I swat her hand away. "Stop fussing, Trudy. I'm fine." I snap the first aid kit shut and shove it at her. "Here, go nurse Layla."

Trudy screws the lid back on the ointment. "I already have. Her wounds ain't nearly as bad as yours. She really whooped your butt."

"Good for her. She should compete for the women's light-weight boxing title. She's certainly mean enough."

Trudy's pallor is off and a sheen of perspiration coats her skin. "Are you okay, Trudy? You don't look like you feel well."

"Humph. After what you put me through today, it's no wonder."

"I already said I was sorry. How else can I make it up to you?"

Her face softens. "You can eat your sandwich like a good girl."

I swivel the chair around to face the desk and take a bite of the sandwich. The combination of mayonnaise and bananas transports me back to my childhood, and I stuff the remainder of the half in my mouth. "When's the last time you made me a banana and mayonnaise sandwich?"

"So, you do remember," she says, lowering herself to the chair opposite me. "I wasn't sure you would. That was your mama's . . . Ivy's favorite sandwich. I could never bring myself to make that sandwich again after she died."

I lift the bread back on the other sandwich half and rearrange the banana to my liking. "Did Layla apologize to you?"

"Nope. Not one word of regret from her. What were the two of you fighting for anyway?"

"I found out from Marcus that she intends to contest Dad's will. She's certain she's Ivy's daughter, the only living Stoney heir, which makes her entitled to the house."

Trudy startles me when she pounds her fist on the desk. "That's hogwash."

"Layla's lost her mind as evidenced by the state of my face. I'm tempted to give her my half of everything. I sold three paintings. I now have money in the bank."

Trudy grins. "That's wonderful, baby. I'm so proud of you."

"I'm proud of me too, Trudy." I rest my head against the

back of the chair. "I've been fighting Layla all my life. I don't have the energy to go another round. I'm not materialistic. I don't have extravagant needs like her. I've been trying to save the house, because it's my home. Even when I rented that apartment over the art gallery, I spent a lot of nights here. I've always felt safe here, like the house is my security blanket. It's the strangest thing, though. Now that the past has been revealed, I suddenly feel like an intruder. There's nothing I can do to keep the house in the family, anyway. Not without Layla's help, and I'd rather die than ask her."

Trudy mops the perspiration from her face with a folded red bandana. "You can't give up yet, Miss Lillian. Your father was hoping to bring you and Layla together. Not tear you further apart."

I reach for her hand. "Calm down, Trudy. It's not the end of the world. It's time for me to find a new home with a clean slate where I can create new memories. *Happy* memories. Because, let's face it, a lot of the memories in this house are bad."

"At least talk to Melanie first," she says in a begging tone.

"I don't have much choice about that, unless I want another visit from Officer Delgado. I admit I'm curious about Melanie, though." I reach for the computer keyboard. "Let's see if I can contact her through her website."

Trudy's eyes are on the screen when Melanie's author photo loads on her website. "Wow. She turned out to be a lovely lady."

I find the contact form and enter my email address along with a short message. I talk out loud as I type. "Melanie, this is Lillian Alexander, Graham's daughter. I have an urgent matter of a personal nature I need to discuss with you. Please call me at your earliest convenience." I enter my cell number and press send.

Trudy rises out of her chair, gathering up the empty plate and first aid kit. "I think I should spend the night here with you girls. I don't trust you on your own."

"And I think you should go home to Isaac and your own bed. You look exhausted. The past week has been hard on everyone. Forgive me if I don't walk you to the door. I'm too sore to get out of the chair."

She rounds the desk and kisses the top of my head. "You promise to call me if you need me?"

"I promise. You don't have to worry about me, Trudy. I plan to stay as far away from my sister as I can get. Besides, I promised Bert I'd update my website. I'll probably work at Dad's desk until I go to bed."

Through the open doorway, I watch her shuffle through the drawing room and disappear down the hall. I would never admit it to Trudy, but being alone in the house with my sister in her current erratic state of mind unnerves the heck out of me. Despite my aching body, I get up from my chair and close and lock the door. For good measure, I push a small bachelor's chest in front of the door. If she tries to get in, I will not hesitate to call my good friend Officer Delgado.

Checking my inbox periodically for an email from Melanie, I focus my attention on redoing my website. I post the photographs of my other paintings to my front page, arranging them in order according to type—historic buildings of downtown Charleston, the beaches of Sullivan's island, the marshes of Wadmalaw. I studied art history in college, and I deem myself something of an expert on paintings. While I consider my technique one of the best among my contemporary peers, the subjects are nothing special. Which is probably why it's taken Bert so long to find a buyer. After spending some time perusing other artists' websites, I come away newly inspired to explore different subjects, to dig deeper, to look for the unusual in my scenes.

When night falls, the light in the study grows dim and a gentle breeze wafts through the open window. I'm putting the finishing touches on my website when a small object lands with a thud on the rug and rolls across the floor. It's a rock with a note fastened to it by a rubber band. I recognize Marcus's handwriting. *Care for a moonlight stroll?*

I go to the window and lean out. The night is lovely with the orange glow of the full moon in an inky sky. Marcus is standing on the sidewalk below, waving up at me. He lifts his face skyward and begins howling at the moon.

"Stop! Marcus. The neighbors will call the police. They've already been here once today."

"The police have been here? Really? Come down and tell me about it." He begins howling again.

"Shush! I'm coming. Give me a minute."

Pushing the chest out of the way, I crack the door and peek into the drawing room. The room is empty, and Layla is nowhere in sight. I make a dash for the hall and hurry down to the first floor. Marcus is waiting for me outside the front door.

"You can't go throwing rocks through my windows, Marcus. You could've broken it."

"My aim is spot on, Lil. I was an all-state baseball pitcher in high school."

"How could I have forgotten? Mr. Perfect." I punch him in the arm.

His eyes widen when he catches a glimpse of my face. "Oh my God! What happened to you?"

"Layla and I got in a fight." Casting an uncertain glance up at the piazza, I hold my finger to my lips and whisper, "She's probably listening to us."

"Come with me," he says, taking me by the hand. We run across the street to the seawall, and as we stroll down the promenade to the park, I tell him about my fight with Layla, Trudy calling the police, and Officer Delgado insisting I contact Melanie.

"Have you heard back from Melanie yet?"

I check my phone again. "Not yet. And there's a very good

chance I won't. She made it very clear to Dad and Ivy that she wants nothing to do with her child."

"You'll hear from her. You told her you have an urgent personal matter to discuss with her. She's not going to ignore that." We pass the park, and Marcus stops suddenly when we get to King Street. "I live in that building."

My gaze follows his finger. "Where? There? I've never known anyone who actually lives in that ugly building."

He scrutinizes his building. "It's not that bad, is it?"

"It's just plain. It doesn't have any particular architectural features. What's it like inside?"

"Some condos are better than others. I got one of the nicer ones, a corner unit on an upper floor. You can't beat the location and the view is incredible. Wanna see it?"

Going to his condo is a terrible idea, yet I don't want to go home to Layla either. "Depends."

He cocks his head to the side. "On what?"

"On whether you have any food." I rub my belly. "I haven't eaten dinner."

"How does chicken stir-fry sound?"

"Chicken stir-fry sounds delicious."

When he steps off the curb to cross the street, I grab his hand, holding him back. "Just dinner, Marcus. Nothing else."

He hunches his shoulders, as if to say whatever you want, but the mischievous look in his eyes tells me he's hoping for more.

His building's lobby is shabby, but when we take the elevator to the fourth floor, I'm surprised to discover his apartment is handsomely decorated and updated with modern conveniences.

"You have great taste," I say, looking around.

"Correction. My mom has great taste."

I laugh. "I remember that about her."

He leads me into the small kitchen where the light is better, and tilting my chin upward, he studies my black eye. "I've seen worse, but you have a bona fide shiner. I can't believe Layla did this to you." Removing his phone from his pocket, he snaps off a few photographs.

"What're you doing?" I ask, covering my face with my hands.

"I'm documenting the fight in case your sister decides to proceed with her lawsuit."

"What if she looks worse than me?"

"She doesn't. I know you. Did you get in any licks?"

"None as bad as this." I pull my hair back and show him my bald spot.

Anger flickers in his green eyes. "Are you kidding me right now? She scalped you, Lil. You are not going back to that house alone."

Ignoring him, I walk over to the sliding glass door. "You're right. The view is incredible."

He slides the door open and we step out onto the small balcony. The warmth of his body next to mine is comforting. I'm too vulnerable to be here alone with him. But I can't drag myself away.

"I've been worried about you all day, Lil. My extrasensory perception was warning me you were in trouble. I knew I wouldn't be able to sleep until I saw for myself that you were okay. I've been wanting to tell you something since that first day at your dad's funeral."

Tiny hairs on the back of my neck stand to attention. "What's that?"

"I realize my timing sucks with all you have going on, and you're not in the best shape emotionally to hear this, but I love you, Lillian Alexander." His breath is hot on my ear. "I never stopped loving you. Spending time with you these past few days reminded me of how good we were together. You're my person. I don't regret going to New York. I needed to find myself, to grow up. I wasn't ready to make a lifetime commitment. But I am now. Once you sort things out with your sister, I'd love it if you'd consider giving me . . . giving us, another chance."

I take a long moment to gather my thoughts. "Today, tomorrow, a week from now, my answer will always be the same. You hurt me deeply when you broke off our engagement. I can't go through that again. I need a friend right now, Marcus. But if you can't be that friend, I understand."

"I can be your friend. I'm here for you whenever you need me. But I'm warning you, I'll never stop trying to get you back. You have no reason to believe me when I tell you this, but I will never hurt you again. Let me prove it to you."

I turned to him, pressing my finger to his lips. "It won't make any difference, Marcus. I'm not going to change my mind. There is nothing of us left." I experience a stabbing pain in my gut and hear a voice inside my head calling me a fool. "I should go."

He kisses my forehead. "Please stay. You've had a rough day. It's not a good idea for you to be alone in the house with Layla. I promise I won't make a pass at you. We'll cook dinner and watch some TV. I'll sleep on the sofa and you can have my bed."

I want so much to stay in the safety of this apartment with him. But I still love him. I know that with absolute certainty. And I don't trust myself, not in my weakened state. "I can't, Marcus. I really must go home."

Disappointment crosses his face. "All right then. I'll walk with you." His lips parted in a sad smile. "But for the record, I didn't expect to win you back the first try. Be prepared for many more attempts. You, of all people, should know I never give up until I get what I want."

"And you, of all people, should know I'm as stubborn as the day is long when I wanna be."

LILLIAN

o calls or emails come in from Melanie during the night, but I receive a long text from Marcus. *I meant every word I said last night. I will eventually win you over.* (Wink emoji.) *In the meantime, I'm here for you. Whatever you need. Call anytime, day or night.*

I get out of bed and throw open the piazza doors. The sky is clear, the sun bright, and I can taste autumn in the crispy air. Layla's rental is parked in the courtyard below, but by the time I've showered and dressed in jeans and a quarter-zip quilted pullover, the car is gone. I grab my camera and set off to find new inspiration for my work. I venture down streets and alley-ways I've previously ignored, snapping dozens of photographs of courtyard gardens, colorful window boxes, and enchanting porches with inviting front doors.

My memory card is full and my stomach rumbling when I head for home a few minutes before one. As I turn the corner from Atlantic onto East Battery, I see a silver SUV with an Uber sign in the window pulling to the curb in front of our house. The back door on the passenger side swings open, and Melanie Hogan gets out with a small rolling suitcase. I stop dead in my tracks. She's even more beautiful in person with hair fastened in a messy bun at the nape of her neck and stylishly dressed in skinny jeans, an oversized cream-colored silk blouse, and ochre suede loafers. Did she fly to South Carolina on my account or was she already here, visiting family or attending a book signing?

When she notices me, she strides up the sidewalk toward me. Removing her designer sunglasses, she says, "You're the spitting image of your father." Her irises are the palest of grays. The combination of alabaster skin, snow-white hair, and translucent eyes is ethereal. Like an angel. I hope she can save my sister and me from ourselves.

"Are you Lillian or . . ." Her cheeks blush pink.

"Layla. My sister's name is Layla. But I'm Lillian. I'm the one who sent the email. I didn't expect you to come."

"When you said you had a matter of some urgency to discuss, I assumed you'd found out about . . . about me. I've waited thirty-three years for the opportunity to meet you girls. I couldn't wait another day."

I'm surprised, not only that she wants to meet us but that she said *you girls* instead *of my daughter.*

She zeroes in on my face. "What happened to your eye?"

"I had an accident." Before she can interrogate me further, I gesture at the house and say, "We should go inside to talk."

Melanie extends the handle of her suitcase. "Sorry about the suitcase. I came straight here from the airport. I booked a room at Zero George."

I understand her point. She doesn't expect an invitation to stay with us.

She follows me down the driveway to the front door and up the stairs to the drawing room. "Please, make yourself at home," I say with a sweep of my arm at the sofa. "I'll ask Trudy to fix us some refreshments."

I dash down the hall to the kitchen where I find Trudy

seated at the table folding a load of laundry. "Trudy! You're not gonna believe this! Melanie Hogan is here!" I point at the floor. "In this house. In our drawing room."

Trudy drops the towel she's folding into the laundry basket. Taking me by the arms, she gives me a gentle shake. "Calm down, Lil. She's just a person."

"She is definitely *not* just a person. She's a world-famous romance author. And she's drop-dead gorgeous. What if she's my mother? What if she doesn't like me?"

"Even if she's not your mother, she's gonna love you. You're a sweet girl with a huge heart."

"Okay." I take a deep breath to steadying myself. "I've got this."

Trudy spins me around, giving me a gentle shove toward the door. "Go back to your guest. I'll bring you something cold to drink in a minute."

My mind continues to race as I hurry back down the hall. I have so many questions, I don't know where to start. Melanie has left the drawing room and is standing at the railing on the piazza.

When I join her, she says, "Everything is exactly how I remember it." She takes a loop around the porch, pausing to look out over the brick courtyard.

"I saw you at the cemetery," I say to the back of her head. "I didn't know who you were at the time."

She turns to face me. "So, your discovery is recent."

"I've only known a few days. Dad left a memoir, about the years he was married to my mother." I motion her to the wicker sofa and sit down in the lounge chair beside her.

Melanie settles back against the cushions. "Ahh . . ." She takes a deep breath and let's it out slowly. "I've missed the salt air. Aside from your father's funeral, I haven't been back to Charleston since . . . since your . . . since Ivy died. How much do you know about that day?"

"Everything, now that I've read his memoir. I know that Dad was with you when she killed herself."

Her lips part in a sad smile. "Your father was the love of my life. I was more attracted to him than he was to me. He was head over heels for Ivy. But I was grateful for his friendship. He helped launch my career. He was a gifted editor. He taught me to dig deeper, to raise the standard for my work." She stares out over the harbor. "That last week we spent together, when I flew to town on a whim to seek his help on a manuscript, I sensed things were not right for him at home. I felt his attraction to me. But he loved Ivy too much to act on it. After she died, I thought maybe there was a chance for us to be together. I tried contacting him a couple of times. But he never returned my calls. He kept his vow to Ivy. And he devoted his life to you girls."

I find her pale eyes hypnotizing, and I lean against the arm of the chair, closer to her. "Did you ever marry?"

"I did. To a man I barely knew. I was in my late thirties and desperate to have a baby. When I failed to conceive, he left me." Melanie lifts a shoulder as if to say it doesn't matter. "We didn't love each other. My life is full. I have my work. My characters keep me company."

This is something we have in common. I, too, relate better to fictional characters than real people. Does this mean she's my mother? Her calm demeanor has an effect on me, and I want to open up my heart to her. But first, I need some answers. "Do you ever think about your baby?"

"Every single day since I gave her away," Melanie answers without hesitation.

"Then why did you give her up? You said yourself, you wanted to have children."

"I was so young when I got pregnant. I wasn't ready to be a parent. I had dreams of becoming an author. I realize how selfish that must sound to you."

"But you saw the pregnancy through before pursuing your dreams. I consider that incredibly unselfish."

Melanie smiles. "Your father was a good man. I knew my baby would be better off with him than with me." She smothers a laugh. "I was terrified of Ivy. She was older than me, so sure of herself and confident of her station in life. At least that's what I thought at the time."

I wonder how much Melanie knows about Ivy's suicide. I'm debating whether to ask her when Trudy emerges from the house with the refreshment tray. She sets the tray down and hugs Melanie like an old friend. "You're looking well, Miss Melanie."

"And you haven't changed one bit, Trudy."

Trudy burst out laughing. "You're telling a fib, but I thank you for saying so."

Melanie looks down at the tray. "Is that sweet tea and —"

"Lemonade mixed. Just the way you like it. And your favorite benne wafers, the only thing I could get you to eat that wasn't grown in a garden. Are you still a vegetarian?"

"I'm a vegan now." When confusion crosses Trudy's face, Melanie explains, "It means I don't eat any animal products including eggs and cow's milk."

"Lord, help us. You don't know what you're missing."

Melanie's plump pink lips part in a smile. "I'm sure you're right, Trudy, but I've been that way all my life. Even as a child, I didn't have the stomach for eating animals."

"We all have our crosses to bear," Trudy says as she shuffles off the porch, and I get the impression she's talking about more than not eating meat.

I feel Melanie's eyes on me as I'm pouring the contents of the pitcher into two glasses. Is she speculating about whether I'm her daughter? Is she disappointed? When I raise my gaze, handing her a glass, her brows are knitted and her eyes locked on my scabbed-over bald spot. I don't want her to think I'm one of those people with an obsessive hair-pulling disorder. I'm tempted to tell her the whole story—about our financial problems and Layla's determination to cut me out of Dad's will—but we don't know each other well enough to share that kind of family drama.

I smooth my hair over the bald spot. "I'm a bit of a klutz. I ran into a bush on my bicycle," I say, but I can tell she doesn't believe me.

"Ouch. You should be more careful."

I fake a laugh. "Tell me about it."

We share bits about our lives while we drink our delicious lemon tea concoction, which I'm surprised Trudy has never made for me. Melanie asks if I have a passion, and I tell her about my painting. When she talks about her career as a romance author, I scrutinize her and see nothing of Layla or me in this woman's features. She fascinates me. Her creativity. Her success. Is it too late for us to have a meaningful relationship if she turns out to be my biological mother? *Stop! Don't go there, Lil. There's only a fifty-fifty chance. All these years, you've gotten along just fine without a mother. Haven't you?*

Layla appears suddenly in the doorway. She's wearing a balloon-sleeved gray top with cropped jeans and high-heeled booties. She's been to the hairdresser, an expensive one from the looks of the sophisticated bob grazing her shoulders. She extends a hand to our guest. "You must be Melanie. I'm Layla. Thanks for coming on such short notice."

Melanie rises to greet her. "I'm delighted to meet you."

"Well then, I've had my few moments alone with Melanie. I'll let the two of you get acquainted. I'll be in Dad's study if you need me."

I leave Dad's study door open. When they've finished talking, we'll need to decide on our next step. And I definitely want to be included in that discussion.

I spend a few minutes at the computer researching DNA

testing centers in the Charleston area. I'm relieved to see the process is fairly straightforward, and I jot the address for the closest center down on a sticky notepad.

Melanie and Layla are alone on the piazza for what seems like forever. I can't help but wonder what lies Layla is telling about me.

I'm sitting with my elbows propped on Dad's desk and my face buried in my hands, wondering how I can graciously extricate myself from my life, when Layla's loudmouth interrupts my thoughts. "Get up, Lil. Time to go for the DNA test."

I spin around in the chair and jump to my feet. "Are you okay with this, Melanie?"

Melanie looks from me to Layla and back to me. "If it's what you both want. But it's an important step. If you need some more time to think about it . . ."

"Nope. We're doing this thing today." Layla shoots me a look, warning me not to disagree. *Or else, what, Layla? You'll give me another black eye?*

I tear the sticky note off the pad and hold it out to Layla. "I was just researching testing centers. I found one that's just west of the Ashley."

Layla snatches the note from me. "Melanie, you ride with me. Lil, we'll meet you there."

Uncertainty and confusion cross Melanie's face. "Can't we all go together?"

My sister's behavior won't win Melanie over. Then again, Layla isn't being rude and bossy to Melanie. Only to me. And the tension between us is natural considering the circumstances.

I smile at Melanie. "We should take two cars. I have errands to run on the way home."

I watch them walk out of the room together, arm in arm, all chummy-like. My sister is up to something. Twenty-four hours ago, she wanted nothing to do with Melanie. Correction: She wanted nothing to do with Melanie's DNA.

The DNA test is quick and painless, a cotton swab to the inner cheek. But it's expensive. Melanie offers to pay the $200 fee, but I insist, clunking down my credit card. I say a silent prayer it doesn't get declined, and I'm relieved when the charge goes through.

"You can call after nine tomorrow morning for the results," the nurse tells us on our way out.

In the parking lot, Melanie says, "I'd love for the two of you to join me for dinner tonight." She flashes her phone at us. "My assistant managed to secure a reservation at Slightly North of Broad at seven."

I feel my sister's eyes on me. She's hoping I'll decline the invitation, but I say, "I'd like that. I'll meet you at the restaurant at seven."

I barely make it out of the parking lot before I burst into tears. I cry all the way home and go straight to my room. I stretch out on the chaise lounge on my piazza, and for the next few hours, I stare up at the blue sky, wondering how my life will change if Melanie is my mother.

I spend longer than usual applying makeup and styling my hair. Several layers of foundation powder on my black eye make it less noticeable. I don my favorite wrap dress and knee-high boots, but I feel like Cinderella when I see Layla, the fashion model, waiting for me at the top of the stairs in snakeskin bell bottom pants and a sleeveless black turtleneck.

I vow to use some of the proceeds from the sale of my paintings to spruce up my wardrobe. Not for Melanie or Layla or even Marcus. But for me.

"We should Uber," Layla says.

"We should walk, actually. It's a nice night," I say, regretting my decision the minute my high heels hit the uneven sidewalk on East Battery.

Layla is beside me and then in front of me. I increase my pace and lengthen my stride to keep up with her, and by the time we reach the restaurant, we're practically racing each other. Everything is a contest with my sister. And that competition continues over dinner. Although I don't stand a chance because Layla totally steals the show. She monopolizes the conversation with talk of her successful fashion business and active social life in Atlanta. And she speaks of Roger, her loving husband, as if he's eagerly awaiting her return home.

I'm noticeably quiet, and halfway through our seafood entrees, Melanie asks if I'm feeling all right. I wave off her concern. "I'm fine. It's been a long ten days."

Melanie offers me a sympathetic smile. "'I'm certain it has, you poor dear."

I'm aware of other diners staring openly at Melanie. One woman has the nerve to stop by our table to ask the celebrated author to autograph her cocktail napkin. Melanie is gracious about the intrusion. "I don't mind," she says to us after the woman departs the table. "After all, where would I be without my fans?"

The waiter takes away our entree plates, and we decline his offer to show us the dessert menu. Once he's gone, Melanie clears her throat and rests her hands on the table. "About the DNA test . . . if you decide not to share the results with me, I totally understand. I'm glad to have had the chance to meet you both and to get to know a little about each of you. I would love to stay in touch, to continue our relationship. Either one-on-one or the three of us together. Whatever we find works best. I don't have any family, and you girls . . . well, one of you . . . well, you know what I mean. You're both Graham's daughters. And he was once important to me. I think he would approve of us being friends."

"I'd like that," I say. And Layla adds, "Fine by me," with a little too much enthusiasm. She's shamelessly vying for Melanie's attention. What is she scheming now?

I'm so totally over the sibling rivalry. I've been battling it out with my sister all of my life. As far as I'm concerned, Layla can have it all—the house and the mother.

While we wait for the check, Layla goes on and on about how hard it was to watch our father wither away from pancreatic cancer. I long to scream out, "You weren't even here." But I sit quietly, inwardly stewing. Like Ivy, I would never cause a scene.

Despite everything I've learned about our childhood, I'm still letting my sister control me. She's toxin to me. If I don't get away from her, I think I might die.

Fog has set in and a fine mist is falling when we exit the restaurant. A chauffeur-driven car magically appears for Melanie. She offers us a ride, but Layla has already ordered an Uber. We say goodnight and promise to call her in the morning with the test results.

Our car arrives within minutes. Layla climbs in, leaving the door open for me. I kick it shut with my knee-high boot and take off running down East Bay Street. My father is gone. I don't know who my mother is. I'm about to lose my house, the core of my existence. I deserve to be happy. And there is only one person who can give me that happiness. One person on this earth who accepts me for me. He broke my heart once, and there are no guarantees he won't do it again, but Marcus is a risk worth taking. He understands me. He will help extricate me from my sister's clutches.

Climbing the steps to the seawall, I stop long enough to tug off my boots and continue running in bare feet to King Street. I enter Marcus's building, and as I pass through the lobby, I catch my reflection in a mirror. My dress clings to my body, and my damp hair is glued to my head. I'm a wet mess. But I don't let my appearance stop me. If he truly loves me, he won't care.

When Marcus opens the door, I'm in his arms pressing my lips to his. "I love you, Marcus Mullally, if you'll still have me."

"Damn straight, I'll still have you." He pulls me inside his apartment. "You're soaking wet. Let's get you into some dry clothes."

He shows me the bathroom and hands me a stack of towels. He leaves, returning a minute later with a flannel shirt, sweatpants, and a pair of wool socks. "I'll wait for you in the other room."

I untie my soaked dress and hang it to dry on the back of the door. His clothes swallow me, and I feel like a clown, but they are warm and dry and smell like Old Spice body wash. I splash water on my face, gently rubbing off the smeared mascara, and use his comb to untangle my hair.

Marcus is stirring a pot of cocoa on the stove in the kitchen when I emerge from the bathroom. He hands me a mug, and we sip the warm thick chocolate. He has froth on his lip, which I find adorable. I can't help myself. I'm overcome with emotion for him. I set down my mug and stand on my tiptoes and lick it off.

Marcus holds me at arm's length, smiling down but with a serious face. "We need to set some ground rules."

"Ground rules?" I shove him away from me. "I'm sorry. I must've misunderstood last night when you professed your love."

"You didn't misunderstand. I love you with my whole heart." He sweeps me off my feet and carries me down the hall to his room, pulling back the covers and setting me gingerly down on his queen-size bed. He strips down to his boxer shorts and climbs in beside me. "Not only do I want you in my bed, Lillian Alexander, I want you in my life. I made a vow that, if I ever got another chance with you, I wouldn't make any mistakes. I want to hold you, Lil. To comfort you. But you're too emotional tonight for sex. I need you to be sure about us. I want you to want me for me, not because you're angry at your sister or confused about Melanie or selling the house or any of the other drama in your life."

I snuggle closer to him. "God, I've missed you. You're such a good person, aside from the part where you broke up with me. But I understand your motivations. Just don't do it again."

He kisses my bald spot first and then my black eye. "I won't. I promise. I'm yours forever if you'll have me."

"I'll have you." I place my hand on his chest. This man has some serious pecs. While I'm eager to explore his grown-up body, I agree we should take it slow. "You're right. I am a mess tonight. I'm confused more than anything. I feel vulnerable, yet I feel this new person evolving inside of me. I want to take risks. To try new things. But there's still something holding me back."

"There's a lot still holding you back. But we'll sort through it *together.* And then we'll do all those things you talked about *together*. We'll live, Lillian. We'll take on the world *together.*"

Pulling me down with him, he settles deeper beneath the covers. "Now, tell me about Melanie."

LILLIAN

$\mathcal{I}$ stay in Marcus's bed long after he leaves for work the following morning. Nine o'clock comes and goes. I'm content to let Layla call the testing center. As long as I don't know the results, I can hold out hope that Melanie is my mother. For a number of reasons, I really want her to be. She's way cool, super talented, and a compassionate person. That's not to say I'd be devastated if Ivy turns out to be my mother. She was remarkable in her own way. But Melanie is alive and Ivy has been dead for twenty-seven years. The idea of having a relationship now with my biological mother thrills me to the core.

When Bert calls my cell phone, he congratulates me on a job well done updating my website, and we speak at length about my prospects for selling more paintings. I tell him about the photographs I took on my walk yesterday and my ideas for a new series, titled *The Hidden Wonders of the Holy City*.

After we hang up, I brew a coffee and meander around Marcus's cozy apartment. When my father died, he took his love with him. Our house on East Battery is now filled with bitterness and hatred. Home means love. And I feel that here with Marcus.

When I can no longer delay, I change out of Marcus's clothes and into my wrap dress and walk home. I sneak in the front door, hoping to avoid my sister. Not because I'm ashamed but because it's none of her business where I spent the night. I make it to the main floor without anyone seeing me, and I'm halfway up the stairs to my room when I hear Layla talking in the kitchen. I pause on the stairs, listening.

"Think about it, Trudy," she says. "Melanie is a successful romance author. She's worth . . . like a gazillion dollars, and she has no family to leave it to. Except, of course, her daughter. Which I'm certain is me."

Tiptoeing back down the stairs, I eavesdrop from outside the kitchen doorway.

"Oh really?" Trudy says, and I hear the sarcasm in her voice. "Just yesterday, you were convinced Ivy was your mother."

"I was wrong. Melanie and I have so much in common. There's no way she's not my mother. We're both creative and talented. Obviously, I look like Dad, but I resemble Melanie a little, don't you think? I'm fashionable and sophisticated like her. Lillian is way too mousy and insipid to be related to Melanie Hogan. Think of the money I'll inherit."

There's anger in Trudy's voice when she says, "I didn't raise you to be so materialistic. All you talk about is money, money, money."

When I hear a gasp, I peek around the doorway in time to see Trudy clutch her breast and fall to the floor with her legs bent beneath her. I rush to her aid, tossing my purse on the table and dropping to my knees beside her.

The color has drained from Trudy's face and I can tell she's not breathing. I place my hands one on top of the other on her chest and begin CPR. Between counting numbers, I yell at my sister to call for help, but Layla is paralyzed, her eyes locked on Trudy.

I take my hand off Trudy's chest long enough to whip my phone out of my back pocket. Instructing Siri to call 9-1-1, I set the phone on the floor beside me. I return to doing compressions, and when the operator answers seconds later, I bark, "I need an ambulance. Fast. My mother passed out. She's not breathing. I think she had a heart attack. I'm doing CPR, but I'm not sure if it's working."

"Ma'am, are you a medical professional?"

"No! I learned CPR years ago. Please! Call an ambulance. Fast!" I say and give her the address.

The line goes silent, and I count fifteen compressions before she returns.

"A crew was finishing up on a call near you," she says. "The ambulance will be there momentarily."

Hands on Trudy's chest, I look up at my sister. "Go out in the courtyard and direct the EMTs to come in the back door."

Layla remains glued to her spot on the floor.

I hear the siren in the distance. "Move it, Layla! Now!" My piercing scream jerks her out of her trance, and she bolts out the side door. Through the window, I watch Layla flagging down the driver, and seconds later, the ambulance comes into view.

Doors slam outside and a team of emergency response personnel enter the kitchen. I move out of their way as they begin working on Trudy. They determine she's in cardiac arrest, shock her heart with an AED, and transfer her to a stretcher, maneuvering it through the door.

Grabbing my purse, I follow them outside. "Where are you taking her?"

A bald-headed paramedic tells me, "The Heart & Vascular Center at MUSC. It's located in Ashley River Tower."

I jump in my Subaru and start the engine. The ambulance

peels out, and I'm rounding the fountain to follow them when Layla steps in front of my car. I slam on the breaks, and she climbs in.

"Are you crazy, Layla? I almost ran over you."

My sister doesn't respond.

I click on my hazard lights and increase my speed to catch up with the ambulance. I tap on Isaac's contact information and press the phone to my ear. He answers on the second ring. "Isaac, it's Lillian. Trudy's had a heart attack. She's on the way to MUSC in an ambulance. Type Ashley River Tower in your GPS for directions."

Isaac's end of the line is silent. "Are you there, Isaac?"

"I'm here, Miss Lillian. And I'm on my way."

No sooner have I hung up when the phone rings again with a call from Marcus.

"Hello, beautiful," he says. "Have you gotten the DNA test results yet?"

"Not yet. I'm on the way to the hospital, Marcus. Trudy just went into cardiac arrest in our kitchen. Thanks to you, I knew how to perform CPR. You may have inadvertently saved her life."

"Jesus, Lil. I'm so sorry. Do you want me to come?"

"Not yet. But thanks. I'll call you when I know more."

I drop the phone in the cup holder and grip the steering wheel with both hands.

I glance over at my sister, who is staring with a dazed expression out the window. "Are you okay, Layla?"

"In the kitchen just now, you called Trudy your mother," she says to the window in a voice so low I can barely hear her.

I shift my eyes back to the road. "Did I? I don't remember."

I feel her eyes on me when she asks, "Why did you say that?"

"Because she *is* my mother in every way that matters."

And, even though she's always been here for me, I let her

down when she needed me the most. My mind travels back over the past few days. Trudy has been exhibiting warning signs — the agitation, exhaustion, ever-present sheen of perspiration on her face — but I chose to ignore them, because I was too distracted by my own problems.

I stay glued to the ambulance's bumper when it circles a tall glass building on the MUSC campus. It backs up to the ambulance loading zone, and I park in a nearby space and kill the engine. With Layla matching my pace stride for stride, we follow Trudy's gurney through a door marked Authorized Personnel Only.

A team of medical professionals dressed in matching blue scrubs swarm Trudy's gurney. I stand on my tiptoes, but I can't see over their heads. The bald paramedic from the house steers Layla and me down the hall, away from the gurney. "Good job with the CPR," he says to me. "You saved her life."

"Is she out of danger?" I ask.

"For now. But she's a very sick woman. She'll be assigned to a team of cardiologists. They'll determine the cause of the cardiac arrest and prescribe the appropriate course of treatment."

He turns us over to a younger nurse with an iPad who asks me a million questions about Trudy. After I provide the answers I know, I say, "You'll need to get the rest from her husband. He should be here by now."

The nurse walks us down the hall in the direction opposite from where they've taken Trudy. She pushes buttons on a wall keypad, and we pass through a set of double doors to the waiting room. Isaac has just arrived and he's still winded from his rush to get to the hospital. He takes over with the nurse, filling in the blanks about Trudy's medical history.

Isaac's height and muscular build have always comforted me, but today, deflated by his wife's sudden illness, he seems small to me. Before I get a chance to speak with him alone, the nurse whisks him through the double doors.

Layla and I find empty seats together in the middle of the busy waiting room, and I shoot off a text to Melanie. *We have not yet called for test results. Trudy had a heart attack. We are at the hospital with her now.*

Poor Trudy. I'm so sorry. Is there anything I can do?

Prayers are appreciated. How long are you staying in town?

I'm booked at the Zero George through the weekend but planning to stay indefinitely. Please keep me updated on her condition.

Will do.

Layla and I don't speak during the excruciatingly long hour that passes until Isaac returns. I jump up to greet him as he approaches. "Did they tell you anything about her condition?"

"The doctors confirmed that she went into sudden cardiac arrest. They tell me you saved her life, Miss Lillian. When did you learn CPR?"

I'm aware that Layla is listening with interest. "In college. One Easter weekend, Marcus and I were staying with friends on Sullivan's Island when one of his fraternity brothers nearly drowned in a rip current. He would've died if not for the doctor who happened to be on the beach at the time. Marcus signed us up for a CPR class the following summer."

"Good old Marcus. I still miss that boy. You give him my gratitude when you see him next." Isaac always had a soft spot for Marcus. He was disappointed when we broke off our engagement.

"I will," I say. "Do they know what caused the cardiac arrest?"

Isaac shakes his head. "Not yet. They're still running tests."

"Is she awake? Did you talk to her?" I'm afraid to ask if there is evidence of brain damage.

"She's awake, agitated but lucid. She's asking to see you."

My muscles go weak as relief washes over my body. "Thank God."

He inclines his head at the same nurse from earlier who is standing at the double doors, shifting her weight from one foot to the other while looking impatiently at us. "She's waiting to take you back."

I hurry off with the nurse, following her through the doors and past a myriad of cubicles. I'm shocked when I see Trudy. She appears to have aged ten years in the past hour. Monitors beep over her head and a road map of plastic tubes are wound around both arms. I swallow past the lump in my throat. I will not scare her by crying.

When I ease down to the side of the bed, her eyes flutter open. "My sweet girl," she whispers through cracked lips.

I place my hand over hers. Her skin is cool to the touch. "You scared me to death. Don't do that again."

"I scared me too. I'm not ready to leave this life yet. Not when those I love still need me." She winks at me, and I don't deny it. I totally still need her. "I've been ignoring the signs. The doctors tell me you saved my life. If you hadn't been there . . . Well, I'm just glad you were. This is a warning that it's time for me to slow down. I want to enjoy my last years."

"As you should. You've been working too hard these past few months with Dad being sick and the funeral. It doesn't help that Layla and I have been such brats." I bring her hand to my cheek. "Oh, Trudy, I'm so sorry. Our behavior is unforgivable."

"Shh, now. It's been a difficult time for everyone." Trudy closes her eyes, and I think she's drifted off to sleep when she suddenly opens them again. "Your daddy had his heart set on you and Layla making amends. I wanted that for you too, but from what I've seen this past week, it's not gonna happen. Your sister is only interested in the almighty dollar. Her heart is cold. She ran off her husband and now she's making you miserable too. I love Layla as much as I love you, but she's a bad seed. Get out of that house, Lillian, while you still have your soul intact."

Trudy is not one for drama, and the intensity of her words gets my attention. I kiss the back of her hand and lay it gingerly on the mattress. "Say no more, Trudy. Marcus and I are back together. I'm thinking of asking him if I can stay at his place until Layla returns to Atlanta."

"Marcus is back in your life? Oh honey, that's the best news I've heard in a long time." She places her hand on her breast. "My heart feels better already."

"Mine too, Trudy. He's a good guy."

"And you deserve happiness, my sweet girl."

Two orderlies come to wheel Trudy off for tests. I kiss her cheek and step back from the bed. I return to the waiting room and sit down in an empty chair opposite Isaac and Layla. Isaac is texting on his phone and my sister is sitting with her head bowed, her shoulders heaving as she silently weeps.

"What's up with her?" I ask Isaac.

He shrugs. "I'm not sure. I reckon she's upset about Trudy. After you left, she started crying. I tried to tell her Trudy will be okay, but that didn't seem to comfort her none."

"Are you texting with Ruthie?"

"Yes'm. She has to clear some things up at work before she can leave Columbia, but she should get here sometime this evening. She's planning to stay for a while."

"Oh good! Trudy will like that. She's been taking care of others all her life. Now it's our turn to take care of her. Trudy told me just now she's ready to slow down. It's time for her to retire, Isaac."

A look of resignation crosses his face. "If you want, I can help you find someone to replace her."

"That won't be necessary. We're selling the house." I'm not sure when I made the definite decision to sell the house. Deep down, I've known all along I would be forced to sell. But now it feels right.

Layla's head jerks up at the mention of selling the house. I glare at her. "I don't know why you're surprised. You're getting what you want."

Isaac, who is visibly uncomfortable with the tension between Layla and me, stands and stretches. "I should get back to Trudy."

"We'll be right here, Isaac. Let me know if I can get anything or do anything for you."

He gives my shoulder a squeeze as he passes my chair. "Thank you, Lil. I'll let you know when I find out more about her condition."

Layla continues to cry as the minutes and hours tick by on the wall clock above our heads. This extreme show of emotion is out of character for my sister, but I don't feel sorry for her. I'm sure she feels guilty for causing Trudy's heart attack. And she should. I know I do.

I haven't eaten all day, and around four o'clock, I go in search of food. They've long since stopped serving lunch in the cafeteria, so I grab two hot teas and two strawberry yogurt parfaits. Layla declines the yogurt, but the warm tea seems to settle her. She stops crying and slips into a catatonic state. She doesn't look up, even when an unruly homeless person causes a commotion and two security guards escort him out of the building. The yogurt is sour and the granola soggy, but I eat every bite of the parfait and chunk the empty container in a nearby trash can.

It's nearly six o'clock when I see Isaac again. The waiting room is empty, and Layla has fallen asleep with her neck bent and chin touching her chest.

I stand to face him. "How is she?"

"Resting peacefully," he says. "The doctors have determined that Trudy has a problem with her heart's rhythm. They called it ventricular fibrillation. She's having surgery in the morning. They're implanting some sort of device inside of her. Ruthie will be here soon. She'll understand it better than me."

What Isaac doesn't say, I hear in his dismissive tone. I'm no longer needed here. Even though she's the closest thing to a mother I've ever known, Trudy is not my real mother. Isaac and Ruthie and her two college-aged granddaughters are Trudy's family. I have no family. My father is dead. My sister and I despise each other. I am an orphan.

"Trudy is a strong woman and she's gonna pull through just fine." I gather up our belongings. "I'd better get my sister home. Please call me if anything changes. I can be here in the morning if you need me. Otherwise, I'll wait to hear from you after the surgery is over." I lean up and kiss his cheek.

Tears fill his eyes. "I'll never be able to repay you for saving her life."

"I'm just glad I was home at the time."

He walks slumped over, with his shoulders bearing the weight of the world, across the lobby and out of sight. He's been a friend of our family's since before I was born. Panic grips me. I'm powerless to do anything about all the changes in my life.

LILLIAN

$\mathcal{L}$ayla doesn't utter a sound on the way home, but she breaks into a fit of hysterics when we enter the kitchen, the scene of Trudy's heart attack.

I cast my eyes heavenward. *What did I do to deserve this?*

She collapses onto the floor in the spot where Trudy lay dying only hours ago. She's sobbing so loud, I cover my ears. "Layla, Jeez. You've gotta calm down. You're freaking me out. Do you want to talk about whatever it is that's bothering you?"

She cries louder, as if that's even possible.

I go to the refrigerator and open the door. "You're bound to be hungry. Can I fix you something to eat?"

She shakes her head.

"I know what you need. Come with me." Taking her by the hand, I drag her upstairs to my bathroom. From the medicine cabinet, I remove a bottle of sedatives my doctor prescribed for me when my anxiety over Daddy dying was at its worst. I shake a pill out in her hand and give her a glass of water to wash it down.

"Now. Bedtime for you." I walk her down the hall to her room. Even though she's been here for ten days, she has yet to unpack her suitcase, a sign she does not intend to stay. Her clothes are folded neatly inside. I grab a satiny negligee, the color of lavender fields in bloom, and hand it to her, averting my gaze while she changes into it. I hold the covers back as she she climbs into bed and then tuck them tight around her.

"Can I get anything for you?" I ask, but her eyes are already closed.

I feel disgusting. I'm still wearing my same wrap dress from dinner last night. I strip naked in the hallway on the way to the bathroom. After a very long steaming hot shower, I dress in sweats and go back down to the kitchen. I make myself a cup of chamomile tea and sit down at the table to drink it. After the cacophony of loud voices and screaming children at the hospital and Layla's hysterical sobbing, the house is blissfully quiet. I send Marcus and Melanie the same text. *Home from the hospital. Trudy will have surgery tomorrow. Grateful she's alive.*

I place the call I've been dreading. My brother-in-law picks up right away. "Lillian, what's wrong?" Naturally, Roger suspects something's wrong. As long as I've known him, I can count on one hand the number of times I've called him. Which saddens me. He's family. I blame Layla. She never encouraged us to bond. I wasn't even a bridesmaid in their wedding.

I release a breath I didn't realize I'd been holding. "So much I'm not sure where to start."

"The beginning's always a good place," he says.

I walk him through everything that's happened since the reading of the will at the attorney's office last week. Roger doesn't speak, but the sound of his soft breathing lets me know he's still on the line.

"I know when your wife is being melodramatic. This is real, Roger. I'm really worried, and I thought you should know."

"I was afraid something like this might happen. I'm sorry you're having to deal with this, and I hated to bail on you, but I couldn't take it anymore. Layla's success has gone to her head. Her priorities have gotten all screwed up."

I grunt. "As if her priorities were ever in the right order."

He chuckles. "True. But she's gotten way worse."

As we talk on, he makes it clear he's still in love with my sister but clueless how to reach her.

"She's vulnerable right now, Roger. Maybe she'll finally listen."

"I hope you're right," he says, and I hear the sound of a coffee maker in the background. "I'm going to drive to Charleston tonight. I want to be there when she wakes up in the morning. Can you leave a key out for me?"

"There's one under the mat outside the kitchen door. Drive carefully, Roger. And good luck."

When I end the call, I check my phone for texts. There is one from Melanie letting me know she's thinking of us, and one from Marcus saying he's in a meeting and will call when it ends. I make myself another cup of tea and dawdle around the kitchen, opening cabinets and looking in drawers. Trudy has been the head of our household for nearly forty-five years. The Stoney home won't be the same without her. But I won't be living here so what does it matter?

At the thought of my uncertain future, that panicky feeling returns, and I'm relieved to see Marcus's face in the window at the door. I swing the door open and throw myself into his arms.

"Is it Trudy?" he asks, alarmed. "Did something happen since your last text?"

I shake my head, but I can't speak for the lump in my throat. With his arms still around me, he backs me into the house, and I cry on his shoulder until his shirt is soaked and I'm all out of tears. But I feel better, like I might survive my future as long as Marcus is in it.

"You know what you need?" he asks, and without waiting for me to answer, he says, "Comfort food."

Turning me loose, he opens the refrigerator and rummages through the contents until he finds a pie dish covered in aluminum foil. "Is this what I think it is?"

"Depends. What do you think it is?" I peel back the foil on my side of the dish so only I can see the pie.

"I'm hoping it's Trudy's turtle pie. I missed you something awful when we broke up, but not nearly as much as I missed Trudy's turtle pie."

"You're in luck. It's Trudy's turtle pie." I open the flatware drawer and remove two forks, holding one out to him. "I see no reason to dirty up plates."

Seated across from each other at the table, we devour half of the pie. "I could get used to comfort eating." Dropping my fork to the table with a clatter, I fall back in my chair and rub my belly. "I think I might be sick."

"I know the feeling." He sinks his fork into the pie for one last bite before returning the leftovers to the refrigerator. "I need to get horizontal. I'm moments away from a food coma." He pulls me to my feet, and we walk down the hall to the drawing room.

We lie down on the sofa with our arms around each other and the afghan over us. "Now, tell me about Trudy."

We talk until well past midnight, about Trudy and Layla and our past, including the ten years we were apart. But mostly we talk about our future. I fall asleep in his arms and wake up alone to the peal of eight chimes coming from the grandfather clock in the hallway. Trudy is now in surgery. I close my eyes and say a prayer.

When I hear the sound of voices compete with the clanging of pots in the kitchen, I get up and pad down the hall on bare feet. From the doorway, with my hair springing out from my head in an unruly mess, I watch the two men working at the stove—Roger ladling pancake mix onto the griddle and Marcus frying bacon in an iron skillet. They are cracking jokes and telling war stories like old friends.

"Did I miss something?" I ask. "I wasn't aware the two of you knew each other."

Roger grins up at me. "Never met. We bonded over coffee."

I give my brother-in-law a quick hug. "I didn't hear you come in last night. Was it very late?"

"Around three. I accidentally woke Layla. We've been talking ever since."

"So, you've been up for more than twenty-four hours?"

"Yep. Pretty much." He points his dripping ladle at me. "A very productive twenty-four hours, mind you."

Marcus hands me a cup of coffee and plants a noisy kiss in the crook of my neck. "Morning."

I wrap my arm around his neck from behind, tugging his head down and kissing his cheek. "Morning."

Layla appears in the doorway. "Lil, can I talk to you alone in the drawing room?" Without waiting for me to respond, she turns away from the kitchen and disappears back down the hall.

I cast a nervous glance at Roger. "Should I wear my body armor?"

Roger laughs. "I don't think you'll need it."

Dreading the confrontation, I trudge back down the hall to the drawing room. Layla is sitting ramrod straight on the sofa. I know that pose. She has something important on her mind, and I'm going to hear about it.

"Whatever this is about, before you say anything, I want to check for messages from Isaac. If I can find my phone."

I'm shocked when my sister actually helps me look for it. We finally locate it wedged between two sofa cushions.

"The battery's dead. I'll just be a minute." I take the phone to my charger in Dad's study and plug it in. The phone comes to life, pinging with a text message from Isaac.

I call out to Layla, "Isaac says Trudy is in surgery," and thumb off a quick reply. *We're praying for her. Keep me updated.*

I leave the phone charging and join my sister on the sofa. Several awkward minutes of silence pass before Layla says, "I'm sorry for freaking out on you yesterday. I honestly don't know what happened to me. I just lost it when I saw Trudy lying on the floor, so still and pale, and you working so hard to save her life. And then you telling the emergency operator that she was your mother. I didn't realize it until you said it in the car, but she has been like a mother to us. I've been so wrapped up in myself all these years, I've taken so much for granted. And you . . . I've been too busy criticizing you to notice what a remarkable person you are. I mean . . . you saved her life, Lil. And you were so calm in handling the situation."

Whatever I was expecting, this was definitely not it. I'm tempted to ask her to repeat it, so I can video it. "People react differently in times of stress," I say.

"I've been such a bitch to you, Lil. Not just since Dad got sick but all our lives. I'm *so* sorry for making you believe you were responsible for Ivy's death. I don't remember that specifically, but I do remember being mean to you when we were little. I don't know what's wrong with me. I'm morally flawed or something. You would think I would've wizened up when my husband left me, but our separation made me behave even worse. I told Roger last night that I truly want to be a better person. He's agreed to give me another chance if I promise to get counseling. I actually *want* to see a therapist. I *need* to see a therapist."

If she's looking for sympathy, she's come to the wrong place. But I soften toward her just a smidge.

Tucking one bare foot beneath her, she angles her body toward me. "I know how much it means to you to keep the house. My life is in Atlanta. I have no interest in ever moving to

Charleston. But I'm willing to give you some time to try and figure out how to buy my half."

I stare openmouthed at her. Is this really my sister? I can't believe she's actually giving me what I want. But is it really what I want anymore? I could give it a go. The money I earned from my paintings is a start. But the house needs so many repairs, I'd be pouring money into a sinking ship. And what about Marcus? If we end up together, would it be fair to saddle him with such a financial burden? There are plenty of other houses on the Battery. Houses with no ghosts.

"We should sell it," I blurt out before I can change my mind. "Especially now that Trudy is retiring." I get up and walk around the room, studying the artwork that belonged to my ancestors. I stand at the window, looking out over the harbor. "A lot of good things happened to our family in this house. But a lot of bad things happened as well." I don't need to say it. She knows I'm talking about Ivy's suicide.

"Are you sure this is what you want?" Layla asks.

"What I want is for a lot of things to be different. But I have no control over sickness and death, any more than I can control the things other people do. I can only control my own actions. It's the right decision, regardless of how difficult it is to make. In the long run, we will both be better off."

"We'll get a lot of money for the house, Lil. You don't have to move out of downtown. You can buy something smaller and more manageable. Are you and Marcus . . . you know, together? I confessed to Roger what I did to you. How I broke up your engagement."

I leave the window and return to the sofa. "Here's the thing, though, Layla. You didn't break us up. You kissed him. He didn't kiss you. Marcus simply wasn't ready to get married. We were too young. He wanted to give law school his best shot without the added burden of having a wife."

Her beautiful face turns sour with disappointment. All these years, she's prided herself on having ruined my chance at happiness. She's going to need a lot of therapy to become a better person.

Layla cracks her knuckles, a surefire sign that she's preparing to attack, but I'm saved from her onslaught when Marcus calls us to breakfast.

In the kitchen, we sit down to a breakfast of pancakes, eggs, bacon, sausage, and toast. The smell of the food makes my mouth water. "You two went a little overboard. There's no way we can eat all this."

"We may have gotten a little carried away," Marcus admits.

"Your refrigerator is stocked with too many choices," Roger adds. "We had a hard time deciding what to cook."

"That's Trudy for you." I smile sadly at the realization that Trudy will never again come through the back door with an armful of groceries.

Marcus offers the blessing, I add a prayer for Trudy, and we dig into the food.

"So . . ." I pop the cap on the syrup and drizzle it over my pancakes. "What do we do about the DNA test results? We can't keep Melanie in limbo indefinitely."

Layla drags her fork through her scrambled eggs. "Do you want to call for the results? Or do you want me to?"

Her tone insinuates that she wants me to make the call. "This is something we should probably do together. I'm going to the hospital as soon as I finish eating, but we can call when I get home this afternoon." I don't ask my sister to accompany me to the hospital for fear she'll have another breakdown.

Marcus breaks a slice of bacon in two and pops half in his mouth. "Why don't I have my assistant call the testing center? I'll have her seal the results in an envelope, and the four of us can read them together over cocktails."

"Making a party out of it might lessen the tension. What do you think?" I ask Layla.

"I like the idea," she says. "Should we invite Melanie?"

I shrug. "Why not? She can always say no."

"Roger and I don't have anything to do today," Layla says. "We'll go to the store and make some hors d'oeuvres. Name the time, Marcus."

"How about six o'clock? I'll come straight here from work."

LILLIAN

*T*rudy makes it through the surgery with flying colors. "Aside from her heart, she's in excellent physical shape," her doctors say. "She's a very lucky woman."

I think we're the lucky ones.

I don't hang around the hospital after the surgery. I will visit her at home when she's feeling better. For now, her daughter and husband will take care of her. Trudy is a part of my life. Whether she's my housekeeper or not, she's a trusted friend.

When I call Melanie to invite her to the results party, she says, "Considering the circumstances, I think it might be awkward for me to be there."

"It's your call, Melanie, but honestly, I think it might be less awkward if you came. Everyone will be on their best behavior with you here. Besides, this would be a good chance for you to meet Layla's husband, Roger, and my boyfriend, Marcus."

"In that case, how can I say no. Regardless of the outcome, as I said the other night at dinner, I'd like to develop friendships with both you girls."

Warmth spreads through my body. "I'll see you tonight at six."

I spend several hours that afternoon sorting and editing the images I took on my walk on Tuesday. Many inspire me, but one in particular—two little girls, identical twins, playing with a black Lab puppy—tugs at my heartstrings. While my art school professors had praised my work in portraiture, none of my prior compositions include people. What does that say about me? Are there no people in my scenes because there are so few people in my life? I aim to change both in the future.

A cold front slides through that evening, bringing no rain but wind and noticeably cooler temperatures. Layla and I have a good laugh when we both show up in jeans and black turtle-neck sweaters.

I snap a selfie of us. "If our mother could see us now."

Layla scowled. "I always resented her for making us dress alike."

I give my sister's hair a yank. "You don't say?"

Roger builds a fire in the drawing room while I help Layla put together a charcuterie tray with meats and cheeses, nuts and fruits. I notice a bottle of champagne chilling in the refrigerator. Will my sister pop the cork if I'm the winner of the coveted prize?

Marcus and Melanie arrive within a few minutes of each other at the appointed hour. Introductions are made and drinks are served. To an outsider, we're having a cozy gathering with friends on a chilly autumn evening. On the inside, the air crackles with electricity in anticipation of the results that are soon to be revealed. Something feels all wrong about this process, this results party, to me. And it's not until Marcus produces the envelope that I figure out what it is.

I look around the room at our odd little group. Marcus, at the fireplace with envelope in hand. Layla and Roger book-ending me on the sofa. Melanie, sitting quietly in a wingback chair. We are all bound together by blood or marriage or love. What if learning the results of the DNA test fosters more resentment between Layla and me? We might never see each other again. I admit there have been times when that's exactly what I wanted. But now, in light of her apology and Trudy's heart attack, I feel obligated to give her another chance. In honor of my father's memory, I'm willing to try one last time to be sisters.

"Wait a minute." I leap to my feet. "Stop the presses. Why are we even doing this? Why does one of us have to get left out? Layla and I are adults, no longer in need of a mother to feed and nurture us. At our age, we need a mentor and a friend. We can both have that in Melanie if she agrees." I turn my attention to Melanie. "You said the other night at dinner that you don't have any family. And we're both Graham's daughters, and he was once important to you . . ."

Three sets of eyes bore holes in me, and I slowly sit back down. "Okay. Maybe not. Just a thought."

"I think it's a wonderful idea," Melanie says in a soft voice. "I have enough love in my heart for both of you."

All eyes travel to Layla whose downturned lips broaden into a smile. "Yes! Of course! I love the idea." She grows serious again and says to Melanie, "Are you sure we're not asking too much of you?"

Melanie places her hand over her heart. "Asking too much of me? My dear child, you and your sister are giving me way more than I deserve. You're answering my prayers."

Marcus holds up the still-sealed envelope. "I'll give this to Ball and Cross for safekeeping in case you ever change your minds."

Roger rises from the sofa. "This calls for champagne. Marcus, I could use your assistance."

I wait until the guys have left the room before I invite Melanie to join my sister and me on the sofa. "I feel like I railroaded you into this decision. One of us was going to get left out. Selfishly, I don't want that someone to be me."

"I don't want that someone to be me either," Layla says in a tone of resignation, as though she's not totally on board but willing to go along with it.

"It's a win-win situation for me," Melanie says. "I get two daughters for the price of one."

"Marcus still has the envelope," I say. "It's not too late to read the results."

"And Marcus will always have the envelope if we decide to revisit the issue in the future." Melanie relaxes back on the sofa. "I'm looking forward to getting to know each of you better. Now that I'm allowed back in the city I love so much, I'm considering buying a condo and spending more time here."

"And that's a win-win for me." I elbow my sister. "It's motivation for you to spend more time in Charleston as well."

"For sure," Layla says. "At least in the next few months while the house is on the market, and we're divvying up the contents. Are you fully on board with calling the Realtor? I hate to push you, but I'll be returning to Atlanta with Roger on Sunday. I've spoken to Bennett Calhoun. He's available, if you're up for meeting with him over the weekend. If it's too soon, we'll wait. I just thought that since I'm here." Layla's lips part in a genuine smile that softens her features. It's a good look for her, one I hope to see more often.

"There's no time like the present," I say. "But I think we owe it to Dad to consult with his real estate agent as well. Maybe we can interview both to see which we like best."

Layla shakes her head, as if this is news to her. "You never told me Dad had spoken to a Realtor."

"I've forgotten her name." I leave the sofa to retrieve the file from Dad's study. When I return, I read the contact information on the business card stapled inside the file. "Midge Calhoun. Wait, isn't Calhoun your agent's last name?"

"Yes, Bennett Calhoun. Duh, Lil. They're a husband and wife team."

"Perfect." I drop the file on the coffee table. "One less decision we have to make."

Marcus and Roger return with the bottle of bubbly, and a celebratory mood falls over our small group. Every time Melanie tries to leave, we beg her to stay longer. Around nine o'clock, we defrost one of Trudy's chicken and wild rice casseroles and gather around the kitchen table to eat it. It's close to midnight when Melanie catches an Uber back to her hotel. Layla and Roger, who have been making goo-goo eyes at each other all night, head immediately off to bed.

I take Marcus's hands in mine. "My days in this house are numbered. Would you consider moving in here with me? At least until we sell it. Layla is going back to Atlanta with Roger on Sunday. She plans to come back often, to help with packing everything up, but the house is so big, she won't be in our way. With Trudy out of the picture, I'll be responsible for all the upkeep."

His face is serious, but he's totally teasing me when he says, "I'm tempted. But I'll need to see the view first. Show me your room."

We climb the stairs and pass through my bedroom to the piazza. "We can move into the master suite. The suite is much bigger, and the view ten times better."

He takes me in his arms. "I would love to move in here with you, in whichever room you choose."

"Are you sure we're not moving our relationship along too quickly?"

"Not at all. In fact, I don't think we're moving fast enough. We've wasted ten years. I don't want to waste another day. I'd marry you tomorrow if I didn't think my parents would kill me. I'm sure you want a big wedding with all the hoopla anyway."

"That's not at all what I want." I scrunch my brow and purse my lips. "Wait, Marcus. What are you saying? Are you talking hypothetically?"

He removes a small velvet box from his jacket pocket and kneels down in front of me. "Marry me, Lillian Alexander. All those years we were apart, I never stopped loving you. The timing is right for us now. I promise I won't disappoint you."

He removes the ring from the box and places it on my finger. I hold my hand out in front of me. It's dark out, but I can see from the soft glow of the moon that it's not the same ring from our first engagement."

As if reading my mind, Marcus says, "I traded the old one in. I can afford a nicer ring now, and I was afraid the old one might hold bad memories for you." He shines his phone's flashlight on the ring, so I can see the large solitaire set in a platinum band of pavé diamonds. I gasp when the light causes the diamond to sparkle rainbow colors.

"Oh, Marcus. It's exquisite."

He rises from his kneeling position. "Does that mean you'll marry me?"

I throw my arms around him. "Yes! I'll marry you."

"The sooner the better," he says. "I'm eager to get on with our lives."

"How does the Saturday after Thanksgiving sound? We can have a small wedding here at the house. Even if someone makes an offer to buy it right away, we won't be able to close until after New Year's. It'll take us that long to clear everything out. The Stoney family will go out with a bang."

"Thanksgiving sounds perfect to me."

"Did you know Dad and Ivy had their reception here?"

"You told me." He tucks a strand of hair behind my ear. "Speaking of your father, there's something I didn't tell you about my meeting with him before he died."

"What's that?"

"He asked me if I was seeing anyone. When I told him no, he wanted to know if there was any chance you and I might get back together. I told him that was my hope, and he gave me his blessing if we ever decided to marry."

Tears fill my eyes. "You have no idea how much that means to me. Make love to me, Marcus," I say, my voice thick with lust.

"It would be my pleasure," he says and plants a kiss on me that weakens my knees. With lips locked and no air between our bodies, we inch our way back inside. The years fall away as we tear each other's clothes off. We're a young couple again, engaged to be married. He lays me down on the bed, and when he enters me, I am whole again after all these years. Our bodies entwined, we move together in rhythm. He brings me to new heights, and my body explodes in ecstasy, again and again and again.

EPILOGUE

*T*wo Years Later

I put the finishing touches on the birthday cake and stand back to admire my work. Although I don't consider baking one of my natural talents, the sheet cake—cream cheese icing on vanilla cake with *Happy Birthday Ivy* scripted in pink frosting—represents my best effort to date.

Layla criticized me when I named my daughter Ivy. "You'll curse her. She'll turn out . . ." Her voice trailed off, and while she didn't complete her sentence, I knew what she was thinking.

"How would she turn out, Layla? With a beautiful soul like our mother's. I certainly hope so."

I circle the downstairs, conducting a final inspection of our house on Church Street, a mini version of the Stoney mansion that Marcus and I were able to afford because it needed some work, most of which we've done ourselves.

I cried buckets when we moved out of our house on East Battery. But I brought my favorite pieces with me. The grandfather clock. The desk from Dad's study. And the portrait of Ivy, which hangs prominently in the dining room. Layla and I both wanted the portrait, but I won it in a coin toss.

The front door flings open and Trudy bustles in, her arms laden with gifts. She's as much a part of our household as she's always been. No longer as a housekeeper, but as a babysitter for Ivy several afternoons a week. I spend my free time in my attic studio painting. My series, *The Hidden Wonders of the Holy City*, was an enormous success, and I currently have a long list of patrons waiting for future works.

I unburden Trudy of the gifts. "For goodness' sake, Trudy. You spoil that child rotten."

"Humph. That's a grandmother's prerogative."

I love it that she considers Ivy her granddaughter, and I kiss her cheek because she's so special to me and I'm so glad she's still alive. She follows me into the dining room. I have eyes in the back of my head, and I know she's running her finger along the tops of the furniture, inspecting for dust.

"The house looks lovely, Lil. You're a fine homemaker."

"That's high praise coming from you. But I learned from the best." I place the gifts at the end of the table where I've positioned Ivy's highchair for the ceremonial blowing out of the candle for her first birthday.

"Who's coming to the party?" Trudy asks, arranging the gifts in a tidy stack.

"Melanie, of course. I asked her to come early. She should be here momentarily. Other than that, Marcus's parents and Dr. Hudson."

She narrows her brown eyes at me. "I didn't realize you were still seeing Dr. Hudson."

"I'm not. At least not professionally. We get together for coffee about once a month. Turns out we have a lot in common. Having a shrink for a friend has its advantages."

Trudy chuckles. "I imagine it does. And Layla? Is she coming?"

"She couldn't get away. She's showing her spring collection at market this week. Considering the situation, I'm glad she can't be here." I tidy the forks, napkins, and plates I've arranged on the table. "Am I doing the right thing in telling Melanie?"

"It's not a matter of choice. She's gonna see for herself whether you tell her or not."

The doorbell rings and we return to the living room, which doubles as a family room, and triples as Ivy's playroom. I open the door to Melanie who looks stunning in a tangerine silk blouse and tan slacks. "I've missed you so much." I press my cheek against hers, kissing the air beside her ear, and then pull back so I can get a good look at her. "Being a world traveler agrees with you."

Melanie has just returned from a three-month publicity tour. Prior to that, she spent five months in Hollywood adapting her latest release for the big screen.

Melanie waves off the compliment. "Traveling is for the birds. I've never been so happy to be home."

It makes me giddy with happiness that she refers to Charleston as home.

Handing me another stack of gifts, she enters the house and welcomes Trudy with a warm embrace. "Where's the birthday girl? I can't wait to see her."

"Upstairs. Marcus is getting her dressed. You won't recognize her. That full head of dark hair she was born with has all fallen out. She's now blonde."

"That's wild. Why haven't you sent me any pictures?"

Melanie's been begging for pics of Ivy for months, but I've been ignoring her request, just as I ignore her now. "I have some exciting news to share with both of you." I motion Melanie and Trudy to the sofa, but I'm too nervous to sit.

"I bet I can guess what it is," Trudy says.

"Because you know me so well." I stroke my baby bump. "I'm pregnant. I had an ultrasound last week. This one's a boy. His name is Stoney Alexander Mullaly, which is a mouthful I know. But we're gonna call him Stone."

Trudy slaps her leg. "Stone. I love it. Your daddy would be so proud."

Melanie's smile is bittersweet. "Yes, he would. Congratulations, sweetheart. When is he due?"

"In early February."

We hear Marcus's voice from above and seconds later he bounds down the stairs with the baby on his hip. Ivy squirms out of his arms and totters on chubby legs over to me. I scoop her up, but she immediately wants back down again. She runs over to Trudy, burying her little face in Trudy's lap.

Trudy says, "Happy birthday, sweet baby girl. Can you say hello to your guest?"

Ivy raises her head, cocking it sideways in curiosity. Melanie's jaw goes slack, her eyes wide. The same pale gray eyes as the little girl looking up at her. "It's uncanny. She's . . ."

"The spitting image of you." My grin is so big, my cheeks hurt.

Melanie fingers a lock of the child's fair hair. "You said blonde. You failed to mention that her hair's the same snow-white as mine. And that nose and those lips. I'd know that cupid's bow anywhere."

I sit down between Trudy and Melanie on the sofa, lifting my daughter onto my lap. "If everyone agrees, Marcus and I think we should read the DNA results for confirmation, but genetics don't lie. She's your biological granddaughter." I pause, letting this sink in.

"Which makes you my biological daughter." Tears well in Melanie's eyes as she puts an arm around me, drawing me close. "Oh, darling, I can't tell you how happy this makes me."

"Me too, Melanie." I rest my head on her shoulder.

"Have you told Layla yet?"

I'm a little jealous that she's thinking about my sister at a time like this. But that's Melanie. If the tables were turned, I

ASHLEY FARLEY

would hope she'd be thinking of me. "I figured I'd let her see for herself the next time we're together."

Melanie presses. "And where and when will that be?"

"On Wadmalaw at Thanksgiving. She and Roger have already said they're coming again." Marcus's parents gave us the cottage as a wedding gift. We're making it a tradition to get our family together for the holiday weekend.

Melanie's tone is firm. "Thanksgiving is two months away, Lil. This is important. We should plan a trip to Atlanta."

Melanie is the glue that holds us together. When we're all in town at the same time, she treats us to spa days and three-martini, soul-bearing lunches. And when we're apart, she schedules monthly conference calls where we talk for hours.

Layla and I are committed to making our relationship work. We grew closer while the house was on the market. Melanie was in Charleston a lot of that time as well, finalizing the purchase of her waterfront condo and working with a decorator to furnish it. They helped me plan my wedding. Melanie walked me down the aisle, and Layla was my matron of honor. While Layla's visits have been few and far between since she drove away with her truckload of priceless Stoney heirlooms, she has been here for the important times—for my baby shower and the birth of my first child.

I have yet to visit Atlanta, despite Layla's many invitations. It would mean a lot to her and perhaps soften the blow when she learns that Melanie is my mother.

"You're right, Mel," I say to my mother, who has dropped from the sofa to the floor and is playing peek-a-boo with Ivy. "We should go to Atlanta, sooner rather than later."

ACKNOWLEDGMENTS

I'm grateful to many people for helping make this novel possible. First and foremost, to my editor, Patricia Peters, for her patience and advice and for making my work stronger without changing my voice. A great big heartfelt thank-you to my trusted beta readers—Mamie Farley, Alison Fauls, Cheryl Fockler, Kathy Sinclair, Anne Wolters, Laura Glenn, Jan Klein, and Jenelle Rodenbaugh. And to my behind-the-scenes team, Kate Rock and Geneva Agnos, for all the many things you do to manage my social media so effectively.

I am blessed to have many supportive people in my life who offer the encouragement I need to continue the pursuit of my writing career. I owe a huge debt of gratitude to my advanced review team, the lovely ladies of Georgia's Porch, for their enthusiasm for and commitment to my work. To my architect, Tim Galvin, for answering my many questions regarding architecture. To Leslie Rising at Levy's for being my local bookshop. Love and thanks to my family—my mother, Joanne; my husband, Ted; and the best children in the world, Cameron and Ned.

Most of all, I'm grateful to my wonderful readers for their

love of women's fiction. I love hearing from you. Feel free to shoot me an email at ashleyhfarley@gmail.com or stop by my website at ashleyfarley.com for more information about my characters and upcoming releases. Don't forget to sign up for my newsletter. Your subscription will grant you exclusive content, sneak previews, and special giveaways.

ABOUT THE AUTHOR

Ashley Farley writes books about women for women. Her characters are mothers, daughters, sisters, and wives facing real-life issues. Her bestselling Sweeney Sisters series has touched the lives of many.

Ashley is a wife and mother of two young adult children. While she's lived in Richmond, Virginia for the past 21 years, a piece of her heart remains in the salty marshes of the South Carolina Lowcountry, where she still calls home. Through the eyes of her characters, she captures the moss-draped trees, delectable cuisine, and kindhearted folk with lazy drawls that make the area so unique.

Ashley loves to hear from her readers. Visit Ashley's Website @ashleyfarley.com

Get free exclusive content by signing up for her newsletter @ ashleyfarley.com/newsletter-signup/

—